121

# DONUTS AND OTHER PROCLAMATIONS OF Love

ALSO BY JARED RECK

*A Short History of the Girl Next Door*

# Donuts AND OTHER PROCLAMATIONS OF *Love*

## JARED RECK

ALFRED A. KNOPF
NEW YORK

THIS IS A BORZOI BOOK PUBLISHED BY ALFRED A. KNOPF

Visit us on the Web! GetUnderlined.com

Educators and librarians, for a variety of teaching tools, visit us at RHTeachersLibrarians.com

*Library of Congress Cataloging-in-Publication Data*
Names: Reck, Jared, author.
Title: Donuts and other proclamations of love / Jared Reck.
Description: First edition. | New York : Alfred A. Knopf, [2021] |
Audience: Ages 12 & up. | Audience: Grades 7–9. | Summary: While his
friends prepare for college, Oscar decides his future is working with his
grandfather on their food truck Hej Hej!, but when Oscar unexpectedly gets
his first taste of adulthood he realizes his plans may be half-baked.
Identifiers: LCCN 2020043185 (print) | LCCN 2020043186 (ebook) |
ISBN 978-1-5247-1611-0 (hardcover) | ISBN 978-1-5247-1612-7 (library binding) |
ISBN 978-1-5247-1613-4 (ebook)
Subjects: CYAC: Food trucks—Fiction. | Grandfathers—Fiction. |
Cooking—Fiction. | Swedish Americans—Fiction.
Classification: LCC PZ7.1.R398 Do 2021 (print) | LCC PZ7.1.R398 (ebook) | DDC [Fic]—dc23

The text of this book is set in 10.5-point Aldine 721.
Interior design by Ken Crossland

Printed in the United States of America
June 2021
10 9 8 7 6 5 4 3 2 1

First Edition

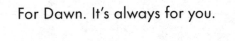

For Dawn. It's always for you.

# DONUTS AND OTHER PROCLAMATIONS OF Love

# HEJ HEJ! RULLEKEBAB & MUNKAR

## Festival Menu

### RULLEKEBAB

1. Original (Rullekebab)
*Shaved seasoned beef, fresh flatbread,*
*lettuce, tomato, cucumber, kebab sauce*
2. Blue Kebab (Rullekebab med blåmögelost)
*Original with blue cheese*
3. Shroom Kebab (Rullekebab med champinjoner)
*Original with mushrooms*
4. Hej Hej! Special Rullekebab
*Original with pineapple,*
*blue cheese, jalapeños*

### MUNKAR

1. Äpple Munk
*Fresh donut, cinnamon sugar,*
*filled w/ apple and sweet cream*
2. Bär Munk
*Fresh donut, sugar, seasonal*
*berry jam, sweet cream*
3. Munkhål
*Baby donuts (holes), cinnamon sugar*
4. Special Munk
*Seasonal specialties*

## CHAPTER ONE

## GOAT CHEESE POUTINE: THE PROMISED LAND

I STILL SMELLED LIKE A DEEP FRYER WHEN I ROLLED OUT OF BED at 6:00 a.m. that first Saturday in September.

We'd been up late the night before, the last Friday Food Trucks of the season at Springettsbury Park, and we'd been slammed—the line snaking from our window to the other side of the gravel parking lot for a good hour, the deep fryer spitting out droplets of oil like angry hornets every time I plopped in another batch of munkar. Swedish for donuts.

I'd already been in school nearly two weeks by that point, it already sucked, and now, with Saturday's festival in downtown York the last big one we'd do for the year, I was looking at the endless slog of just school through the fall, winter, and spring.

Senior year. A hundred and seventy-two more days.

"Ready, Gubben?" Farfar called from the kitchen, where he'd just finished packing up the last cooler from the emergency cook-fest the night before. Barely five hours before, really.

"Ready."

Two travel mugs of thick, dark coffee waited for me on the island counter—mine turned light by a healthy pour of heavy cream and sugar, Farfar's the color of roofing tar.

We thought we'd prepped enough earlier in the week to

handle back-to-back events, but we didn't plan on the Pee-Wee football scrimmage, overlapping with the free concert for that Eagles cover band, wiping out our entire stock of munkar dough. We were lucky we didn't blow a fuse that night, trying to reload for the festival in the morning.

"Did you get all those extra kebab sauces I packed last night?" I asked, taking a first, cautious sip from my coffee.

"Already took the cooler down to the truck."

"You shouldn't be lugging coolers down the stairs, Farfar. Seriously. I told you I'd get them."

"Eh." He waved me off. "You spent so much time dolling yourself up in the bathroom, I had no choice."

I held my arms out, stared down at my ratty clothes. Even after multiple washes, all my Hej Hej! shirts smelled a little like a deep fryer.

Not unpleasantly so, but still.

Farfar hefted another cooler into my arms, which nearly pulled me to the floor.

"There you go, Gubben. You can carry this one down. Spare an old man his aching back."

*Gubben* (rhymes with Reuben) is actually Swedish for "old man," but kind of like you'd call a little kid *big guy*. It's what Farfar's called me since I moved to Gettysburg with him—to this country with him—when I was four.

Koopa laced between Farfar's legs, meowing and purring aggressively for attention, like she knew we'd be out for the entire day. Whenever Koopa saw the coolers, her separation anxiety kicked in.

On cue, Farfar scooped her up in his arms.

"Min lilla bebis sötnos, ja. Lilla kattkatt."

His gray ponytail swung over her gray face while he prattled on in his ridiculous Swedish baby talk, Koopa yowling and batting at the end of his hair.

"That's enough," I said, straining with the handles of the cooler, loaded down with dough and backup fruit filling. "It's getting uncomfortable."

"Aww, Gubben, there is enough love to go around." The two of them snuggled up close to my face, Farfar babbling Swedish baby talk to both of us now, Koopa purring like an outboard motor, burrowing her gray face into mine.

"That's nice. Thank you," I said, blowing cat hair from my lip.

Farfar gave Koopa one last nuzzle with his short-trimmed beard before setting her on the floor, Koopa twisting and yowling incessantly between Farfar's feet, begging us (him) to stay.

"Okay. Come on, Gubben—to the truck!"

We drove, like always, with the windows down, Farfar's NPR station cranked, my arm resting out the window, barely conscious for the forty-five-minute ride into downtown York.

This was our third year at the What the Food Trucks Festival, my favorite of our circuit. Short drive, great turnout, cool vendors, live music, York College girls still clinging to summer. Everything. And with our weekly trips to Springettsbury just a few minutes away, we got more customers who knew us, which I loved. It made me think about opening a café someday, maybe, to go with the truck—somewhere regulars stop in, know where they're going to sit, what they're going to order. I wondered if Farfar had that—or, I guess, if Amir had that—back in Åland. If that was how they met, where they fell in love.

We had our same spot for the third year in a row, right in the middle of everything. People walking to the park from nearby lots had to come right by us. And I loved hearing passersby sounding out our name—*Hedge hedge? Oh, hi hi! Nice! Is that Swedish?*—followed by some variation of *Is it a meatball truck?* or *Do they sell fish? Isn't that what people eat in Sweden?* And followed again by audible confusion blending into palpable intrigue over our menu—*Rullekebab and munkar? Is that, like, gyros and donuts? Hmm.*

We must have sold thousands of donuts that weekend.

And yet Farfar still wanted me going to school all day senior year. What a waste.

We got to work as soon as he parked the truck and got us all hooked up, Farfar firing up the spit and prepping vegetables at his station, me rolling out the first batch of dough at mine. I could cut two dozen out of an entire batch, thirty to forty munkhål rolled from the pieces left between the circles, all set on trays to rise again before hitting the deep fryer closer to go time.

I knocked out four batches—I figured around a hundred was good to get us started—before making sure all the day's fillings were ready, waiting in giant piping bags in the mini-fridge.

This was always one of my favorite times, the quiet work early in the day, before any customers showed up. The focus on a job you know you're good at, and knowing—in a few hours—everyone else is going to know it, too. The truck is always warm, but not the sweltering box it becomes later in the day, when the sun beats down on us, and the deep fryers are cranked, and the spit reflects heat from Farfar's kebab station, a meat-scented space heater. (Gross or delicious, you decide.)

"I'm going to take a lap," I said, toweling off my hands when all my prep work was done.

"Be good, Gubben," Farfar replied, like always, without looking up from the pyramid of cucumbers he was dicing for the day, his wire-rimmed glasses resting on top of his head.

"Two-beer limit. Got it."

A piece of cucumber bounced off the back of my head as I crawled out through the passenger seat up front.


That morning, I took my lap with a focus.

All three years, Windswept Café's retrofitted bread truck had been in the same spot, like ours, theirs near the far-end corner of the park. So beelining for their truck let me get a good look at some of the other offerings: Tot to Trot, Uncle Tommy's Stuffed Pretzels, Three Hogs. Intriguing options, sure, but not what I was really looking for:

Goat cheese poutine.

Fresh-cut fries. Thick, rich beef gravy. Some other secret goodies splashed in. And creamy, tangy goat cheese.

Jösses, the stuff was life-changing.

Carl and Cathy, the husband-and-wife owners I'd cyber-stalked, were bickering back and forth inside the truck when I stepped up to their window, both already frantic and sweating with less than an hour before the official start time, Carl with a Phillies hat turned backward and a one-week scruff-beard, Cathy with light-brown frizz in braided pigtails beneath a yellow bandana. Just like in their pics from other events.

I scanned their menu board before deciding whether or not to interrupt them. And sure enough, there it was, at the bottom of the board, listed as an event special with the note *While goats and gravy last!!!*

"Hey, what can I do for you, boss?" Carl said over his shoulder after I knocked on the frame of their open window. "We don't open for a little while yet."

"I know," I replied. "I just wanted to thank you for bringing the poutine back today. I've been thinking about that stuff for two years." Here I was, fanboying over gravy-cheese fries to complete strangers. But it needed to be said.

"Wait, are you the guy that's been badgering us on Instagram?" Cathy said, sidling up to the window. I couldn't tell if her smile was genuine or not—I'd been pretty relentless in my pursuit of goat cheese poutine.

"Yeah," I said, forcing a laugh. "Sorry about that. It really is the greatest stuff I've ever had at a festival, though. Like, ever."

Carl turned around then, too, stepping closer to the window beside Cathy.

"Hej hej?" he said, wiping his brow on his arm and squinting at my shirt.

"That's our truck," I said, pointing vaguely back through the park.

"Wait, are you Erik's grandson?"

I nodded, and Carl's face lit up. Cathy leaned into his shoulder, beaming at me now, too. For real this time. All traces of bickering vanished.

They gushed for the next ten minutes, how they'd met Farfar as college students years ago at Gettysburg, where they both got addicted to his rullekebab, and used to stand around chatting with him, sometimes skipping an afternoon class in the process.

"We were both bio majors," Cathy said, while Carl turned back to mess with more preparations, still chiming in over his shoulder. "But here we are. . . ."

I tried to picture it—how many years before? Farfar'd never told me this story.

"We got jobs in labs after we graduated, back in Jersey. Pharmaceuticals. Great pay."

"Hated it," Carl called over his shoulder, shaking his head.

"Hated it," Cathy agreed. "We emailed Erik—your grandfather—a few years ago, when we got the crazy idea to start this."

I was just about to beg for an early sampling of poutine then—at double the market value, if necessary—when Carl turned back to the window, a basket in each hand.

Two heaping baskets of the Promised Land.

"Take one back for your grandpa. Let me know what he thinks."

I stared at the steam curling off the gravy, grinning like a little kid, playing it cool. "What do I owe?"

Carl waved me off.

"On me, boss. Tell Erik we said hi."


"Whatcha got there, O?"

Jorge, my best friend. Grinning from inside the window, his too-small Hej Hej! shirt faded from countless washings, his rolled bandana identical to Farfar's, pushing his thick black hair up from his forehead.

As usual, he'd gotten there less than a half hour from go

time. Though, to be fair, I guess there's no reason to be up at the butt crack of dawn just to run the window—not when you drive there yourself.

"Goat cheese poutine. Don't touch."

I set the two baskets on the window counter and climbed back inside the truck. Jorge had a mouthful of fries within those eight seconds, sucking gravy off his fingers, a goat cheese crumble stuck to the corner of his mouth.

"Dude, O, that's crazy," he said through his hand while the other reached for another clump of fries.

"I know, right?"

Farfar just smiled when I told him about Carl and Cathy, putting the untouched poutine down beside him.

"Good kids, Gubben."

I waited for more of a story, but that was all he said before stuffing a pair of dripping gravy fries into his mouth and turning back to his station, releasing a sound like a satisfied bear.

He did manage to work in his typical joke about Jorge being the "eye candy."

"*I* used to be the eye candy, Gubben," he said, grinning—a new addition to the joke. "Now . . . I am more . . . *visual fiber.*"

"Good for shit," Jorge said, laughing and lightly backhanding Farfar's shoulder before snatching another pair of fries.

Farfar laughed back, beaming. "That is a good one!"

I shook my head. Had I said the same thing, Farfar would have frowned and tsked me about inappropriate language.

I left the two of them chuckling over their brilliant new eye-candy material to get the first tray of munkar started in the deep fryers—get a head start before the first customers lined up.

And then the day began in earnest, and the next four-plus

hours were mostly a blur—a very hot, very greasy, very sweaty blur.

I loved having Jorge as our third—not only because he really did seem to be effective eye candy for customers, with his blinding smile and his stupid gorgeous hair and his easy way of small-talking every customer like they'd already met, but also because he knew exactly how to manage the workflow inside the truck.

He knew, for Farfar at the kebab station, to slide written tickets down the line so Farfar could see them and check them off.

He knew, for me at the munkar station, that written tickets would never work, that he could just call them out to me and I'd remember.

He knew how to take four or five orders in a row, then pause and chat up customers while we finished orders before starting again.

He was eye candy *and* good for shit.

His joke, not mine. Doesn't count.


When the last of the sunburned, beer-happy patrons had finally cleared out, Farfar handed Jorge a wad of bills.

"Don't go spending it all in one place," he said, slapping Jorge's back.

"Won't be spending it anywhere," Jorge replied, tucking the cash into his old Velcro wallet and shoving it into the back pocket of his camo shorts. "Hopefully it'll cover a textbook or two next year."

"Oh, have you decided where you want to apply?" Farfar asked, and I swear, I could feel him trying not to glance at me.

"We checked out a few places this summer. I'd love to stay

here in Gettysburg. Jesus is looking to go a little farther away, I think. Dickinson and E-town were really nice. Loyola's D1. He talked to one of the coaches there."

"Are you both playing soccer? Package deal somewhere, maybe?"

"We'll see. Jesus for sure. Depends who gives us enough in scholarships."

Not that they needed the athletic scholarships. Jorge was sitting at the top of our class, Jesus not too far behind him, though I'm not sure anybody else really knew that. He never said a word about class rank, even as other seniors talked about it incessantly in the commons during senior privs, comparing SAT results, humble-bragging weighted GPAs, these bizarre, passive-aggressive fishing competitions to see who could self-deprecate themselves into the most compliments. Lou—Farfar's precious precious Lou—was the worst of them all.

I handed Jorge a giant bagful of leftover donuts before he split after the last few stragglers. He and Jesus had a game at the Y at seven, and I knew he'd spend all day Sunday—and probably most of Labor Day Monday—on homework and studying.

"Tuesday, O," he said, walking backward from the truck, holding the paper bag up in front of him. "Reveal the *true Oscar.*"

I grabbed a napkin from the dispenser in the truck window and held it in front of my other hand, slowly revealed my middle finger. Jorge laughed and waved and walked toward his car.

"Homework this weekend, Gubben?" Farfar said on the drive home, the sun low and ember-orange, like we'd drive right into it by the time we pulled off Route 30.

I groaned into my hands, exhausted, pretending not to hear him. "I can't believe this is the last festival of the year," I said instead. "You sure there are no more you want to do? I don't mind longer drives—I can even drive some. . . ."

"Someday, Gubben."

Someday, Gubben.

I'd gotten a lot of *Someday, Gubben*s.

"You know, I could've taken English, speech, gym—could've even done *online* gym—and been done. Taken D.O. and spent most of the day on the truck with *you*." I paused for effect. I'd been dropping hints about Diversified Occupations—basically work release for seniors—since my freshman year. "Is this your way of telling me you don't want to spend time with me?"

My play for cheap guilt. Which he ignored.

"How does one take online gym?"

"I don't know, record yourself doing jumping jacks and push-ups?"

He reached over and squeezed my arm.

"Can I record you trying to do push-ups, Gubben?"

"Only if I can record you trying to do crunches," I replied, poking the side of his belly.

"No poking the driver, Gubben. Safety first."


I wish I'd known that would be the last festival we drove home from together.

## CHAPTER TWO

# I GUESS WE'RE BOTH
# KIND OF BROODING

THE USUAL CREW WAS SITTING ON THE BACK STEPS OF THE Council of Churches when we pulled up in the alley that night.

"Santy Claus is here! All right!"

Farfar chuckled as he slid out of the driver's seat, and I swear, it sounded like *ho ho ho* was hiding in his throat.

"Everyone has been a good boy today, yes?"

"Shit, I'm out!" one of the men yelled, Tommy, like he did every time.

It was mostly older men, in and out of shelters, halfway houses. Some had clear disabilities, others it was hard to tell.

"Lots of addiction, Gubben," Farfar'd told me once. "No control and nothing left."

So this was the little bit of humanity we could offer.

We gave each one a rullekebab—Farfar knew what kind each of them liked best—still warm and wrapped in foil, along with a bag of donuts. He knew most of the men by name, too, though new guys would show up from time to time, looking hollowed out and skeptical of our offerings.

"I try to picture them as kids, Gubben. At some point, they were all sitting in a classroom like you, playing at recess."

I wondered if he pictured my dad in those moments. His

son—as a kid, where he ended up, the path in between. My dad died when I was only a few years old, back in Åland, where I was born. An overdose. Farfar had already been here in Gettysburg for more than a decade, living with Amir, no clue what was happening an ocean away.

We took the rest of the leftovers inside, where Rhonda was tidying up the kitchen from the dinner line earlier in the evening, her long braids tied into a huge bun on top of her head. She smelled like sweat and baby powder and a little like instant gravy, and I've always found that weirdly comforting. Like that's exactly what someone *should* smell like if they've been trying to make sure the whole world's been fed.

"How's the school year treating you so far?" Rhonda asked, throwing her arm over my shoulder. "I can't believe you're a senior already."

I shrugged. "Still school."

Rhonda nodded, smiling at Farfar, and turned to the boxes of leftovers we'd set on the counter. "Make any decisions for next year? College?"

"Probably this," I said, willing away any other mention of school. "He doesn't like to talk about it, but he really misses me during the day."

Farfar chuckled. "Yes. Many many tears, Gubben."

"Well, I think that's sweet," Rhonda said, tapping Farfar's arm with one of the sacks of leftover munkhål. "Your truck means a lot to this community. More than just donuts." She pulled a sugared donut hole from the bag and took a bite between finger and thumb, closed her eyes. "Mm, they are good donuts, though."

Another few Santy Claus jokes on the way out, now with

kebab sauce on the guys' lips as they laughed, and that was it. We hopped back in the truck and rumbled the last few blocks home.

Farfar had the Wii already fired up when I stepped out of the bathroom from my shower, the menu music from *Mario Kart* blaring from the living room TV. Koopa—the cat, not the character—was curled up on Farfar's lap in his spot at the end of the couch. One hand held his beer on top of his stomach, the other ran through Koopa's gray fur, both of their eyes closed in bliss.

I sank into the other end of the couch and grabbed my controller.

"All cleaned up and ready for your whooping?" he asked, pronouncing it, like always, with long *OO*s, like the crane. He raised his beer to his lips with his eyes still closed. This was probably number two already.

"Not tonight, old man. I'm in the zone, and you're looking tired."

His eyes were open then, a smirk on his face, and he produced his special blue remote—the best Lillajul gift I'd ever gotten him—from the cushion beside him.

"Do you need to ease in with Mushroom Gorge, or are you ready to play for real?"

"I'm ready for any course you want," I said, smirking back.

He just chuckled—without the jollity he gave the guys outside C of C, I noticed—went straight to Rainbow Road, and promptly destroyed me.

Afterward, after sinking back into the couch with a third beer and a number of victories under his belt, he let out a long sigh.

"You did good today, Gubben."

I smiled.

"I'm picking a new character."


I was never sure if they immigrated here at the same time, Far-far and Amir, or if one came first and persuaded the other to join later. Farfar's never been great at filling in the details. But I know they both eventually left everything behind in Åland to come to America. For Amir, that meant the family business with his brothers and parents, a popular kebab shop in Marie-hamn. For Farfar, that meant his job as a civil engineer for the island, and more importantly, his family. A wife and a son—my farmor and my father.

I know I was born there—lived in Mariehamn as a little little kid, briefly with my mom and dad, but mostly with Farmor—but I only have a few fuzzy memories of it. Farfar was already here in America, in Gettysburg, into his second life as a food truck entrepreneur with Amir.

We were both kind of a mess when he first brought me to the US. Each of us with this new world thrust upon us. Farfar was already grieving the loss of Amir, who had died less than a year before. And now, suddenly, his son had died as well. And with me, he had a tiny, pathetic daily reminder of the shame of leaving his old family behind. I was too young to understand that it was Farmor's turn to claim a new life, that sometimes there's a limit to how long a person can live in the aftermath of things beyond her control.

The truck had been withdrawn from the circuit for probably a decade, other than local spots Farfar eased back into on his own, before he decided to dive back in with me as his number two. And I swear, that first festival we hit together, it was like looking at a completely different person. Chatty and charming, with a wide smile and a booming laugh for our customers. Like maybe I was getting my first glimpse into the life he left his old one for—his life before I showed up here. A maybe twenty-year window that, when he looked back, he'd call *his life.*

I always wondered what version of him people saw in Åland. In his engineer life. Or what version Farmor fell in love with when they were young. Was he charming and wide-smiled then? Or was she drawn to the tall, brooding type? Did she get to know and love both?

Did she even have an inkling of what was to come?

When we got back that night, after our first festival, that summer after eighth grade, I'd never been so exhausted in my life. Nothing like the lunch runs and small events I'd helped him with up to that point. Eight hours, on my feet, manning a hot fryer inside a sweltering truck, scrambling to keep up with endless orders of munkar. I felt like I had tiny burns up and down my arms from oil droplets that flew out of the fryer, those invisible hornets. And also like my entire body was coated in a film of fat.

And I remember him grinning at me from across the couch, his gray hair still pulled back in a ponytail, a beer in his hand, still with that . . . opposite-of-brooding look he'd had all day in the truck.

"You did good today, Gubben," he'd said.

"Seriously? I felt like trash. I could hear people complaining about the wait."

He waved me off after a swig of his beer, still grinning.

"That's a good thing, Gubben—people couldn't get enough of your donuts. They sold nonstop, all day long."

And I realized right then that he was right. Even though I was completely wiped, felt completely disgusting, I also felt really good. People couldn't get enough of our donuts—*my* donuts, he had said—and it was the first time I'd ever had the feeling on such a large scale: not just that he and I liked my food, or that our neighbors Maggie and Juliet did, but that literally thousands of people liked my food. Were willing to wait twenty minutes in line in the blistering sun for it.

And I've loved cooking on the food truck ever since.


Farfar's the one who first taught me to cook, obviously. As far back as I can remember, long before the truck, he let me be a part of it every night. My first little Moomin apron's still on the hook beside the fridge in the kitchen. It doesn't fit anymore, but it's still there, beneath two well-worn aprons that do. One for each of us.

When he realized one morning when I was maybe five, not long after I'd moved in, that not only did I love cooking with him, but I was also pretty good at it—careful with measuring, good at following his directions—it became our thing. That first day it was just pancakes—chocolate chip, because chocolate chip—but it's been everything imaginable since then. Still plenty of pancakes, though.

You don't grow out of pancakes.


Farfar did good that day, too.

## CHAPTER THREE

# PAPER BAGS HOLD
# MORE THAN GROCERIES

I NEVER TOLD FARFAR ABOUT THE PAPER BAG SPEECH. I THINK, really, I was doing my best to pretend none of it was happening. Not only would I have to suffer through one more year of English, but Central Adams required every senior to take an additional credit of speech. Which seems excessive, right? Like we couldn't find any way to combine these somehow? We couldn't squeeze a Paper Bag Speech between any of the twenty-eight units of vocabulary?

The worst part, though, aside from having to stand up and give actual speeches, was being next to this girl I couldn't stand—and who clearly thought I was beneath her.

Mary Louise Messinger. Lou for short.

It was the Tuesday after that last festival. Jorge leaned over from his desk on the other side of me.

"O, what's in your bag?"

"You'll have to wait for the speech," I whispered back. "That's when I'll *introduce you to who I really am*. In three objects."

Lou ignored us, reading over her prewritten notecards, her hands twisting the end of her typical long braid, her lips moving silently through the words, though I'm sure she had it perfectly memorized already.

Her paper bag, a white lunch sack, was folded neatly down from the top. *SPEECH* was written carefully in purple Sharpie, and I couldn't help but think of her cabinet at home, ultra-organized, rows and rows of white paper lunch sacks, all folded the same, all with the same purple Sharpie labeling their contents: *SPEECH, TUESDAY LUNCH, SEVERED BIG TOES OF VICTIMS.*

"Let's get started," Mrs. Sommers said from the front of the room. Then she looked right at me, half grinning. "Find out who you really are. In three objects."

My whispering needed work.

"And so I don't have all of you volunteering at once, we'll employ the help of the Select-O-Tron 3000."

She lifted an overturned baseball cap from her desk and shook it in front of her, the pile of numbered Popsicle sticks clacking against each other inside.

She stepped forward, past the front row, and stopped in front of my desk.

"Oscar, reach inside the Select-O-Tron 3000 and reveal your destiny."

She gave the hat one more cursory shake and winked at me.


You might think I was panicked about pulling stick number one from the Select-O-Tron. But the truth is, I didn't mind speech nearly as much as I expected—not the way I loathed English classes, anyway. No cold reading in front of people. No study guides with floating letters and endless blanks to fill. No completely irrelevant books from dead white guys. Just time to plan, time to practice, get up and speak. Easy. Like talking to customers.

And Farfar would've been proud. I could sell it. People were *rapt*. You did not want to have to go second—not after I produced my third item from the bag: another bag full of munkhål I'd whipped up the night before.

"Munkhål?" Mrs. Sommers asked, unable to maintain her own rule of no questions until the end of a speech. She even looked embarrassed, apologetic, a hand over her mouth, but clearly intrigued.

"*Munkar* is the Swedish word for donuts," I explained. "That's my job on our food truck—manning the munkar station while my grandfather"—I explained *Farfar*, too—"makes the rulle-kebab. A single donut is a *munk*. And *munkhål* . . ." I held up one sugared donut hole between my thumb and forefinger for effect. "Baby donut." And I popped it into my mouth before circling the room with the bag to offer a munkhål to everyone.

Like I said, you didn't want to have to follow that speech.

I'd started with one of my Hej Hej! shirts, explained the magical, if unorthodox, combo that is rullekebab and munkar. And I took my little Moomin apron, too, which had everyone leaning forward, trying to get a better look at the cast of characters lined up across the front.

"I've always been partial to Thingumy and Bob," I said, pointing to the twins I've always loved.

Mrs. Sommers was *beaming* at me. *Beaming.* I didn't know what she knew about me, or what she might have heard from the other English teachers about my consistent struggles—my "total apathy and complete lack of effort" from Mrs. Claybaugh from junior year. If maybe she saw my name on her roster in August and thought, *Oh, great, I've heard all about this kid.*

But she was beaming.

20

"Well, that was an amazing start," she said through a mouthful of munkhål, brushing sugar from her hands.

Mrs. Sommers really was one of the few bright spots of senior year.

She had this giant, life-sized *Twilight* cutout in the back of her room, along with book posters of *The Invisible Man* and *Slaughterhouse-Five,* show posters from Shakespeare performances and *Hamilton* and *Dear Evan Hansen,* other Broadway shows I'd never heard of. A bulletin board of fan art by students for books they'd read and loved.

So much to look at when my brain started to go.

"Edward, they just couldn't understand," she'd say sometimes, at random, to the cutout in the back. I think it made Bryce Heiland deeply uncomfortable, which made me enjoy it all even more.

Anyway, Jorge chucked his number two Popsicle stick at me when I sat back down, shaking his head.

"Thanks, O," he said, unfolding himself from his desk and grabbing his paper bag from the floor when Mrs. Sommers asked for the next speaker.

"You want another munkhål?" I replied, holding the nearly empty bag out for him in apology.

"Yes I do."

He popped two more into his mouth before stepping to the front of the room to stand behind the small tabletop podium. He swallowed his donuts, brushed his hands on his jeans, gave me a small nod of thanks, and then dove right in.

Jorge was phenomenal, of course, despite playing up how hard it was to follow me. Our boy flipped on the charm that makes him so good at the serving window, and while he was smooth and flawless in his delivery, smiling and making eye contact with people the entire time, I knew it was because he'd spent hours on our off-day Monday practicing this.

He first pulled out this old canvas bag, big, with a heavy strap and open at the bottom, thick strings hanging from each corner. He held it out, smiled at it.

"My abuelo first came to this area as a migrant worker, decades ago, to pick apples. He'd go from one orchard to the next and send money back to his family in Mexico." Jorge glanced at me then and grinned. "He still brags about how fast he was."

"Eventually, he found a way to stay permanently. Took the nastiest job ever conceived, slinging parts at the turkey processing plant over in New Oxford. Sixty hours a week. Over twenty years. All to give my papi and his brothers a better life here," Jorge said, still clutching the canvas apple bag.

"My abuelo eventually was able to bring his whole family back with him—my abuela and their three sons, all three coming here to Central Adams speaking no English. Papi was in sixth grade. He doesn't talk about it much, but I know it was hard.

"But if my abuelo was willing to sling turkey parts sixty hours a week, Papi was willing to work hard to get through school. And when he graduated, Abuelo made sure he understood that he could go for more, so my dad enrolled at the community college to learn plumbing. And when he started his own business a few years later"—Jorge held up his second item, an old wrench, frayed duct tape around the handle—"Abuelo bought him his first set of tools."

Jorge paused, staring for a moment at the wrench.

"I know none of this has really been about me, but this is

who I really am. . . ." He flashed another grin in my direction. "I am the product of *generational sacrifice*. People whose dreams had nothing to do with their personal aspirations, but who were willing to wish on the possibility of more, decades into the future.

"So my dream," Jorge said, smiling his brilliant smile at everyone before reaching into his paper bag for the last item, "is to become a doctor—and to have my abuelo see me graduate from medical school."

He pulled a toy stethoscope from the bag and hung it around his neck.

I held out my fist for Jorge as he came back to his seat next to me, his stethoscope still hanging from his neck.

"Okay?" he said, back to his quiet self in his desk again. I just nodded and held out the bag with the last two remaining munkhål, extra sugary at the bottom.

Seriously—not trying to brag—but after those two first, no one else's speeches even came close. Just a lot of old sports trophies or ribbons won for this or that, a bunch of family photos.

And yeah, Lou's was really good—of course it was really good. But where Jorge's was all about his family—about *generational sacrifice*, as he called it—Lou's was, predictably, all about herself.

She was number eight in the lineup, and I swear, she didn't look up from her notecards once through the first seven speeches, not for mine—she'd politely said "No thank you" to the munkhål, which annoyed the crap out of me—not during Jorge's, nothing. Not until it was her turn to go up front and stand behind the podium, where she took a deep breath and plastered a smile on her face and looked up at everyone in the same moment (check, check, check on the rubric).

Her voice was smooth and her body language was polished, but I just kept thinking throughout her entire three minutes: *Cyborg.*

The first thing she pulled from her white paper bag was (not severed toes) her certificate for being a National Merit Scholar, "for my performance on the PSAT," she said. She didn't share her exact score, shockingly, but she did share what percentage of high schoolers reach the level she reached (very, very small—in inverse proportion to the size of her head, I'd guessed at the time).

Then she pulled out her old Brownies sash, completely covered in badges. "I'm still a Girl Scout," she said proudly. "I'm currently working on my Gold Award—it's like the equivalent to getting your Eagle Scout in Boy Scouts . . . minus the homophobia."

Okay, that was actually a pretty good line. Bryce Heiland openly scoffed. Also not surprising.

Lou said something else about her Gold Award project, something to do with food preservation that I wasn't completely paying attention to, before she pulled out her last item. The last Harry Potter book, her favorite from the entire series. I guess I couldn't beef with that, either.

But I knew it before she even said it: "I'm a Ravenclaw."

Because of course she was.

Bryce was the last to go. Popsicle number fifteen.

He started with a bang, pulling a Confederate flag patch from his bag. He explained how his grandfather was a reenactor at the Battlefield, and he even explained how even though some people mistook it for a hate symbol, for his family, it was about heritage.

Jorge shook his head, and I might have heard Lou mutter something inappropriate under her breath—which scored her her second points of the day, in fairness—and I looked back at Mrs. Sommers to gauge her reaction. I could see her lips purse a little bit, but otherwise she gave no indication that this was all BS, like she struggled whether or not to call him out during his speech, too. So Bryce kept going—now, I worry, with the silence as some kind of validation for his warped ideas. But it was from his grandfather, after all, and who can look at their grandfather with disdain?

Next, he pulled out an old football jersey from his youth team that went undefeated in sixth grade. Yippee.

And lastly, a Nerf gun.

"My cousins and I used to have these epic battles at Thanksgiving, and this one time my mom and all her sisters ambushed us with a whole arsenal of Nerf guns they had hidden away."

There was so much joy on his face as he told the story. And I'm ashamed to admit, in that tiny moment, part of me was jealous. I remembered wanting that exact Nerf gun one year, and instead getting a book of Swedish folktales, full of trolls and ogres, and trying, unsuccessfully, to hide my disappointment from Farfar. I ended up loving the troll book—almost as much as that old one that was my dad's—and nearly wore the cover off in the years after Farfar got it for me.

But I could still feel a little twinge of guilt as Bryce slid back into his seat and Mrs. Sommers let us start packing up.

"Phenomenal first speeches, everyone. Tomorrow, I'll introduce your second speaking task, but know that you've now set the bar ridiculously high. Well done."

She hung close to me and Jorge when the bell rang.

"Guys, both of your speeches were incredible. Seriously. I knew yours was going to be amazing," she said to Jorge, and I noticed Lou glancing back at the three of us on her way out the door. "I'm familiar with your work. But, Oscar . . . I've never had you in class. That was legitimately one of the most engaging Paper Bag Speeches I've ever heard. And, for better or worse, I've heard *a lot* of Paper Bag Speeches."

Jorge and I both laughed, and I could feel my face burning— for once for a good reason.

"God, I wish I'd thought to record them—I'd love to use them as examples next year."

I'm gloating a little bit now, I know. But she really said all those things.

I got an A on it: 100%. That was the first A I'd gotten in an English class since, what, seventh grade? Which was the *first* time I'd gotten one.

Mrs. Cunningham was the only teacher I'd ever had who counted audiobooks as reading, and she figured out what Farfar had years before. If you left me alone with a page, I'd drown in the letters swimming across the surface. But if you let me hear it, gave me something to do with my hands while I listened, I retained all of it. I finished forty-two novels that year, and for the first—and only—time ever, had a teacher call me "a reader."

Now, I guess I could add "engaging Paper Bag Speaker."

Could've just ended the school year right there.

## CHAPTER FOUR

# I MIGHT BE
# A CUPCAKE NINJA

SINCE FARFAR WOULDN'T LET ME TAKE D.O. AND SPEND MY
senior year working alongside him, I figured out the next-best
option: over half my day in Mrs. Bixler's culinary lab, with Independent Study Foods, Advanced Pastry Arts, and Foods I as
her teaching assistant, along with my lunch period and senior
privs study hall. Not bad.

I've got to be the only kid in our school's history to take
Independent Study Foods, and it was the best part of my day.
Mrs. Bixler became my adoptive school mom the first week of
freshman year, and—despite her mildly disturbing infatuation
with Farfar—I'd've spent the *entire* day there if I could, even
beyond the three-plus periods I finagled into my schedule.

She'd call Farfar her "tall Swedish drink of water," and I'd
make sure I cut her off before she got too far into the source
of those crystal Scandinavian springs. Mrs. Bixler likes a good
metaphor, and her metaphors about Farfar—though certainly
vivid and creative—could also be unsettling. She read a lot of
romance novels, might have even tried her hand at writing some
of her own—I'd see her smirking sometimes, hear her devious
little chuckle to herself over a spiral-bound notebook while I
was in her room cooking lunch.

Which was one of the perks of independent study falling at fourth period, actually, right before my scheduled lunch. Mrs. Bixler let me *cook lunch* every day. Sometimes I'd get a recipe—a printed-out page from the internet, or an old hand-written card, or sometimes just a cookbook with a Post-it inside. Other days, she'd let me come up with something myself. It was like my own little cooking show challenge—she was like my Paul and Prue rolled into one.

I could skip the cafeteria (not that I was a food snob—how many times had Farfar and I gone on late-night Hardee's runs for Monster Thickburgers?), throw in an audiobook, and keep on cooking.

When I walked into the culinary lab that Friday after the festival, though, my Paper Bag Speech victory behind me, there was no recipe of any kind waiting for me. Just a laminated art print from a calendar—the flip side showed the grid from some random May—with a painting of four frosted cupcakes. Push-pin holes dotted each corner, likely from somebody's bulletin board, though I had no idea whose.

"How's my brooding little baker today?" Mrs. Bixler said, sweeping in from the hallway. Her nickname for me—which always made me picture some gray old man with a heavy mustache who only makes dry, heavy loaves of pumpernickel that no one quite understands. His bakery's this drab storefront squeezed between an old textile mill and a store that sells discount mattresses. I might have been spending too much time by myself.

I held up the print in response, raising my eyebrows.

"Oh, good, you found today's assignment."

"Cupcakes?"

"Cupcakes," Mrs. Bixler confirmed, setting her empty mug down next to me on the stainless-steel lab table. "Thought I'd give you a focus today, Oz. Our own little *Cupcake Wars* challenge. Even though you're not competing with anyone."

"There's no recipe with this," I said, palming the back of my neck. "It's just a painting of four cupcakes."

"I know, and don't they look amazing?" Mrs. Bixler grinned down at the painting while she talked. "Doesn't it look like you could dig your finger into that icing and sneak a taste?"

We both stared at it for a moment, ideas forming.

"So I want these for real," she said, putting a hand on my shoulder. "We have a baby shower for Mrs. Crockett, the art teacher, after school, and you're in charge of the cupcakes. Four flavors. You can do one pan of each. The rest is up to you." She gave my shoulder a squeeze, picked up her coffee cup again, and left the room—to where, I had no clue. Probably for more coffee. But mostly to get out of the way and let me flounder for a few minutes, I think.

Mrs. Bixler's big on floundering. She says you only really learn by screwing up. And there's an awful lot of that in the kitchen. It drives some of her students nuts in her foods classes—I saw it firsthand as her teaching assistant for Foods I, when they clearly didn't understand what they were doing, or how to actually perform a technique she'd already demonstrated, and she'd refuse to help them before they tried. Before they floundered and tried to figure it out on their own.

What really gets them is that she makes them come back until they get it right—until the product is *plateable*. On their own time, too—lunches, study halls, after school. She demands the same level of rigor, or more, as any honors class, and I love that. Love that people can't coast through and goof off and eat a few shitty brownies and expect to get credit for it.

So I got down to floundering. I could've just gone for looks, kept the recipe simple, uniform. I could've done one big batch and just colored the frosting. That would've been easiest.

But where's the floundering in that?

The white one would be classic wedding cake—white cake, white frosting—but maybe kicked up a notch with flecks of vanilla bean.

Definitely lemon for the yellow, with fresh lemon zest in the batter.

Devil's food for the brown one, a rich, decadent chocolate bomb of a cupcake.

And the last one, pink, I was thinking maybe a strawberry cheesecake cupcake, if I could pull off the alterations to the batter.

I always kept in mind Farfar's devotion to *simplicity*—simple ingredients, simple techniques, done right. It makes him sound like a hipster burrito chain or something (the gray ponytail's not helping). But it's true. People really just want straight-up cupcake—moist, delicious cake; thick, sweet frosting.

So that's what I did. Simple white-cake batter times four, each with a simple element blended in: vanilla bean, lemon zest, cocoa powder, and, because I couldn't find fresh strawberries in September, Nesquik strawberry syrup (not even remotely adhering to the simple-ingredients rule, but I didn't think anyone would complain). Buttercream frosting, same additions, with a tiny bit of coloring to match the colors in the painting.

I had the batter divided into four separate glass bowls when Mrs. Bixler came back.

"Already diving in, I see?"

I pulled out my earbuds; I'd been listening to the Stephen King fantasy Jorge had recommended.

I gave her my plan, even Farfar's philosophy on simplicity, which I knew she'd love. She let out this guttural chuckle, grinning. . . . *Oh, that Mr. Olsson.* . . . Then, after whatever weird fog finally lifted from her brain, she said, "That sounds perfect, Oz—do you need me for anything?"

"I think I got this," I replied, smirking and popping my earbuds back in.

I slid all four trays into the industrial oven and stacked the empty mixing bowls in the sink for cleanup later, and turned my attention to the buttercream.

Listen, I do have to brag, just for a second. That buttercream? *Transcendent.* Mrs. Bixler audibly moaned after swiping a fingerful of the lemon from the spatula.

So I was doubly surprised when she chose that moment, lemon finger still in the air, to blow up my whole world.

Lou.

"I don't know what I'm supposed to say," I replied, soapsuds dripping from my forearms into the sink. Four perfect trays of cupcakes sat in the racks across the room—one dozen per tray, same white-yellow-brown-pink pattern in each to match the painting.

"Well, for one, you could say, 'Thank you for this unique

opportunity—on top of so many other unique opportunities just for me and me alone—to not only better my culinary skills, but to do so with a greater purpose in mind . . . to help a wonderful classmate and to help my community.'"

I stared at her blankly, my hands still submerged in the hot dishwater.

"*That*, Oscar. You could say *that*, if you're struggling for the right words."

I let out a long breath. I did not say those words, even if most of them were true—everything but the *wonderful classmate*, really.

Instead, I said, "Is she going to be in here with me every day?"

"You're welcome, Oscar. That was so thoughtful of you to point out."

"Seriously," I said, ignoring her sarcasm. "Is she going to be here every day?"

Mrs. Bixler sighed.

"Of course not, Oz. I'm sure she's in AP something-or-other that period. This is still *your* independent study. This class is still all about *you*. I just thought it was an interesting challenge for you that also helps out the community. And being able to collaborate is a good thing," she said, building up righteous steam again. "You won't always be able to just do exactly what you want in the real world."

I dropped the bowl I was rinsing back into the dishwater, splashing suds all over the front of my apron.

"I didn't choose to make those cupcakes," I said, wiping a sudsy hand on my apron and snatching the laminated print from the raised counter in front of me. "I didn't just decide to struggle through a mille-feuille yesterday on a whim. I didn't just have a burning passion to keep those freshman morons from slicing their thumbs off into the pico de gallo the other day."

Foods I yesterday had been a shit-show. I must've been the exception or something, because no fourteen-year-old boy should be allowed to wield a kitchen knife. They wouldn't stop giggling and . . . touching and . . . jabbing each other's kidneys.

Mrs. Bixler didn't reply to me at first. She took another deep breath, one hand pinching the bridge of her nose, the other on her hip. Then a slow sip from her coffee before setting it back down, gently this time.

"They really were idiots yesterday, weren't they."

"What's with the short one?"

"Terrance." She shook her head, her eyes closed.

And then we were both laughing. She had the same secret ninja skills as Farfar, somehow pulling me back to calm when I'd gotten myself worked up.

She picked up the cupcake print after a moment and looked at it.

"Mrs. Crockett's going to be blown away, Oscar. Thank you. Really."

I took a breath and suppressed a smile.

"So tell me more about this stupid project idea."

## CHAPTER FIVE

# THE TRUTH ABOUT
# MARY LOUISE MESSINGER

MRS. CROCKETT DID LOVE THE CUPCAKES, THOUGH. LIKE, *REALLY* loved them. She was waiting outside the door to the culinary lab with Mrs. Bixler the following Monday, and when she saw me, her eyes got huge, and she placed both hands on my shoulders, gripping them with the emotional intensity of an expectant mother. (I'm not positive that's a thing, but it sounds like it, right?)

"Oscar. Oh my goodness, Oscar, thank you so much for my Thiebaud cupcakes!" I had to ask Mrs. Bixler later what *Thiebaud cupcakes* meant—the name of the artist, apparently. Mrs. Crockett held tight to my shoulders, staring directly into my eyes, her near-term belly almost touching mine. Her eyes were even starting to well up.

They were *really* good cupcakes.

"Uh, no problem. I'm glad you liked them. . . . And, uh, congratulations on the baby. . . ."

I'd like to point out that I'd never actually spoken to Mrs. Crockett prior to this moment—wasn't even one hundred percent sure which teacher she was.

But she wasn't the only one moved by my cupcakes, apparently. I had different teachers stopping me in the halls for the next two days, hardly any of them teachers I knew or had had in class, whisper-yelling to me about how much they loved the cupcakes, like they were confiding in me.

"I ate four of them," one of them said to me. *"Four."*

But no amount of cupcake love could protect me from what was coming next. Lou's project.

Really, *I* should've gotten a Girl Scout award for that thing. At least an honorary bronze or a box of Samoas or something.

"Food preservation," Lou said to me that Monday afternoon, nodding as she said it as though the whole thing were obvious enough from just those two words.

I stared at her, brow furrowed, looking from Lou, to Mrs. Bixler standing over her shoulder, nodding at me encouragingly, back to Lou.

"Like . . . making jams and canning tomatoes?"

She looked at me then like *I* was the idiot. As though those weren't, like, concrete examples you'd find by Googling *food preservation.*

"No. Food preservation, as in *eliminating food waste,*" Lou said.

*Well, those are two completely different things,* I thought, but held myself back from saying so out loud. Mostly because of Mrs. Bixler's tilted head and raised eyebrows.

And then Lou went into her pitch as though she were rehearsing a presentation and not just explaining what the heck she wanted me to do.

"Have you ever noticed how much food gets mindlessly thrown away in the cafeteria each day?"

"I don't really eat in the cafeteria," I said, but she continued with her spiel before I even had the period on my sentence.

"This is just from Friday." She produced a whole apple still in its tape-tied plastic baggie, an unopened carton of milk, and a bag of Sunchips. "From one student's tray. Thrown away untouched."

"Has that milk been in your book bag since Friday?"

Mrs. Bixler pursed her lips, but I thought it was a valid question—food safety and all.

Lou shook her head and said, "It has not." Undeterred, emotionless. Robotic, even. Then she continued.

"Nearly a thousand students go through the cafeteria lunch line each day, hundreds more for breakfast. I spoke with the custodians on duty in the cafeteria. Their rough estimates are that more than half the students throw their apples away, unopened, every time they're served, which, looking at the school lunch menu, is roughly twice per week."

I didn't even try to interrupt by this point. I knew she was going to hit me with precalculated numbers next whether I opened my mouth or not.

"With these conservative estimates—just using lunch, mind you—of five hundred apples per day, twice per week, we throw away roughly a thousand apples . . . over *four thousand apples in a month.*"

Okay, I admit, I tried to picture four thousand apples, and she was right—that's a ridiculous amount of apples. A mountain of apples, each week. What I didn't yet know, however, was Lou's plan for Mount McIntosh. Some kind of campaign to convince teenagers to eat their apples?

*Umm, excuse me, are you going to eat that? Because you should really consider eating that. . . . An apple a day, am I right? Ha ha!*

That seems like a good idea, right?

Or was she planning to save them all for some kind of

redistribution? I remembered Mrs. Wetzel, the one really nice custodian in middle school, used to sometimes put out a box for the uneaten apples, to take home and feed the deer. Were we going to drop four thousand apples per month to fatten up the local deer population?

With deer hunting basically a religious holiday in this part of PA, making all the deer fat and lazy seemed a little messed up. I feel like, at some point, you're just shooting someone's pet, right?

Mrs. Bixler finally chimed in.

"I told Lou what an unbelievable cook and baker you are, Oscar. That you'd be able to offer some . . . unique solutions to her problem."

Lou smiled, but I couldn't tell if it was genuine or still her polished presentation smile, and realization was starting to creep in.

"So. Oscar. Since you have all this open time in your schedule, what could *you* do with four thousand apples in a month?"

Two things went through my mind after Lou's condescending question: one was an image of me, standing at the base of Mount McIntosh (the first peak—the foothills, really—of the Great Red Delicious Range), a single, rudimentary apple peeler in my hand.

The other thought was *Open time in my schedule?* Typical Lou. Dismissing everything I did—anything anybody else did, it seemed—as unimportant. Not that I'd made a schedule where I could focus on my own ambitions, to keep getting better in all different areas, to run a business of my own before she was even out of college.

She didn't see that.

Lou only saw a big block of free time in my day, and a better reason to fill it up. For her own benefit.

I've always hated the "real world" talk from teachers, because that's never what they really mean. You can't do this in the real world. You won't be able to do whatever you want in the real world. It's really code for *You're not doing things exactly how I want.* As though the "real world" is just an endless stream of angry bosses, fed up with you for not doing exactly what they want.

I let out a long, defeated sigh in reply to Lou's and Mrs. Bixler's expectant faces. Because this was clearly the "real world" now, too, where someone with more authority and more important ideas tells you what to do.

"My advice to you, Gubben," Farfar said that night, setting his Wii remote down on the coffee table and grabbing his ice cream bowl to join me in the kitchen, "is to know when to step back and let things happen."

I paused for a moment, the heel of my palm pressed deep into the ball of dough that had come together.

"I'm not sure that's even good advice," I said.

He grunted, mumbled something in Swedish as he set his empty bowl in the sink, and opened the fridge for a beer.

"We've had assemblies on being an *up*stander since, like, first grade. And you're telling me to just let things happen?"

"Take a breath, Gubben. You make me sound like an idiot." (He said it the way it always came out, like there was a long *O* at the end. *Idiote.*) "We are not talking about social injustice. We're talking about not getting along with this girl you like."

"Now you're definitely being an idiote," I said, slapping the dough on the counter and pressing my palm in again, while that giant turd hid his grin behind his first sip of beer. "It's not *a girl I like* and you know it. She drives me freaking crazy."

"I can see that," he said, and winked. *Winked.*

I kneaded harder before stopping myself, my forearms burning from the strain, not wanting to work all my frustration into the ball of dough in front of me. If I wasn't careful, that dough was going to be too tough to bite through—teeth wouldn't even be able to reach all that rejected-apple goodness I was bitterly testing out.

Farfar chuckled and laid a hand on my shoulder.

"Let that chill for a little while, Gubben. Come play Rainbow Road with me."

Of course he beat me.


I remember my freshman year, first day of high school, walking into Foods I, breathing my first and only sigh of relief in that huge, terrifying building, because, finally, I was around things I knew. I'd get to *create*. And *eat,* for god's sake. But when I sat down in the assigned seat Mrs. Bixler had pointed me to, this girl Mary Louise Messinger was already there at the stool in front of me, a deep scowl on her face, her ruined schedule crumpled in a ball at her feet.

She was supposed to be in Honors Geometry because she was doubling up on math as a freshman, because of course a sane person would choose double honors math at fourteen, right? But instead, because of some scheduling glitch, she got put in Foods I with all the no-try losers like me, I guess.

That whole first class, while Mrs. Bixler had the rest of us laughing along with her bellowing cackle, Lou stared at her desk, scowling, looking like she was somewhere between crying and strangling a kitten in cold blood. All because her unplanned elective didn't carry the same weighting for her GPA.

We didn't even *have* a stupid GPA yet.

She was only there for like the first two weeks or so, until she must have had her parents complain enough to get her way. I had no idea what class she ended up switching into—if she finally got the Honors Geometry she so desperately craved—but I'm sure it was considerably more rigorous than Foods I.

But here's the secret I knew about her: she failed. In there, in Cooking for the Aimless, Mary Louise Messinger failed. Despite what people might think about the academic rigor of a foods class, Mrs. Bixler did not mess around. She treated her classes like we were all honors students in an AP math class. The expectations in the kitchen are high, and if you mess up—which you will—you're going to do it again until you get it right. There's no A for effort—effort is just assumed. And I loved that. You screw up a chicken breast, you could put somebody in the hospital.

Those two miserable weeks Lou spent in there at the beginning of freshman year, thinking it was a fluff class full of idiots, she *failed.* Not like she bombed a test or flunked the whole course or anything, but her first time in the kitchen, she messed up the ingredients in our batch of basic cookies—switched the sugar and the salt, probably because she was too busy moping or fuming or imagining her carefully crafted Ivy League dreams crumbling before her eyes.

And Mrs. Bixler, after one bite of cookie, called her on it.

After a drink of water. She wasn't mean—didn't scold her for a simple mistake. She just expected Lou to come back on her own time and do it correctly. Because it matters, you know?

The look on Lou's face—if it was torn between crying and murderous before, I didn't know what it was now. Just . . . intensified. Like that poor kitten would have turned to dust in her hands. But like she was struggling to keep it blank, too. A couple of other people took a bite of her cookies right after Mrs. Bixler. Because freshmen. And each in turn made the same disgusted face, laughing and gagging and reaching for water of their own from the sink.

I watched that day as Lou finished rinsing her dishes, Mrs. Bixler talking to her quietly and setting a pink redo card on the counter next to her. Lou dried her hands, her jaw set, and slid the card into her pocket without looking up. Then she silently walked to the door, filled in the sign-out sheet, grabbed a bathroom pass, and left.

I don't know if she ever came back to redo those cookies.

By the following Monday, she was gone. Finally into the promised land of Honors Geometry or whatever.

That was the last time I was ever in a class with her before Senior Speech.

So that's the truth about Mary Louise Messinger. Farfar's precious precious Lou.

At least as I understood it at the time.

## CHAPTER SIX

# THE ARRIVAL (500 APPLES IS AN AWFUL LOT OF APPLES FOR A THURSDAY MORNING)

THE FIRST SHIPMENT OF APPLES ARRIVED FROM THE CAFETERIA that Thursday.

Lou brought them in on a flatbed dolly she must have commandeered from the custodians, beaming, like she couldn't believe the treasure she'd stumbled upon and couldn't wait to show someone. I was that someone.

"What are you going to do with them?" she asked breathlessly.

No greeting of any kind. No question about what I was currently—clearly—making. Just *What are you going to do with them?*

Do you know what five hundred apples looks like?

I will tell you, a lot of freaking apples. It's four bushels— I looked it up.

Four bushels. In one day.

Part of me understood the magnitude and the urgency of the problem she wanted to address. (And don't worry, she spelled out that urgency in great, number-driven detail. Sit tight.) But the other part of me was like . . . *What the hell am I going to do with four bushels of passed-over apples on a Thursday morning?*

I mean, I know my way around an apple. We'd been making

homemade apple filling for munkar for years. But we'd never needed *four freaking bushels*.

Here's some more math for you.

Four bushels of apples—again, the amount sitting on a custodian's flatbed cart in front of me, if I haven't made that clear—is enough to make at least sixty quarts of applesauce (I looked that up, too). There are sixty-four tablespoons in a quart, and let's say that I generously squeeze two tablespoons of apple filling inside each of the munkar.

60 qt = 3,840 Tbsp = 1,920 munkar.

160 *dozen* donuts.

On a Thursday.

I didn't have any of this math figured out in the moment, of course. And let's remember that I didn't have sixty quarts of apple filling, either. I still had five hundred unwanted apples and Lou.

"Uhh . . ." That was my initial reply, mixing bowl in hand.

"I thought you were already planning out ideas," she said.

The truth is, I hadn't been thinking about those stupid apples at all, other than that overworked pie dough from a few nights before that I ended up throwing out. Nobody wants pie crust the texture of jerky.

Instead, in the few days since Mrs. Bixler had roped me into this and Lou had given her well-rehearsed presentation, I'd gone back to my normal routine in the culinary lab, hoping that none of it would ever really happen. I mean, what school official signed off on some high school girl collecting *five hundred* uneaten apples from the cafeteria and wheeling them away on a custodian's flatbed?

So no, I was not planning out ideas. Not for apples. I was

instead obsessed with perfecting gourmet sandwiches and paninis. Farfar and I had watched that *Chef* movie about the food truck, and I had ideas. And maybe I'd been making an extra batch of cupcakes for Mrs. Crockett and the rest in the faculty room, too, because fine, I'll admit—I'm not ashamed—the sudden adoration from all these teachers was pretty nice. Definitely not the norm for me. And who am I to withhold that kind of joy if the opportunity is right there in front of me, right? Farfar raised me better than that.

"I'm kind of in the middle of something," I said, giving the wooden spoon in my hand a cursory turn about the bowl.

A long, awkward silence followed, me holding this glass mixing bowl of cupcake batter that I really needed to get into pans, Lou gripping the handle of her cart, eyes fixed somewhere above my head, with that same look from freshman year—that halfway-between-crying-and-kitty-obliteration look.

Mrs. Bixler strolled in sometime in the span of that awkward moment with her coffee mug and paused. She took one look at the five hundred apples, then one at my face, and started cackling. Set her coffee on her desk, as it was in serious danger of sloshing over, and continued cackling at the two of us.

"Holy smokes, Lou," she finally said when she'd settled down and wiped the last tear from her eye. "This is amazing. What a fantastic idea. Are these all from the leftovers last week?"

Lou forced a smile, still frustrated with me for . . . what? Not immediately knowing what to do with five hundred apples?

"Yesterday."

"*What?*" Mrs. Bixler yelled. "These are from *one day*?"

Lou gave a small, smug nod.

"My goodness." Mrs. Bixler shook her head at the cart. "This is a way bigger problem than I realized." Then she looked back up at Lou in awe. "Great job, Lou. Seriously. This is going to make such a difference."

Then she looked back at me, at the expression on my face, still staring at the reality of five hundred apples in one day, and busted out cackling again.

"Come on, Oz," she said. "We can do this. When are apples on the menu again?" she asked Lou.

"Monday."

*"Monday?"*

I thought she was about to bust out the cackle for the third time, but I caught just a flicker of the same panic I was feeling. The panic of being buried alive by a butt-ton of secondhand apples. But Lou took the opportunity to roll into presentation mode, releasing the flatbed dolly to get her fact-hurling hands in front of her.

The dolly lurched forward slightly, the wheels settling, and Mrs. Bixler and I both jumped a little.

Presentation Lou did not notice.

"Can you imagine all these in the dumpsters outside the cafeteria?"

I realized in that moment that I had no concept of where the school dumpsters were even located, and I wondered how—or why—Lou was privy to this information.

"And again on Wednesday? And Friday?"

*"Three* days next week?" I blurted.

Lou nodded solemnly, mistaking my panic as environmental and not personal.

"Roughly two thousand apples in just over a week. To the landfill." And this is where Lou's eyes gave off a weird glint behind her glasses. "Did you know that food waste—like these apples—releases methane when it decomposes in a landfill? And that, as a greenhouse gas, methane is more than *twenty-eight times* more potent than carbon dioxide?"

She gave us a show pause—not really expecting an actual reply yet, just a dramatic break long enough for Mrs. Bixler and me to audibly blink in unison.

"But it's not *just* the greenhouse gases from landfills. Think about all the energy wasted along the way. The energy and the water and the resources it took to *grow* these. The underpaid, often exploited personpower it took to harvest them, to transport them, to package them. All of it. Wasted. And then it pours methane into the atmosphere. We can't even measure the full scale of the damage."

Lou plucked an apple from the top of the box closest to her.

"And we're only talking apples."

She took a bite. Which, I'll admit, would have capped off a flawless presentation. But I saw her mouth and neck muscles recoil slightly and her chewing slow for just a moment.

The school apples did kind of suck.

Mrs. Bixler let out a deep sigh. "Well, that was uplifting."

Lou, having swallowed her unfortunate bite, gave a sad smile, sheepish—proud of having achieved the desired effect, despite the bleak, crushing reality of her argument.

"Well, it's good I didn't let them get rid of that extra refrigerator," Mrs. Bixler said, taking hold of the dolly. "You are going to rule the world one day, Mary Louise." She started pushing the apples toward the storage room between the culinary lab and the separate classroom next door. "At least I hope so. For all our sakes.

"Oz, I'm guessing you haven't figured out what you're doing with all these," she said, containing one more cackle as she dollied them past me. "So I'll get them in storage for the time being."

Lou raised a smug eyebrow—yes, even her stupid eyebrows were smug, I'm telling you—and crossed her arms over her fluorescent-green Student Council Convention T-shirt.

"Have you?"

I looked down at the mixing bowl still cradled in my arm, the batter drying out around the edges, and I could feel my ears burning magenta the way they do.

"Can I think about it while I finish these cupcakes?"

She left—to go back to AP whatever, I guess—without replying.


Farfar grinned when I came in the door to the apartment that afternoon, the handles of the reusable grocery bag nearly tearing from the weight of the school apples. (Schooples?)

"Much smoother approach, Gubben."

"Stop it. Right now."

He chuckled and uncurled himself from the couch, Koopa dropping from his lap to the floor with a yowl, while I dropped the bag to the floor with a grunt, uncurling my locked-up fingers.

"Were you making new Mii characters?" I asked as he set his blue Wii remote on the coffee table and switched off the TV without shutting down the Wii.

"Just playing around. Wasting time," he said, stretching

his arms above his head without meeting my eyes, his blinding white belly peeking out from beneath his faded blue Hej Hej! shirt.

"Were you out on the truck today?" I asked, pointing to his shirt.

"Just the college over lunch. Busy today, though."

"Lucky. I could've helped."

"Someday, Gubben. Soon enough."

*Soon enough.*

"What is the deal with all of these?" Farfar asked, nudging the schoople bag with the toe of his white sock. Koopa inspected the bag as well before weaving between our feet, ramming her head into our shins in succession.

I let out an exaggerated sigh as I slid my book bag off my shoulders and tossed it behind Farfar to its usual spot behind the couch, where I planned to leave it untouched until the next morning.

"How many apples do we typically use to make filling before festivals?"

"Maybe a few dozen."

"That's what I thought," I said, hanging my head and leaning my hands on the kitchen island.

I'd done the math by that point. The bushels to quarts to tablespoons to donuts. I'd gone back to Mrs. Bixler's room at the end of the day and stared at the overfilled boxes stuffed into the spare refrigerator in the storage room. Mrs. Bixler'd had to remove shelves to get them all in. My cupcakes were done and delivered (and devoured, and I was adequately praised and gushed over by euphoric staff again), so I had no other excuse beyond not wanting to do it.

I couldn't have cared less about telling Lou to forget it. But there was no way I could have let Mrs. Bixler down like that. So I stuffed that reusable grocery bag full of apples from the box on the top and lugged them out to the OG Prius. Mrs. Bixler chuckled from her desk on my way out.

"Thank you, Oz. You're a good person."

I grunted.

"Well," I said to Farfar at the counter, letting out a long sigh, "I'm going to start with a pie. See if my apple calculations are close."

He reached down and plucked one off the top, rubbed it against his shirt. "Maybe two, Gubben." He took a bite and immediately made the same face as Lou. The bad-apple recoil, followed by slow, frowny, regretful chewing. "Red Delicious," he said after swallowing. "One of you is a lie."

"Maybe a little more brown sugar than the recipe calls for."

I redid the pie crust from the night before, this time without the anger—or at least with the anger kept to a simmer, on the back burner, cooking cliché, yadda yadda. Test runs still have destinations, after all: two pies meant two recipients, so I did it right.

Once they'd cooled enough to handle, one went upstairs to Maggie and Juliet (with a Milk-Bone for Winston from the box Farfar kept by the door for whenever they came by from an evening walk). The other to Rhonda at C of C, who was getting ready to serve chicken corn soup to the evening's patrons, as she called them.

Farfar was in the kitchen, staring at the bag of apples, when I came back in around seven.

"How many did you use?"

"Twelve."

"Hmm."

I wasn't even halfway through the bag of apples that hadn't even put a dent in the stash of apples at school. That was an impossible amount of pies.

"We need a new plan, Gubben."

"Mm-hmm."

"We should get some Monster Thickburgers."

"That's a good plan."

## CHAPTER SEVEN

---

# INTO THE APPLES

WE BRAINSTORMED A LIST THAT NIGHT. SPRAWLED ACROSS THE couch, digesting Monster Thickburgers like pythons digesting capybara (they weren't going down without a fight, either), talking through rounds of Battle Mode in *Mario Kart*.

When I walked into Mrs. Bixler's room the next morning before her Foods I class, before I even had a chance to share our list, she'd already solved our biggest concern.

Two old-fashioned mechanical apple peelers sat on the counter. An apple secured in each one.

"I had some gift cards to burn."

"Oh, thank god."

"Terrance already got to one of them."

Sure enough, one of the apples had a strip of skin hanging loose, like a wet Band-Aid, and Terrance was sitting alone at his table, smiling at us sheepishly, trying to contain a giggle.

"Actually, do you think it's acceptable to use him?" I asked. "That wouldn't be considered, like, corporal punishment, right?"

"Hmm."

Mrs. Bixler kept staring at him, hands on her hips. Terrance scratched the back of his head, glanced at one of his friends in their designated kitchen area, mouthed something inappropriate, then looked back at us, attempting to look innocent again.

Honestly, you should've seen the kid. Hair gelled up high in the front, freckles. The whole works. And my god, that giggle. His voice hadn't dropped at all yet, so he could've been anything from a big fourth grader to . . . whatever he was now. But he giggled after *everything*. Like it didn't even register that he was, in fact, in trouble. Or that Mrs. Bixler was *actually* about to hurt him.

"Terrance. Come here."

He did. Giggling.

"Turn the crank, Terrance."

Terrance hesitated, glancing at me for a second, the primitive part of his moderately advanced brain sensing a trap. (He'd been ball-tapped enough times by his friends to smell danger.)

"It's okay, Terrance. Turn the crank."

He did. He seemed pleased at the ribbon of apple skin he'd produced.

"Good, Terrance. Now keep doing it. Faster."

He cranked faster, with a mix of glee and determination, and in a matter of seconds, the first apple was completely peeled. Mrs. Bixler showed him how to take the apple off and held the spiraled fruit up in front of him.

"Dude! It's like an apple Slinky!"

"It is," Mrs. Bixler replied, handing him another apple from a box on the floor and setting the first peeled apple Slinky in a plastic bin next to her on the counter. "Now do it again."

We watched Terrance stab the new apple into place and deftly peel it with another burst of cranks, his eyes lighting up a little with each rotation. He smiled proudly at us, holding up a second apple Slinky.

"Perfect, Terrance. Now keep doing it."

He did. It was our best class of the year to that point.

"I feel kind of bad," Mrs. Bixler whispered to me when they filed out at the end of the period, Terrance jumping to slap the top of the doorframe.

"I don't know. He seemed to like it," I replied, looking at the two huge plastic bins on the counter filled with peeled, cored, Slinkied school apples.

"He did, didn't he?" She was quiet a moment. "I think I've at least found a way to justify passing him."

When I showed up again a few periods later for independent study, I was like a man possessed. Terrance's impassioned peeling was a huge boost.

With the room to myself for a while, I could do some serious damage. I had our list taped to the counter, my school iPad propped up next to it with tabs to recipes Farfar and I had looked up the night before.

I had my earbuds in, relistening to the first Harry Potter—thinking if I was going to be working with school apples for the foreseeable eternity, at least I'd relive some favorites along the way.

I decided to start with the cider—our plan to wipe out as many mediocre apples as possible with minimal effort. Quartered, peels on, into a giant stockpot. Boom. Chuck in a few cinnamon sticks, a scoop of cloves, a few oranges, and brown sugar. Cover with water. Get those puppies simmering for a few hours, and I'm on to the next thing.

I had eight giant stockpots going at two different stoves

around the room before firing up the oven, and in no time I had Terrance's entire supply of peeled apples mixed with lemon juice and sugar and flour and into foil pans and a huge bowl of oats and goodies mixed up for apple crisp.

With a bajillion trays of crisp in the oven and another bajillion gallons of cider simmering away on the stoves, I was back to peeling the remainder of the original bajillion apples. Harry was awestruck at Platform 9¾, and I just kept thinking, *I can really do this*. Not the apples—but *this*. Farfar would have been proud of me, running that entire show on my own, no stress, no getting overwhelmed—granted, no customers waiting in line—but dammit, I was ready for this.

I didn't see or hear Lou come in. I nearly flipped the peeler off the counter when she finally tapped my shoulder.

"What are you listening to?" she said. Not *Sorry*, you'll notice.

"Metallica."

She curled her lip for a second, like she was smelling a fart, and then jumped right back into her own thoughts.

"You know what we should do?"

I looked around the room—I couldn't tell if she'd even noticed the eight giant stockpots steaming, or the dirty mixing bowls in the sink, or the overwhelming perfume of baked apples and cinnamon hanging in the room like a delicious fog.

"What should *we* do?" I finally said.

"I was thinking some kind of healthy apple muffins—something you can grab and eat on the go."

I blinked. Healthy apple muffins.

"I read this article," she continued, my silence an invitation apparently, "about that school LeBron James started in Akron. Did you read it?"

I did not.

"Every day when the kids walk in, all kinds of breakfast options are just waiting for them. No cost, no strings, just good food if you need it. So I was thinking, what if we did that, too? What if we had muffins in the lobby or in the commons?"

All I could think about was Lou, showing up even more, wondering if I'd finished the muffins. Every single day.

"Do you know what they could grab and eat on the go?" I said. "An apple." I held one up for effect, Lou style.

Lou raised her eyebrows, unimpressed. Today's T-shirt: HAPPY VALLEY GIRL SCOUT CAMP, SUMMER 2017. It was pink. She folded her arms across it.

"Go ahead." She nodded at the apple in my hand, calling my bluff.

I took an obnoxiously large bite and willed my facial muscles not to betray me.

How could an apple—in September, in the heart of freaking apple country—be bitter?

I imagined a giant, dreary orchard, all the trees gray and gnarled and crooked on the side of a hill overlooking the same textile mill that's belching out smoke next to my pumpernickel bakery. They're all picked by Gringotts goblins in denim overalls and thrown into the back of old panel trucks headed for the school distribution center.

Lou smiled the whole time, taking great pleasure in watching me swallow that apple.

"Good?"

I rolled my eyes and threw the rest of it into the trash.

"That's going on *your* carbon footprint."

She was doubly annoying, because not only was she right

55

about the stupid apple, but her muffin idea was a really good one. I loved the idea of offering breakfast—delicious breakfast—to students, with no strings attached. Just grab one if you're running late, or hungry, or out of money, or whatever.

But "we" had to figure out apple muffins now, too.

"Don't you have class now or something?"

She waved me off.

"Statistics. It's a hybrid course, so I can do most of it online, and I'm way ahead."

Right, right.

"I already have AP Calc BC, so I didn't really need it, but I thought it'd be easy and look good on my transcripts, and the hybrid means I don't have to show up to class if I'm ahead, so I can use the period to work on other stuff."

It seemed I was the other stuff for the time being. I thought about that first week of freshman year, the extra math.

"I cannot imagine ever choosing to take double math," I said, shaking my head and setting another apple in the peeler.

"If I'm going to get into a top college, I don't have much of a choice. The College Board site says most schools look at difficulty of schedule over everything else."

"Wait, so do you even like math?"

"I like it as much as any other subject, I guess. And it weighs more than other electives for my GPA."

I laughed to myself, thinking back to that first week of freshman year again. The beginning of Lou's epic GPA quest.

"What?"

"Nothing," I said. "That just sounds terrible, personally."

She pulled at the end of her long braid. "I don't see anything wrong with wanting to work hard and do my best."

"Speaking of which," I said, tossing another apple Slinky into the bin and wiping my hands on a dish towel to go check on the cider. I also checked on the trays of crisp, which still had a good twenty minutes, before glancing up at the clock above the door behind Lou's head. There was still a lot of period left, and it appeared she wasn't planning on leaving. I grabbed another apple and set it in the peeler.

"So what colleges are you applying to?" I asked, knowing that this was a question seemingly against my own self-interests. But that's just the kind of guy Farfar raised, isn't it?

As she was about to answer, I slid the peeler toward her and grabbed her hand, putting it on the handle of the peeler.

"Oh," she said, looking startled at first, like she'd never seen it before—despite the fact that I'd literally been peeling apples with it right in front of her since she came in. But she gave it a few cranks, seemed moderately pleased with the results, and kept going.

I pulled over the second peeler while Lou talked through every college visit she'd taken that summer, and I will tell you, it was a ridiculous number of visits—enough to break into categories. Small, selective liberal arts schools: Franklin & Marshall, Swarthmore, Bryn Mawr—I'll be honest, I'd never even *heard* of most of them. Huge research universities: Pitt, Temple, Maryland. (I'd heard of them.) And the dream, "the Ivies": UPenn and Princeton.

I got the pros and cons of each one, the highlights of the tours, the average SAT scores for incoming freshmen, everything. I didn't understand or care about most of it. But once she got going, she went through some serious apples. Maybe not Terrance's level of productivity, but between the two of us, we were well into the last bushel when Mrs. Bixler finally popped in toward the end of the period.

"It smells amazing in here. I could get used to this."

I pursed my lips, and she freaking winked at me.

"Mary Louise, nice to see you again. Here to keep Oscar in line?"

Lou smiled.

"He seems to have everything under control," she said, placing another apple on her peeler. "I'm better at ideas."

I didn't know whether it was a compliment to my competence in the kitchen or an unintended slight, an acknowledgment that I was the manual labor behind her vision—or in her world, if it could be both. But she laid out her whole argument again for muffins and grab-and-go breakfasts, and watching Mrs. Bixler's face, I imagined this was exactly how I'd gotten roped into this in the first place.

"That *is* a great idea," Mrs. Bixler said, nodding appreciatively and looking to me for confirmation. "What do you think, Oz?"

"Muffins are next," I replied, lifting the new bin full of apple Slinkies.

"We're going to have to figure out what to *do* with all this," Mrs. Bixler said. "Besides the muffins, of course."

"I've already got a list of ideas," Lou replied.

"Of course you do." Mrs. Bixler smiled warmly, shaking her head.

"Do you have time to meet up after school today? We probably shouldn't slip into the weekend without a plan."

"I can stay for a bit today," Mrs. Bixler replied. "Oscar?"

". . . Yup." I let out a deep breath that neither seemed to notice.

The bell rang, and Lou had to head off to lunch, and for a few minutes, I finally had my kitchen back. Even if it was technically my lunch, too. I had muffins to make, apparently.

I'd just gotten into the flow of Harry when Mrs. Bixler returned, a grinning Terrance in tow.

"Pulled this one out of lunch detention. Mr. Thoman was more than happy to release him into my care."

Terrance gave me a small wave, still smiling.

"You know what to do," she said, nodding toward the peelers on the counter. "I'll be right back."

And damned if Terrance didn't rub his hands together and dive right into cranking out more apple Slinkies at an alarming rate. I stared for a moment before deeming it safe to put my earbuds in to start dicing up the finished Slinkies for muffins.

When Mrs. Bixler returned, she had a Subway bag, three subs swinging in the bottom.

"Terrance, you strike me as a meatball guy," she said, pulling out one of the subs from the bag and holding it up.

"I love meatball!" he replied, slowing his cranking just slightly.

We ate together, Mrs. Bixler engaging Terrance in a string of questions about his life outside school—baseball and video games and, not surprisingly, his weekend pass to Adrenaline, that trampoline place in York. But also, get this, helping his grandmother with yard work and household chores multiple times a week.

I felt like I was staring at a gelled-up version of myself as a fourteen-year-old—hates school, hates having to sit still, can't (or maybe won't) focus on tedious book work. And really, I could get just as lost in their chatter while I worked. It wasn't terrible.

By the end of the period, we were down to a big grocery bag of unpeeled school apples—about the same size I'd brought home the night before—and I had a dozen trays of apple muffins ready to go into the oven.

"Can I come back for lunch detention next week?" Terrance asked when the bell rang.

"Terrance . . ." Mrs. Bixler sighed but smiled warmly at him. "That, I am sure, is a distinct possibility."

Terrance gave a little fist pump, waved, and jumped and slapped the top of the doorframe on his way out.

## CHAPTER EIGHT

---

# PLANS

THAT EVENING, I CLIMBED THE STEPS TO THE APARTMENT, READY to rant about Lou and apples and pointless meetings. An hour and a half after school on a Friday to discuss what she'd basically already decided: cider to the football game, crisp to the community, muffins for Monday. Then another hour to transport cider—via cart and very careful steps—down to the stadium concession stand.

But when I swung the door open, my eyes landed on Farfar's ponytail, hanging over the back of the couch, and the *Mario Kart* menu waiting on the big screen.

"Order a pizza, Gubben," he said, lifting his beer can in the air without turning around. "It's Race Night."

There'd been a lot of Race Nights over the years.

All through elementary school, when more often than not I'd slump off the bus at the end of the day, exhausted and defeated, trying to will the tears not to spill from my eyes, Farfar would be there. Waiting on the sidewalk with a grin on his face and a Wii remote already strapped to his wrist.

"It is about time, Gubben," he'd say, as though it weren't the same time every day. "Are you ready for a whooping?"

He'd waggle his eyebrows, and I'd go tearing past him to the little stoop next to Maggie's gallery, the walk-up to our apartment. "Ha! You're the one who's going to get a *whooping!*" I'd say it how he said it, with that long double *O*, and just like that, I could put the emotional drain of the day behind me.

Somehow it still worked.

"Okay, Gubben, this time you have to pick your least-favorite character with your least-favorite vehicle."

I picked Peach, to which he raised his eyebrows.

"You hate Peach, Gubben? Seems a little . . . misogynistic."

"What are you talking about? Princess Peach is a horrible representation of women—how many times does she wait for Mario to save her?" I realized I sounded a little like Lou. You know, if Lou's rants ever extended into classic Nintendo characters.

Farfar picked Toad.

"Seems a little . . . *mycogynistic,* doesn't it?"

He just chuckled. "Stupid mushrooms."

I picked the Super Blooper for Peach, Farfar picked the Booster Seat for Toad, and we spent the next hour laughing and yelling disparaging things at the screen.

Afterward, with Toad still standing atop the podium, the volume now way down, and an empty pizza box on the coffee table, the week finally started bubbling out of me.

Farfar's eyes were drooping, and I didn't mean to rehash the same argument I'd been having with him for months, not after another perfectly timed Race Night. But after consecutive days with Lou, I still felt like people looked at me and saw some kid struggling with his future. I wasn't *lost*. I wasn't struggling with what path to choose.

"I can *see* the damn path," I said, betting he was beyond calling me out for swearing. "I know *exactly* what I want to do. I'm ready to do it."

His eyes slid to mine, bleary.

"And don't tell me *Someday, Gubben.* I could be doing it right now, and we both know it."

He was quiet for a second.

"I know, Gubben. I know."

He laid his head back on the cushion, and closed his eyes, and I thought he was out. But then he finally said something different. Quiet. Up toward the ceiling.

"I don't know how you can be so sure, Gubben. . . . When I was your age, I wasn't sure about anything." Then, "I'm still not. . . ."

And then he really was out.

I sat there, thinking for a few minutes while his snoring grew more pronounced and rhythmic, Koopa's heavy breathing filling in the gaps, three kitty snores for every one of his. I cleaned up a little bit. (Fine. I moved the pizza box from the coffee table to the kitchen counter.)

Then I went into Farfar's room to grab the thin quilt he kept folded at the foot of his bed. And—I don't think I'd ever told him this, but—like I did often when he was out somewhere, I sat on his bed by his pillow.

We don't really have any photos—family photos—hanging up around the apartment, beyond my yearly school pictures magneted to the fridge.

But this one—this old photo of Amir, I'm not even sure from

where—taped to the side of his dresser beside his bed. You can't even see it when you walk by the room, and even if you're *in* the room, it's usually partially hidden by the side of his pillow. This one single picture of Amir, years and years before—years and years before I even showed up—smiling and squinting into the sun.

I looked at it all the time, this little part of Farfar he mostly kept to himself. I don't know why. Or why I never mentioned it to him or asked about it. I wish I'd asked more.

Before I switched off the Wii and the TV, I hit the home button on the Wii remote, glanced back at Farfar, and put the TV on mute. I pulled up the Mii gallery. Just to see.

Me and Farfar, obviously—with his gray ponytail and beard, his looked remarkably close to real life. Maggie and Juliet, from when they came down for Little Christmas the year after Farfar got me the Wii.

Our weird, humanized attempts at Koopa and Winston.

Moomin characters and Harry Potter characters and random weirdo characters I thought were funny at the time.

And then, there they were, at the end of the line. His new additions.

First, Amir—also remarkably close to the real thing—at least, the real thing in the picture taped to his dresser.

Filip. My dad. His son.

Linnéa. Farmor. A younger version than the one in my memory.

Older-looking characters, Lars and Gunilla, I was pretty sure were his parents. Leo and Marianne, I thought were maybe Farmor's.

*I'm still not. . . .*

I didn't know what it all meant, if it was just some strange way of torturing himself. Part of me wanted to delete them all from the gallery, pretend they were never there. Instead, I turned off the Wii and the TV, laid the quilt over just Farfar's legs so I didn't disturb Koopa, and went to bed thinking about what he'd said. How, at seventeen, I was so sure of exactly what I wanted. And at seventy-five, after a lifetime of choices, Farfar still sometimes felt lost.

He's never felt lost to me.

By the time I got up that Saturday, there was no trace of Race Night. The pizza box and the beer cans were all down in recycling already, I assumed, the living room was all straightened up, and Farfar was at the stove, humming along to the radio turned low on the counter.

"About time, Gubben," he said, placing a chocolate chip pancake on the stack of six on the plate next to him. "I thought you were going to sleep the whole day away."

I checked my phone: 8:22.

"I thought *you* were going to sleep in," I said, grabbing a plate from the cupboard and taking the top three pancakes off the stack. "After the *whooping* you took during Race Night."

He just chuckled and poured the last of the batter into the hot pan with a satisfying sizzle, one of my favorite sounds in the world.

"Someday, Gubben."

I was three bites into my pancakes, scrolling mindlessly through my Instagram feed—mostly other food trucks and chefs and food bloggers, an occasional pic from Jorge or Jesus.

"Ready to work the college today, Gubben?"

"Oh, god." Farfar turned back from the stove, stunned, I think. "Not you," I clarified.

The text from Lou: what's your address? I can be there in 15 Then: no need for 2 cars 🌑💜

Again, even with the reality of having peeled five hundred apples, having made eleventy-billion quarts of cider, twenty-plus trays of crisp, and over a hundred and fifty muffins—in two days, mind you—I was still pretending none of it was happening. Even if I kind of liked the focus and intensity required to create so much in so little time.

What I *didn't* want was to spend more time with Lou. At school. On a Saturday.

"Lou's coming," I said into my hands, which were at the moment covering my face.

"What does that mean, Gubben? *Lose-coming?*"

He sat down next to me with his own stack of pancakes, Koopa leaping up onto the table to purr and watch him eat.

"Lou. Mary Louise. She's picking me up. We have to go to school and get all the apple stuff."

I filled him in on our marathon session the day before, the meeting after school I didn't want to talk about when I got home and he'd saved the day by announcing Race Night.

"You did all that in one day, Gubben?"

I nodded. He was quiet for a moment while he took a bite of pancakes.

"That is impressive."

I nodded again, trying, despite myself, to contain my smile.

"And this Lou girl is coming here in . . ."

"About ten minutes."

He was quiet again. Took another bite.

"I should probably put pants on."

"We should probably both put pants on."


I was sitting on the stoop next to Maggie's gallery in the bright morning sun (with pants on) when Lou pulled up along the curb in her tan Malibu. She held her hand up in a quick wave and then just stared at me, the Malibu still running.

I sighed and got to my feet, then stood at her passenger-side window until she finally rolled it down.

"You have to come inside," I said, admittedly without the charm or smile Farfar was expecting of me. Lou, understandably, looked skeptical.

"This is not my plot to kill you," I said.

"It's not much of a plot to get me inside, either," Lou replied, and with some amount of surprise, I laughed.

"Farfar, my grandfather, he said I have to invite you—guests—inside."

I've never wanted to not be talking so much in my entire life.

Lou checked the time on her phone, looked at me funny again, and finally turned off the car.

Farfar was at the stove—with pants on—when we walked in. Koopa, somehow sensing visitors, was right next to the door when we stepped inside, and Lou jumped a little when Koopa immediately butted her head and rubbed her flanks into Lou's shins, meowing for attention from the newcomer.

Our furry little welcoming committee.

"Hello! Hello! Come in, come in," Farfar said. He turned around with another plate of chocolate chip pancakes he'd somehow managed to whip up in no time, his smile wide, his charm turned up to festival levels. For what should have been just a quick, polite intro before we took off.

"Lou, this is Farf—my grandfather."

"Erik," he said, setting the plate on the counter and smiling even wider. Farfar shook her hand with both of his around hers. "Lou?" He said it the same way he said *whooping,* a long double *O,* like he was pursing his lips for a kiss. *Loooo.*

"Lou," she confirmed, beaming back. "Nice to meet you."

"Did you have breakfast yet, Looo?"

"I . . ." She hesitated, unable to lie over such a dumb little thing. But Farfar pounced on it.

"Sit, sit. You have to have breakfast before a big day."

"We're just going to sch—" I started to say, but Farfar shot me a quick, stern look I didn't get very often, so I shut up.

Lou, for once unable to argue, slid onto one of the stools on the other side of the counter looking into the kitchen. "These look amazing," she said, "but I definitely can't eat three of them."

Farfar was quick to make people feel comfortable. Besides me in that moment, I guess. He grabbed two more plates and forks.

"How about one for each of us, then," he said, taking the top two off the stack with a fork and putting one on each plate. "I can always eat another chocolate chip pancake."

I could, too, in truth, so I slid onto the stool next to Lou. Farfar grabbed the butter and syrup, watched the two of us awkwardly prep our pancakes with this audience of one, grinning at us across the counter.

"So I have a proposition for the two of you," he said after we'd each taken our last bite. "You have many many trays of apple crisp to deliver, yes? And only one regular car?"

We both nodded. I hadn't figured out exactly what he was up to yet.

"How about if we all take the truck to your school? They will all easily fit on the munkar racks, right, Gubben?"

"Wait . . . the truck . . . as in the food truck?" Lou asked, looking at me now.

It was an excellent idea, actually—we'd be done in no time. Plus I'd have Mr. Charm-Britches here to handle most of the chatter. And my little denial of reality wouldn't mess up our prep time for the truck. You see, I thought for a sly, sneaky moment that *I* was using *him*. Oh-ho-ho, I was a fool.

But it wasn't *Lou's* idea—not how she had it planned out in her head, and I could see her struggling with that at first.

"He's right," I said to Lou, helping—with what little influence I had—to nudge her into Farfar's plan. "It would be way easy . . . and no chance of apple goop getting in your car."

It wasn't until we were pulling into the school parking lot—Farfar driving, Lou in the passenger seat, me on the small bench behind it—that he revealed the next part of his dastardly plan.

Farfar would argue later that it was a business decision—that good help was hard to find. *You'll understand someday, Gubben.* That I'd already established how bright and hardworking and ambitious Lou was. And the eye candy had a soccer tournament outside Lancaster that day.

"So this seems like a pretty one-sided proposition so far," Lou noted, smiling warmly at him now from the passenger seat—now that Farfar'd spent the whole ride asking pointed questions about college visits and future plans. "You just offering to help and feeding me pancakes. Not that I don't appreciate it," she added quickly.

69

"Happy to help," Farfar said, smiling. "I am sure you will return the favor one day."

I stayed silent during that ride. Not sure if either one of them noticed.

Mrs. Bixler was waiting on the sidewalk for us when Farfar backed the truck up to one of the side entrances near the culinary classrooms. This was the best change of plans ever for her, and it was all over her face.

"Mr. Olsson!" she exclaimed when we hopped out of the truck. "I didn't know you would be here today!"

Farfar waved—a little sheepish, maybe?—and said, "Happy to help," for the second time.

We had to wait on the sidewalk while he and Mrs. Bixler gushed about what amazing kids we were, and such big hearts we had for wanting to help and—okay, so that part wasn't the worst. I'm sure Lou received that kind of praise all the time, but it was not the norm for me. It was all right.

Once we were finally inside, Lou and I got the trays of crisp from the fridge, all covered with foil lids and stacked in a tower where Mount McIntosh once stood. We pushed them outside on carts while Farfar and Mrs. Bixler continued chatting on the sidewalk in the sun, Mrs. Bixler cackling more each time we came by.

"What happened to all the cider?" I asked when we went back for the last load of trays.

"What do you mean?" Lou said, pausing to give me a confused look, one hand on the fridge door, the other on her hip. "You helped wheel it down to the stadium."

"They went through *all* of it?"

"They went through all of it. The Music Boosters couldn't

believe we were just donating it to them for the concession stand—especially after they tasted it." Lou smiled then, somewhere between smug and genuinely excited. "They begged for us to do it again. If they sold out on a warm night, imagine how much they could go through when it gets colder."

I will tell you, I did not imagine. I was, in that moment, incapable of imagining more.

"Are you annoyed? Because you're also kind of smiling." I looked up at Lou, grinning back at me. "It kind of looks like it hurts, actually."

I shook my head, feeling my lips betraying me and my ears getting warm.

We pushed the last of the crisp outside and loaded it onto the racks inside the truck. Farfar was right. Plenty of room. Lou looked around the truck as I slid the last one into the munkar rack, like she was just now considering what actually went on inside the truck.

"It's a lot cleaner than I expected," she said, her nose crinkled, her hands on her hips.

"Um. We clean it."

"No, I know. I just always pictured food trucks in general to be much dirtier on the inside. All the grease and stuff." She kept looking around the kitchen space, as though she might spot our hidden stash of rancid safety violations.

I just shrugged. "I mean, if this were your business—your profession—you'd want to take care of it."

Lou just nodded, ran a finger along the racks with our trays of crisp. "Yeah. I guess you're right."

I don't know that she was doing it as a more rigorous inspection, her absent gesture, but that's what it looked like, and I was—too sensitive or not—suddenly ready for her to be out of our truck. Out of my space.

By ten-thirty, that was almost a reality. All crisps delivered, Lou gone (for the rest of the weekend, at least). Despite Lou's extensive list of possible places to donate our apple crisps, we knew Rhonda could make good use of all of them at the Council of Churches. Between hot lunch and dinner service seven days a week and Meals on Wheels, there were plenty of apple needs to be filled.

And Rhonda said she'd give extra trays to volunteers who delivered meals throughout the community. A lot of these volunteers, she said, had been there for meals themselves at one time or another, so the crisps would surely be appreciated.

Boom. Apple crisps done. Cider done. Muffins on standby for the Monday-morning test run of Grab-N-Go. Five hundred apples had been headed for the landfill. Instead, in two days (of an unimaginable amount of peeling and prepping and cooking and baking), those five hundred apples were back out in the world, spreading joy instead of methane.

Lou had C of C somewhere on her list, but she had no idea they'd take care of everything in one shot. And she really had no idea Farfar and I would be greeted so warmly there—or that Rhonda's warm hugs would be automatically extended to her as well.

I couldn't tell at first if she was relieved when we climbed back into the truck, or if she was still trying to figure out what had happened.

"How does she know you so well?" she asked, in the passenger seat again.

"We stop there all the time," Farfar said, navigating the truck through the narrow alley the last few blocks to the apartment. "Oscar takes food to them almost every night."

"Food . . . that you make?" she asked, turning to look at me. "Like the apple crisp?"

I nodded. "I don't get any kind of hours for it, but yeah."

It didn't feel as satisfying as I thought it would, my swipe. And not because I caught Farfar's disappointed eye in the rearview—though that felt pretty awful, too. Lou's face remained blank as she nodded, but her cheeks darkened.

"I drop off any leftovers from the truck," I said, trying to push past the moment and pretend it hadn't happened—kind of my specialty this year, really. "Rhonda says the Meals on Wheels folks love finding donuts in their boxes."

Lou, then, looked back to Farfar without responding and put on her presentation smile.

"So that was five hundred apples we just saved," she said. "Five hundred apples that were headed for the landfill, all that energy, all those resources wasted, just to rot and pump more methane back into the atmosphere."

"That is very impressive," he said. "You should both be very proud."

I *was* really proud. I'd worked my butt off to make that happen. I'd put those five hundred apples back out into the world spreading appley joy instead of methane. My carbon footprint was practically *nonexistent*. Like my feet were made entirely carbon-free, which led to some strange images in my head.

And that *should* have been the perfect place to leave things. Lou goes home to track her hours and upgrade her résumé and transcripts, and I do not. Perfect.

"We might be a little shorthanded today, Gubben," Farfar said as the truck pulled into our garage space behind the building. And there it was—the final piece. Like he was just casually moving on to the next item on the day's agenda. No ulterior motive in mind at all.

"Shorthanded with what?" Lou asked, on cue.

"We're working the truck over at the college today. Should be lots of people out. Beautiful day."

"We'll be fine." I jumped in, finally realizing what he was doing—what he'd been planning all morning.

"Can I help?" Lou asked before I could finish.

"Jorge usually helps run the window on busy days. Take orders. Handle money," Farfar said. "But he is so busy with soccer in the fall."

"I could do that," Lou said, glancing at me but primarily talking to just Farfar now. "I mean, I'm probably no help cooking anything, but I think I could take orders."

"No no," he said, waving her off. "I'm sure you are very busy. Oscar has told me how involved you are."

"I'd love to help. You helped us out so much this morning, and I'm really not too busy today. . . . I can work on application essays and AP stuff tomorrow."

She glanced at me one last time.

"And honestly, it sounds kind of fun."

---

## CHAPTER NINE

# IT'S A HARD STORY TO TELL

IT WAS A LITTLE CLUNKY AT FIRST, WITH LOU AT THE WINDOW. SHE was a little slow taking orders, a little too thorough in making sure she had all the rullekebab toppings right, which confused some of the customers more than anything.

But mostly, she just didn't know our preferences the way Jorge did. At first she kept sliding me tickets, which took some serious effort to decipher, and I was starting to get frustrated.

"Can you just yell these out to me?" I said after the fourth ticket came my way, one with half a dozen munkar on it. "Your handwriting's impossible to read."

She stared at me for a moment, confused, looked down at the ticket in her hand, then back up at me.

My face burned and I turned back to the fryers with a quieter "Please."

"Keep writing mine, please, Looo," Farfar chimed in, sliding a rullekebab order onto the window counter next to her. "Yell his. Write mine. My old-man ears can't hear you anyway."

Farfar kept praising her, coaching her up, as if she really needed additional self-assurance to be our cashier.

"You are a natural, Looo," he said at least three times in the first half hour.

And, point of fact, she was *not* a natural. Not that first day. Jorge was a natural, with his easy smile and quick pleasantries. Lou was, at best, presentation polite.

"Are these supposed to have cinnamon sugar?" she even asked me once, after being anointed *a natural.* "Or just plain sugar?"

I pulled another tray of proofed dough from the rack and dropped it onto my workstation, pretending not to have heard her. Farfar jumped a little bit at his station, squirting kebab sauce onto the counter, then giving me the side-eye. I took a deep breath to pull myself together.

She was doing fine, I tried to tell myself while I dropped the next basket into the fryer. No mess-ups. Not overwhelmed. Engaging enough with customers. And she did seem to enjoy it. I could see it on her face when I finally turned around with another handful of orders, like she was genuinely excited to hand off hot donuts to waiting customers. And when she looked up at me with this flushed smile, there was no trace of Presentation Lou.

We sold out of munkar by midafternoon. Farfar had spent a lot of time at Gettysburg over the years and had a good sense of the best times to show up—one of the things I would have *loved* to learn from him senior year instead of sitting in school all day.

"Pretty good day, Gubben, eh?" he said, slapping my shoulder while I cleaned up my station.

"I can't wait to get to college," Lou said then, leaning out the window. Even though I didn't remember Gettysburg even being on the list she'd rattled off while we were peeling apples, she'd been transfixed for the past fifteen minutes, pointing out the redbrick castle-looking Glatfelter Hall and the more modern Science Center, and all the smiling students traversing the lawns in between.

"I guess you don't need to go to school for this?" she said, straightening up again inside the truck. "I mean, I guess a business degree could be helpful . . . or culinary, obviously. . . ."

Was she really asking, or just monologuing?

"But Oscar seems to be able to do everything already. . . ."

Somehow her words felt good and bad at the same time.

"No. No special degree for this," Farfar answered. "Just hard work. And love. . . . But I did all of that. University." Lou turned around then, leaning back against the counter to look at him. "I was a civil engineer in Mariehamn."

"So you went to college. . . ."

"In Sweden. Uppsala University. Founded in 1477. Very beautiful . . . and very hard."

"So you were a civil engineer in Sweden. . . ."

"In Åland," he corrected. "Technically part of Finland, but a Swedish-speaking island. The boat ride to Stockholm is much shorter than to Helsinki."

He loved talking about Åland to new people, and Lou was hanging on every word he said. Truthfully, I liked hearing it all, too.

I still want to go back and see everything. Farfar promised, after graduation.

"So . . . what made you decide to come here?" Lou looked around, arms out, indicating not just here as in America, but here as in the food truck, when he'd clearly had a much more prestigious career—one that could have easily transferred across the Atlantic.

"Just following my dreams," he said, his head down now, his voice quiet.

It broke my heart a little, watching it. No one should be hiding that much shame and guilt on their faces when the answer is *following my dreams*.

To Lou's credit, she didn't push for more of an answer. She only had a very small part of the story.

*I* only had part of the story for a long time, really.

It's a hard story to tell.


It came out to me in pieces over the years, our story—how Farfar got here. How I got here later.

Farfar lost his son (my dad) when I was only four, though I didn't know much about the details around it. My dad wasn't exactly a permanent fixture in my life.

Farfar told me about the overdose years later. That night we stayed up late talking, after a really miserable food truck festival in Harrisburg.

But I could tell, even then, that his information wasn't first-hand, either. That it'd been told to him by Farmor, after the fact. Because he'd lost his son years before that, by his own doing—which I know sounds harsh, but I'm just repeating his words.

He'd moved to the US years before, before I was even born, before my dad's problems really spun out of control.

Some run-ins with drinking, Farfar'd said, throughout high school. Stashes of pot he'd found in my dad's room, then ceremoniously flushed down the toilet in front of him. Some other things, too, but he wouldn't go into it any further with me. He waved me off at that point, remembering, going dark and quiet the rest of that night—not his typical chattiness after a few beers. I didn't bring it up again for a while after that.

Maybe things were spinning out of control even before Farfar left. Maybe that's a big part of the guilt.

Because I know that's a big part of it. The guilt—of leaving, of blowing up his family, even if the fuse was already lit.

I know that.

But he has to know he doesn't need forgiveness from me. Ever. I would never change the fact that I'm here. With him.


There was a lot to unpack from Lou's question, though—*So . . . what made you decide to come here?*—a lot of complicated story.

I was so young when I came here—so lost—that for most of our years together, *I* never even thought to ask that question. *Here* was just where we lived, and in my limited memory, things had fallen apart where I lived before. My mom was gone before I was even a year old. Found a job on a cruise ship—a big industry there—and never came back. My dad was a mess.

As a little kid—once I was here, with Farfar—here was just home. Where else would you be, right? As a little kid, you don't have that sense, those layers of before and before and before, you know? And even Farmor's pained birthday cards faded after a few years. She needed to start over, too.

Farfar fit in the biggest piece for me, years ago, after some kids on the bus said some ugly things about the building we lived in—the Pride flags and the lesbians upstairs. I was maybe ten, eleven at most. Probably a little earlier than he'd originally intended—if he'd planned it out at all. Or if maybe he'd intended to keep those parts, those chapters of his life, entirely separate, separated by pages that would never overlap.

I remember hearing somewhere—I think maybe a show we watched together, a comedian—how you don't just come out *once*. That after that first big time, there's still every single time you meet somebody new, or talk to another family member, or an old roommate or whatever, after that.

But grandfather to grandson is not one he could have planned for, is it?

"You don't have to say anything, Gubben. I just wanted you to know. I didn't want to live with the lie anymore."

He looked deflated that night, like he could've disappeared into the couch, like Koopa was just resting on a cushion, not his small globe of a belly.

"I lived with that lie for so long," he said, more to Koopa than to me, it seemed. Or to himself, maybe. "I gave up my whole family to tell the truth. Lost them all . . . and then I got you. It was like a second chance. And I haven't screwed it up, Gubben, I haven't. I've been good. . . ."

His voice was thick, his accent even heavier through the emotion.

"But I don't want to pretend, Gubben. Not again. Not to you."

I knew that somewhere in that mess, he was asking for forgiveness. I just wasn't sure why. I mean, he was right. He'd been good. Better than good. He was my whole life.

At most, I wondered if maybe my parents would have been happy with this life of cooking and baking and *Mario Kart* and quiet contentment. From the little I know of my mom and dad before, they could've used *quiet contentment,* I think.

I just can't imagine how hard it must've been for Farfar to live that lie—to have lived with it for such a long time. To live that lie all the way into a family.

Guilt on top of guilt on top of guilt.

A lot to unpack.

He's never told me much about Amir. I don't know if it's too hard. Or (what scares me, honestly), he really *didn't* intend for those two worlds to ever overlap.

Maggie's told me, though. I wish I could have seen it, even if the idea is too weird for Farfar.

"I don't believe in soul mates," Maggie said to me, just recently. "There's not one perfect match for you out of the eight billion on this planet. Relationships take work. It takes time and energy and patience and forgiveness and more patience to maintain love over a lifetime."

Then she smiled.

"But I've never seen any two people make it look as effortless as Erik and Amir."

That's something I'd like to have witnessed.

---

## CHAPTER TEN

# A RARE FIGHT

I HAD A ONE-DAY REPRIEVE FROM LOU AT SCHOOL ON MONDAY and a one-day reprieve from apples, which were being collected that very moment in the cafeteria. One day to throw my earbuds back in and return to my gourmet sandwich experiment.

Which was promptly interrupted.

"O. Tell me these are your muffins, man." Jorge's head was in the doorway, half-eaten muffin in hand.

I grinned, slid my knife through the onion I was preparing to caramelize, then jumped a little as Jesus's head appeared from the other side of the door. He held a muffin in each hand. "Please tell me this isn't just today."

I thought of Lou, stationed by the trash cans in the cafeteria. "I don't think it's just today."

Jesus took an enormous bite from his right-hand muffin and disappeared into the hallway again. Jorge stepped inside, took another bite of his own.

"Dude, these are amazing. The attendance secretary had to yell at kids sneaking out to get them on bathroom passes."

I smiled, noticed the wooden hall pass tucked beneath his arm.

"Would you be one of those kids?"

"Not important," Jorge replied, pushing the last bite into his mouth and tossing the wrapper in the trash. "But I should probably get back to class." He paused on his way out the door. "Is this in any way connected to Lou harassing people in the cafeteria?"

I let out a long sigh. "It is."

"They really are terrible apples."

"They really are."

"You're a magician, O." Then, "If you have extra time, grab-and-go donuts might be nice, too."

The onion slice just barely missed his head.


On Tuesday, during independent study, Monday's haul of second-hand apples showed up in the culinary lab, an annoyingly satisfied Lou behind the cart, and the whole process started over again.

Which is basically how it went for the next month.

Though I will say, on that Tuesday we established a pretty impressive rhythm. With the Booster Club's pleas for more cider for Friday night, I more than doubled the number of stockpots I had going at one time, which knocked out a huge chunk of the apple supply.

Terrance was back to help, too, both during his Foods I class and during "lunch detentions" with Mrs. Bixler. Give the kid a meatball sub and he could do anything. Or, at least, a hell of a lot of cranking. I decided to teach him some basic knife skills, which he was surprisingly okay at. He didn't lose any fingers.

And the muffins—well, it turns out Jorge was right: high school kids like free muffins. "They're the talk of the school, Oz," Mrs. Bixler confirmed over lunch, Terrance nodding enthusiastically beside her, sauce at the corner of his mouth.

So not too bad, honestly. People loved my muffins. My cider. My crisp was going out into the community and doing its crispy-gooey thing for people who probably deserved a little more crispy-gooey in their lives. And my interactions with Lou were minimal outside of her dropping off a new mountain of apples, once she must have figured out I didn't need to be micromanaged.

And then Farfar changed all that.

When I walked into the apartment after school on Thursday, he asked about crisp deliveries.

"Lou said she put towels down in her backseat and her trunk," I explained, thinking it was perfectly reasonable for her to handle the deliveries after I'd spent almost my entire week on apples again. With all the cider and the increased muffin demand, it wasn't nearly as many trays as before.

"Gubben. Text her. Right now."

"What? No. Why?"

"Gubben. Text her. This is your project. This is the job you agreed to. You should be there helping. Not here. . . ." He held his arms out, looked around the apartment, like he couldn't even imagine what I might be up to.

I stood there, mouth open, trying to process *your project, the job you agreed to,* that I was somehow shirking *my* responsibilities.

"I know you did all the cooking, Gubben. But the job is more than just cooking." When I still couldn't manage a reply, he grabbed his keys from the basket on the counter. "Did she stay at school?"

"I don't know. . . . I think she said she had to run home for towels first. . . ."

It sounded worse out loud, which made it that much more frustrating, knowing Farfar was right.

He stared at me, one eyebrow raised, hands on hips.

"God. Fine," I finally said, huffing, as Koopa hopped down from the top of the couch and brushed against my leg, yowling.

"I know, lilla kissemissen. I don't know what he is thinking, either." And Farfar scooped her up so they could both stand there and judge me.

My phone buzzed a few seconds after I hit Send.

"She says that's too much to ask. She's fine."

"Tell her you're learning to drive the truck, if it makes her feel better."

"I already know how to drive the truck."

"Good, then I'll drive. Let's go."


Okay, so the truth is, I knew I was being selfish. But it had been a long week. Farfar wasn't aware of this yet, but with all my focus on Lou's project, I was sinking big-time in my other classes. Even if the apple situation was starting to work pretty well, it still felt like every different person had a different idea of what I needed to be doing, and not a single one of them was what I really wanted to be doing.

So yeah. I should've stayed after that Thursday to help Lou with the crisps. But when I hit my locker at the end of the day, fresh off a lecture from Mrs. Shue after English and another blank reading packet tossed onto the top shelf, I needed to just go home. Be done. At least for a little while.

Instead, I was riding in the passenger seat of the truck, my arm draped over the open window, staring at the too-familiar buildings on the trip back to school. Back to Lou. Back to apples. Back to a parking lot that was still probably half full of teachers' cars.

Lou already had the trays of crisp on carts when we pulled up, waiting by the side doors we'd used the last time. She stood with Mrs. Bixler on the sunbaked sidewalk, each of them munching on one of the muffins I'd made over lunch that day.

Farfar honked the horn in greeting, as if this were some fun little adventure, while I slipped out of the passenger side to start loading up the trays without a word.

"Do people know it is two teenagers behind this whole apple business?" Farfar asked, once we were loaded up and pulling out of the parking lot again, with another little farewell honk to Mrs. Bixler.

"You know, I've been thinking about that," Lou said, turning in her seat to face him, her arms out in front of her—they had plenty of room to move inside the truck, I'd noticed. "And it's actually really frustrating. Because everyone's happy about free muffins, and hot cider at football games, but those are just selfish outcomes, you know? I'm not sure they really know or care about the environmental impact—or the *community* impact," she added, waving an arm toward the trays behind her. "That there's a much bigger benefit than *Hey, free muffins!*"

Farfar nodded, inviting her to continue.

"I don't know how to create that *awareness*, of *here's why we're doing this*. I'm—we're—creating all the change and no one else really has to change their behavior at all, you know? Besides *throw your apple in this box instead of that trash can*, which, honestly, I still have to remind people of every single day."

"Mm. Sounds like you need better marketing," Farfar said. "Maybe some rebranding. Some . . . enlightening signage maybe."

"Methane-Reduction Muffins?" I suggested from my perch behind Lou's seat.

Farfar chuckled. "Sounds like muffins that make you stop farting."

"Not-in-a-Landfill Cider?"

"You really have a knack for this, Gubben. Our business is in good hands."

Farfar and I went back and forth with more terrible marketing ideas, but Lou's brain was spinning with legitimate plans.

"Maybe some poster-sized signage behind the muffin baskets with actual figures on methane reduction," she said, looking up at the roof and tapping the end of her braid against her chin.

"Eat a muffin, save a polar bear?" I was on a roll.

"Hmm. That might actually be a good sign header," Lou replied, more to herself than to me.

"But you don't think *Hot Landfill Juice* will sell at football games? I bet Terrance and his buddies would be all over it."

I've spent a lot of time with Terrance since then. I stand by that statement.


Rhonda hugged us all again—including Lou, who seemed a little more prepared for it this time—when we dropped off all the crisp trays.

"You should've seen it," she said, shaking her head and smiling. "I had my husband run out and get a few buckets of vanilla ice cream to go with it, and people couldn't stop talking about it at dinner that first night. Everyone laughing and talking over each other about favorite desserts and what their grandmothers made when they were kids. . . ."

Stories. Everyone wants to tell their stories.

"That's some good apple crisp, mister," Rhonda said, pinching my chin like a loving aunt. "Keep 'em coming."

That was the best thing I'd heard all week—the one thing that felt like my doing. My decision.

"Maybe we can meet with Mrs. Bixler tomorrow after school again to brainstorm," Lou said on the ride back to school, still thinking about how to make a bigger impact—how to move people to understanding, to action, beyond eating a recycled muffin. And I just thought, *Of course, what's another hour tacked onto the end of another week to hear you talk?* Because it's not like I could've just said no thanks with Farfar right there.

And then, as we pulled back onto the high school campus to drop Lou at her car, Farfar tacked on even more.

Jorge and Jesus were walking back across the parking lot from the soccer fields at the end of practice, laughing and shoving their younger brother Javy between them, when Jorge spotted the truck and waved.

"How is the eye candy today?" Farfar asked after Jorge trotted over from his car.

"Feel more like the visual fiber right now." Jorge smiled and wiped his face with his sweat-soaked shirt. "What are you guys doing here in the truck?"

"Just delivering more of Looo and Oscar's apple goodies."

Jorge looked past Farfar, noticed Lou in the passenger seat, me on the bench behind her. His smile instantly widened.

"More muffins tomorrow, right?"

Lou smiled and nodded. I stared coldly back at Jorge.

"O told me he's thinking of doing grab-and-go donuts next week, too."

Farfar and Lou both turned to look at me before I had time to flip him off, which made him smile somehow even wider.

"Another away game this weekend?" Farfar asked, leaning out of his window again.

"Yeah, over in Lancaster, like an hour away."

The two of them chatted soccer for another minute—we never missed their home games—until Javy honked the horn from the backseat of their car. We watched Jorge jog back and throw his soccer bag to Javy. Jesus honked again as they pulled away, and Farfar made his move.

"It is supposed to be another beautiful Saturday, Looo, if you are available to help."

"Really?" Lou replied.

"Parents' Weekend at the college. Lots of people. Lots of paying parents."

"I would love to!"

"Then we can do like last week," Farfar said. "Come early. I'll make pancakes, we'll deliver to Rhonda, then go to the college."

"Okay!" Lou said, beaming. "Thank you!" She climbed out of the truck, looking up again after opening her car door. "See you Saturday!"

Farfar waved, smiling back so that the sides of his eyes wrinkled into pronounced crow's-feet, and I waited until Lou was in her car before I climbed back into the passenger seat without a word, relieved that Farfar turned on NPR to fill the air.

"You really had to invite her again?" I finally blurted that night, sitting over a plate of frozen meatballs and mashed potatoes Farfar had whipped up when we got back from dropping Lou off at the school.

"What do you mean, Gubben?" he asked, his last meatball pausing midflight to his mouth. "Why does she irritate you so much?" Then he grinned this stupid grin. "I am starting to think . . ." He waggled his stupid eyebrows, and honestly, I wanted to slap them off his stupid forehead before his meatball completed its flight.

"Would you stop it?" I said, white-knuckling my fork. "This isn't an act—*I don't like her.*"

His brow furrowed while he chewed, shaking his head; then he let out a deep breath.

"Gubben, I am just teasing you. I am sorry. Only teasing. Because you are sometimes fun to tease, Mr. Brooding Baker Man. But," he said, pausing to stand and grab a beer from the fridge and popping it open with a hiss. "Now that we are having, as you kids would say, *real talk* . . ."

"Kids don't say that."

He waved me off.

"We do need a third person on busy days, Gubben. And Jorge is not available during futball season."

"Soccer season."

"Yes, I will let the rest of the world know."

He settled into his spot on the couch while I cleared our meatball plates.

"You might not know this yet, Gubben, but it is not easy to find reliable, hardworking people to help."

"I get that—not that you've really wanted to teach me any of it yet, but—"

He cut me off with a wave of his Wii remote. "And yes, Gubben, I like Looo. She is engaging, and polite, and hardworking, and very intelligent. And even if you are for some reason annoyed, Gubben, look at the amazing things she has gotten you to do this year."

I couldn't even look at him. It was like, if someone else made the decisions for me, maybe I could do amazing things. Just not on my own.

"If you really hate her so much, Gubben, I will look for someone else to help. . . . Or, better yet, maybe *you* could find somebody else reliable to help. But that is one of the first things you will learn, Gubben—one of the first things I learned from Amir—how hard it is to find good help."

Farfar rarely mentioned Amir, even just their time on the truck together, and it threw me. I had this strange thought that Farfar was once the Padawan to Amir's rullekebab Jedi. *He* was the one, coming from engineering, who had a lot to learn. I wondered if Amir was ever a dick to him about it.

"It is not just a fantasy, Gubben, just driving around and making donuts and making people happy. Do you know what to do with the wastewater from the truck? How to dispose of and replace the fryer grease? Do you know how to fix the engine if the truck breaks down, Gubben? Do you even know how to change a flat tire?"

I didn't look up, and he kept going.

"Do you know how to order more supplies and ingredients, Gubben? To do bookkeeping? To do taxes? Do you have any idea how to pay taxes, Gubben?"

I'm not sure if he could tell that I was crying by that point. It took all my willpower to keep my voice steady and my eyes clear. I felt like a stupid little kid, again, coming in from the bus after a day of stuttering over words, only now Farfar wasn't making it better.

"There is so much to learn, Gubben. I know you are ready to take the truck out every day, but there is so much to learn."

I stayed quiet for a moment, trying to compose myself, steady my voice—because every time I went to open my mouth, I could feel the back of my throat close up and my nose burn.

"That's *my* whole point, Farfar. Why aren't I learning all this, instead of stupid school? I know it's not a fantasy. . . ." I had to stop there—that track, for some reason, was leading back to tears.

Farfar took a deep breath, and I couldn't tell if it was controlling his frustration or something else, but I didn't like it.

"Because you *must* finish school, Gubben. Non-negotiable. This food truck is not a sure thing. This is not a guaranteed living. And I do not want you to be . . . stuck, Gubben . . . if something happens."

He took a long swig of beer, emptying the can, and wiped his other hand down over his face.

"I am trying to do this right . . . to raise you right, Gubben. I did not do so hot the first time, you know. . . ."

That prompted another trip to the fridge, and in that moment, I kind of wanted to join him—to have something quick and easy to reach for that would blur out the rest of the night.

92

I didn't. But I saw the appeal—and it actually kind of terrified me.

"Maybe Looo is right, Gubben. Maybe you could go to culinary school, or get a business degree. . . ."

That was enough to shake me out of my longing look at his stupid beer.

"Now? *Now* you're telling me I need to go to college? Are you serious?"

He wouldn't look at me at first, which made me even angrier.

"A few months from finally being finished . . . from starting *my* dreams—even if I clearly don't know anything—and you're telling me I should pay money for another nightmare?"

"Don't be so dramatic, Gubben," he said, taking another long pull and now flipping through characters on the screen. "College is not a nightmare."

"Not for you, maybe! Or . . . your precious fucking Lou!"

His head snapped from the screen to me, his nostrils wide, but for some reason, he didn't say anything about my swearing, which threw me, honestly, because I'd used the big one on purpose. Instead, after a moment, he took one hand off his Wii remote and placed it on my knee.

"HACC has a culinary program right here, Gubben. Less than five minutes away." He gave my knee a shake. "You would be *phenomenal*.

"They have business, accounting classes, marketing, Gubben. . . ."

He seemed like he was getting excited talking about it, revising my plans for me, which—and I know he didn't intend to—only made me feel worse.

"Shippensburg is a short drive. Penn State Mont Alto. All have good business programs, Gubben, if you wanted to get a bachelor's. And I am sure you could get in, even if you wanted to start at HACC first, save a little money."

"Have you been researching this?"

"Sure, I've looked into it, Gubben. I like to know the options. I like to do the research. It is important to know these things—to be aware of different possibilities."

He'd gone into full-on sales pitch, it felt like, and I could just hear Lou's presentation voice behind it all.

"You have to think of it as an investment in your business—in *our* business, Gubben. To ensure your plan works . . . and to have options if it doesn't. It is investing in your future, Gubben."

"I don't learn that way," I said, quiet, finally selecting my character. Finally agreeing to the game. "Why can't you just teach me these things? I'm ready to learn. From you."

"Gubben . . . ," he said with a long exhale.

Not *Someday*. Just *Gubben*.

It felt like for so long he'd been trying to slow me down, that I was pushing too hard and that our time would come. Just be patient.

But now the time was almost here, my someday now imminent, and he wasn't ready for it.

## CHAPTER ELEVEN

# A DIFFERENT SIDE OF LOU

LOU PULLED POPSICLE STICK NUMBER ONE FROM THE SELECT-O-Tron 3000 the next morning, Friday. Demonstration Speeches. And from the very beginning, she was different.

When she stepped in front of the podium—not behind, in front—she calmly stated that she would be demonstrating how and when to administer Narcan, or naloxone, and that she would need a model for the demonstration. Her friend Meredith was absent, and she locked eyes with me as soon as she started talking. And so, after looking around the room for a minute, hoping for eager volunteers that didn't exist, I raised my hand a few inches off my desk and joined her at the front of the room.

She had me lie down on the floor on my back in front of her, and she explained that I was a potential overdose victim, and my mind swirled. I was almost positive the two of them, she and Farfar, had never discussed it—the reason *I* was here, with him, four thousand miles from where I was born.

She knelt down beside me then, clinical, holding up the bottle of Narcan she said she kept in her purse. "You insert the nozzle into the nostril, until your fingers touch the victim's lips and the bottom of his nose."

It was a weird weird feeling, having her fingers resting there, this thing in my nose—this thing, I realized, that maybe could have prolonged my dad's life, some fourteen years earlier. What would my life have been then?

I noticed also, stupidly, that Lou's fingers smelled a little bit like chocolate, and I got this picture of her, sneaking mini–Hershey bars at her locker before class, and I kind of had the urge to smile, which would have been wildly inappropriate at the moment, obviously.

She rolled me onto my side then, making sure my left hand was tucked under the right side of my face. Lou explained all the signs and symptoms of an overdose.

I'd thought for sure her demo would be something with the apples—with food-waste reduction and the environment and everything. I mean, the apples were all-consuming, right? And I was prepared to sit there and seethe over the credit she'd take for all my work. Like I was looking forward to it, even, which I realize seems kind of sick. Was this for some kind of Girl Scout badge? Her whole presentation was un-Presentation-Lou-like. Not the usual prepared animation and eye contact. This was calm, serious, detached, even.

(And yet her fingers still smelled like chocolate.)

"So, Lou, I've thought about this for a long time, but I've just never done it," Mrs. Sommers said, almost sounding disappointed in herself. "How do you *get* the Narcan? Can anyone just get it and carry it on them?"

Lou nodded, still businesslike. "Most pharmacies will give it to you without a prescription. I get mine at Target."

And then Bryce decided to pipe up from his corner of the room.

"So, do you just, like, walk around waiting to come across a junkie to save?"

". . . Yep."

"Doesn't that, like, encourage drug use?"

"Nope."

And then she just sat down. Without further argument. Without a battery of facts and statistics, because I knew she had to have them.

I was still up front, on my side, propped up on my elbow now. Mrs. Sommers seemed surprised, too.

You take for granted people like Lou, to speak up and call things out—to be the conscience for the room, even if you roll your eyes at it, even if it sometimes goes overboard into obnoxious territory.

"Two of my uncles are EMTs," Bryce continued then in our silent affirmation. "They say it's a joke. The same people OD'ing and getting saved again and again. I mean, if people want to waste their lives, let them."

Again, silence, a few nods of approval, until Lou finally spoke, without even looking up from her desk.

"The *DSM*-5 classifies addiction as a disease. I doubt you'd say the same thing about cancer."

Bryce, feeling like he'd gotten the upper hand, swelled in his chair. "Except you don't choose to give yourself cancer. You make the choice to shoot up."

"Does anyone in your family smoke?"

"My grandpa does, but—"

"So when he gets lung cancer, we should just let him die, right?"

"How about you shut up about my grandpa."

Lou didn't raise her voice. Didn't glance at anyone else for confirmation, not even Mrs. Sommers, who still looked like she was deciding on the right thing to say as the official adult in the room. I was still on the floor, watching Lou.

It was all wrong.

Lou got an A, I'm sure, just like I did when I gave my speech later.

But it was all wrong.

Jorge followed her presentation, which was awkward at first—and maybe it *should've* been—but he's such a natural in front of people. We were ready to smile, and Jorge delivered.

"I've loved Garfield since I was a little kid," he began, behind the podium, and it was like the whole room exhaled at once. Lou stared out the window. "My abuela always read the newspaper, and she'd save the comics for Jesus and me. And one summer, when I was trying to help my mom shelve books at the library—I was not much help, believe it or not—I stumbled upon the entire collection of Garfield treasuries."

And Jorge proceeded to teach us all how to draw Odie.

"He's much easier to draw than Garfield, actually."

Then he drew two different Garfields on the whiteboard—one how we all know him, the other how he looked in the very first strips.

As a Moomin fan, I was into it. Honestly, everyone was, except for Lou, who drew her Odie without any affect whatsoever.

Bryce's effort to be funny a few speakers later landed with way more people than I expected, but I don't know, maybe if someone else had given the same demonstration, I would've laughed, too. Lou definitely did not laugh at his "How to Pick Up Chicks" demonstration, though.

He also needed a "volunteer"—Teegan Sponseller, the girl he'd been flirting with, obnoxiously, every class since the beginning of the year, and who wholeheartedly obliged, laughing three clicks above normal and slapping his arm at least once a period. (I could usually catch Mrs. Sommers shooting an imploring look at Edward in the back of the room each time.)

But at the end of "Bryce's Five Surefire Moves"—which included "The Wink and the Gun" and dropping his pencil in front of Teegan's desk and slowly bending over in front of her to pick it up—as Bryce concluded with "The ladies cannot resist" and one last wink-n-gun, Lou put her hand in the air.

"What if she's a lesbian?" she asked before waiting to be called on.

"Uh, I don't know. Ask if I can watch?"

Teegan's mouth dropped open and her eyes went wide with fake, gleeful shock before she busted out laughing, along with half of the rest of the room.

Lou flushed, looking like she was about to lunge out of her chair. "Do you ev—"

"It was just a joke, Lou. God," Bryce said over her as he returned to his seat.

Jorge rolled his eyes without laughing. I shook my head, seething, but also—I'm sorry to say—silent.

Mrs. Sommers let out a long sigh. "Stick around after class, please, Mr. Heiland." To which Bryce rolled his eyes and shook his head, as though he were the one being unfairly targeted.

I thought of Maggie and Juliet, what they would think if they'd witnessed the whole thing. If they'd be disappointed that I didn't call it out. Just Lou. Again. They'd told me stories, the two of them and Farfar, of driving down to DC for the Millennium March together, when Amir was still alive, of demonstrating on the capitol steps in Harrisburg for marriage equality more than once. I'd even attended the first Women's March with them in DC a few years ago, Farfar and I both in pink hats Maggie had crocheted for us. And yet here I sat, silent at Bryce's *joke*.

I can't figure out what I would do if I could redo that moment. But I want to think I'd do something besides wish I could be done with all of it.

I wish I'd done *something*.

But maybe I'm not the only one. I don't know what Mrs. Sommers said or did when she held him for a few minutes after class, but I bet maybe she wished it were more, too. Because even if Bryce got in trouble, I knew his ignorant comeback to Lou would be mythologized in his group by lunch.

I was last to give my speech this time, after Teegan's present-wrapping demonstration, and by that point, everything felt wrong.

I got an A on it. I was on a roll.

I could do the whole thing without really even thinking about it. How to use an apple peeler and prepare an apple crisp. I had my ingredients already measured into small containers, a couple of school apples from the perpetual stock, everything I needed to run my own little cooking video. Basically, what I'd be spending the entire rest of that day doing in the foods room.

But the whole time, I kept thinking about how stupid this was. Doing this mindless thing for an easy A in speech?

As I was literally demonstrating *how to turn a freaking crank*, all I could think was how I had no idea how to fix an engine. I had no idea how to safely and legally dispose of fryer grease.

As I demonstrated how to press a knife down to make slices, all I could think was how I had no idea how to "do bookkeeping" or "do taxes." I didn't even know what "the books" looked like.

But I could peel the hell out of an apple.

"Nicely done, O," Jorge said at the end of the period, right after my speech, popping a raw apple slice into his mouth and giving me a fist bump.

"You too," I said.

And even if that was true, nothing felt right about it.

# CHAPTER TWELVE

## DOUBLE WHAMMY

"I LOOKED UP UPPSALA UNIVERSITY," LOU SAID THROUGH HER first bite of pancake the next morning, no trace of the strange detachment or the disgust from speech the day before. "It's, like, one of the top one hundred universities in the *world.*"

"Very hard," Farfar said, trying not to smile. "I wasn't sure I was going to make it sometimes."

And then she asked another million probing questions about classes and college life and the university system in Sweden, all through our drive to school, to C of C (with hugs from Rhonda), and back to the apartment for a pit stop before we hit the Gettysburg campus for Parents' Weekend.

"*Sötnos?*" she whispered to me, her brow furrowed, while Farfar was in the bathroom. She was crouching to scratch his lilla sötnos beneath the chin.

"'Sweet nose,'" I explained. "It sounds weird, but it's a little . . . lovie term you'd use for a cat."

Her face lit up, and she even tried cooing "Lilla sötnos" to Koopa, which somehow caused this eruption of purrs out of her, like Lou had unlocked some secret code.

Lou looked up again, grinning, her long braid hanging in

front of her so that Koopa could bat it playfully with her paw. "And *lilla . . . missy kissy?*"

"*Lilla missekissen*—kitty cat. *Lilla* is 'little.' "

When Farfar came out of the bathroom and saw what was happening, his face split open into this wide, goofy grin. He picked up Koopa and rattled off the longest, most ridiculous string of Swedish baby talk he'd ever produced—to Lou's stunned delight.

Honestly, it was the weirdest flex I'd ever seen.


"I looked up Åland, too," Lou said, back in the truck, one arm out of the passenger window where mine usually rested, on our way to the campus. "And I saw that it's really an archipelago, but can you get to all the little islands? Do people live on them?"

Farfar burbled with information the whole ride over, and somehow the two of them kept this up all day, even through a heavier lunch rush than we expected and a steady flow of parents and college students throughout the afternoon. Lou never wrote a single ticket down for me—remembered to just call them out—and still somehow kept their conversation going. Hours of it.

I mean, I was supposed to be annoyed. Here she was. All day. Again, in my space. But it was like listening to an interview—and okay, a really good interview—full of all these details about Åland and Sweden I didn't know and all these stories from Farfar's childhood and teenage years I'd never heard before.

I pumped out munkar order after munkar order and listened.

I could kind of start to understand why he liked her so much. I'm not saying *I* did. But I could understand why *he* did.

———

I was in the middle of cutting butter into a bowl of flour to make pie dough on Monday when Lou came in. No apple cart—just a book bag over her shoulder and a T-shirt from *Pippin*, last year's musical.

I had my earbuds in, but she didn't really say anything anyway—just a small wave as she sat down at an empty table and pulled out a binder and got to work on . . . something.

And she just . . . *stayed*.

I kept glancing up at her while I kneaded my pie dough in the bowl, while I rolled it out on the counter, while I rinsed things off in the sink, but she just stayed and worked.

I kept waiting for the catch, for her to dive into her next presentation.

But she didn't.

She just kept showing up and staying then, whether she arrived with a flatbed of secondhand apples or just herself, day after day.

It was weird.

But it was kind of fine, too.

I didn't tell Farfar that.


It was later the following week, the beginning of October, when Terrance showed up early to lunch detention. That's just the kind of reliable go-getter Terrance was. Honestly, I wasn't even sure if he was getting lunch detentions every time or if he just showed up.

These people just kept *showing up*—my study was getting

less independent by the day. It was hard to brood with all those stinking people around. It's physically impossible, actually, to brood next to a meatball-sub-consuming Terrance.

Anyway, that day when Terrance rolled in early for apple-peeling duty, Lou was still in the room, finishing up something that involved binders.

Terrance stood next to me, staring, silent. When Lou finally finished what she was doing a minute after the second bell and packed up all her stuff, she left without a word to either of us—just a small smile and wave and she was out the door to lunch.

Terrance had an apple placed in his peeler before he finally looked up, one eyebrow raised.

"You like her?"

"What?"

"She's pretty hot." He was whispering, conspiratorially, one side of his mouth curling up to match his one eyebrow. "And isn't she, like, super smart or something? Double whammy."

Double whammy.

"Uh, I'm not sure you're her type," I said, hoping to end this conversation quickly.

"Dude, I have a girlfriend," Terrance replied, as though that were an obvious, well-known fact.

"You have a girlfriend?"

"Of course I have a girlfriend," he said in his high-pitched voice. He looked genuinely confused. "She goes to Franklin. Eighth grade. She's smoking hot. She lives two houses down from my grandma."

That was such a scattershot of oddly fitting facts—his grandmother's smoking-hot eighth-grade neighbor—I just nodded slowly and gave him an awkward thumbs-up and tried to get back to muffins, hoping *that* was now the end of the conversation. Or at least that Mrs. Bixler would roll in and relieve me of the conversational burden.

But a minute later, with a new apple in the crank, Terrance looked up again with the same one-eyebrow/one-sided grin dealio.

"So, *do* you like her?"

"Um. No."

"Man," he said, shaking his head, disappointed. "*Double whammy.* There's something wrong with you."

And there was. That very next day, there was definitely something wrong with me. Because stupid Terrance had to point out how hot he thought Lou was, and now I couldn't stop . . . *looking* at her. Trying to see what he was seeing. Like one of those old Magic Eye things where you have to kind of cross your eyes to really see it, which, you know, was awkward when she glanced up and caught me staring and I nearly banged my face on the counter, reaching for another apple.

I didn't want to. Honestly. I just wanted to work in my kitchen with my earbuds in and Harry playing and ignore that she was again sitting at that table with her head down and her binders open, a Mini-THON T-shirt on with the sleeves rolled up a couple of times.

And all right. I don't really know how to say this next part, but . . . okay.

When she was working again, and I could safely sneak glances at her and regain my composure, she kind of had her arm out in front of her, like she was leaning forward to write, you know? And with her sleeve rolled up and stuff, I could kind of . . . *see*. Like, under her arm. Up her sleeve. And (oh, söte Jesus) . . . okay, so . . . I could see her *bra*. And it was *green*.

Which is completely irrelevant information—and in no way makes it acceptable—I know. I'm sorry. But it was too late. I saw it.

And then, I don't know, I couldn't stop seeing it.

She just kept *writing*, and I just kept *seeing*.

It was like my brain finally saw the stegosaurus in the Magic Eye, like it jumped right out at me, which, god, is not meant to be some pervball code—*I finally saw the stegosaurus, boys, heh heh heh* . . . God. Sorry. Again.

And then, even when I tore my eyes away, forced them back to the apples at hand (again, not a euphemism; Jösses), my brain just kept running (like it does), trying, *against my will*, to imagine her in just her underwear, which is ridiculous, because, I mean, who does schoolwork, *in school*, in just their underwear? That's like some kind of nightmare.

As was this.

"Tell me how this sounds," Lou said, without looking up, thankfully, as I was in the middle of what must've been a minutes-long gaze at the stegosaurus (well, it *has* to be the euphemism now, doesn't it?), and I nearly took off my thumb with the paring knife that lurched back into action.

I have no idea what she read to me, maybe a college application essay. I just know, when she was done reading, I said, "That's really good. Really. Good."

Which somehow, against all laws of Lou, was enough to appease her, and she went back to work. And I did, too. Really. I willed myself to focus on the rest of the prep work for the day's load of crisps, and I did not look up again at all until right before the end of the period, when Lou paused to stretch her arms above her head and then twist around in each direction in her chair to crack her back, which should have a zero percent likelihood of causing someone to picture that person in their underwear, but there it was again. *Green.*

Which is also when Terrance strolled in, early again, for lunch detention, and saw me staring. He leaned against the door-frame with his arms crossed while Lou packed up. I could feel my face and ears burning while I tried desperately to busy myself with anything not facing either one of them—which meant opening a random cupboard full of plates and drinking glasses, pretending to consider them, then closing it again.

"Thanks for your help," Lou said on her way out the door, and I turned around to wave a wordless *You're welcome*, but she was already in the hallway, her Mini-THON T-shirt disappearing out of sight.

Terrance kept grinning at me, still leaning against the door-frame, before finally entering the room without a word. He set his book bag on the table Lou had just vacated, stretched his arms above his head, then twisted his stupid soup-can torso side to side before walking up to the counter and grabbing an apple from the box.

"How's it going?" he asked, turning the crank slowly and grinning at me.

Stupid Terrance.

## CHAPTER THIRTEEN

---

# FARFAR'S BUSINESS
# SCHOOL: FIRST LESSON

"GUBBEN. I NOTICED THE TIRE IS FLAT ON THE PRIUS."

"What? What time is it?"

I will tell you what time it was, because I remember the numbers on my clock: 5:03. In the morning. A full hour and forty-two minutes before I'd normally get up for school.

It took a while for my head to clear, even with Koopa yowling around the side of my bed between Farfar's feet. My head was swimming with *green,* and it was deeply unsettling.

"Wait . . . why are you in here?" I rasped.

"Your tire, Gubben. On the Prius. It is flat. Get up."

". . . Can I go to the bathroom first?"

"Yes. Brush your teeth. And don't forget pants, Gubben."

Pants. Right.


My head still wasn't totally clear after a stressful trip to the bathroom and a few sips of the coffee he'd already brewed— what time was he even up, anyway?—probably not helped by the fact that I was standing in our back alley at quarter after five, under the incessant orange hum of the streetlight.

"See, Gubben?" he said, his travel mug in hand with the lid

off. "Flat tire." He blew on his coffee, the steam disappearing in swirls.

"What happened? It was fine yesterday."

"I don't know. Maybe you ran over a nail on your way home. But we've got to fix it before you go to school, yes?"

"I could just skip school."

"Don't be an idiote, Gubben. Get the manual from the glove compartment."

"Wait, don't you know how to do this?"

"Yes. But you don't. Get the manual."

I stared at him for a moment, my wheels barely starting to turn (ha). He was awfully demanding this early in the morning, definitely not his usual easygoing self—I figured he probably could've used another hour and forty-two minutes of sleep himself.

I somehow found the right pages in the manual under the pale glow of the overhead light, but I did not have the patience to try to decipher the text while Farfar calmly sipped his coffee on the back bumper of the truck, just inside the open garage door. The diagrams showed to tear apart the trunk, so that was where I headed.

The trunk was emptier than I remembered—I'd thought I still had a pretty good compost pile of old locker debris going in there, but there was nothing, which should have been a clue, but again, 5:15 a.m.

And I will say, lying on the damp patchwork of asphalt and cracked concrete of the alley under a streetlight is not even remotely pleasant. But it does wake you up. With Farfar's minimal guidance, I had a pretty good sweat going by the time I had the back end in the air with the little jack and had wrestled the nuts off the wheels.

"Look how tiny that is," I said when I'd gotten the spare on and the car back on all fours.

"Tiny ones work, too, Gubben."

"That's not right," I said, shoving him away by his shoulder. "Dirty old man."

"Tires, Gubben. Tires. Teenage hormones cloud your brain." But he couldn't keep that stupid childish grin off his face.

"What do we do with the flat?"

"Just put it in the trunk. We'll take it to get patched after school."


No Terrance in lunch detention that day, thank god. I don't think I could've handled his stupid grin, too, not after my brain had gone totally haywire on me overnight and Farfar had me in the alley at five.

No Lou either, during independent study, for the first time in nearly two weeks. I didn't know if she had a test in statistics or what. I just knew I had a full day to pull myself back together.

Which didn't actually happen, of course.

I'd decided to whip up munkar dough—something I could do without even thinking about it—to try my hand at apple fritters. See if they might be a worthy addition to the seasonal munkar menu. Or—stupid Jorge—how feasible they might be as a grab-and-go option. But between . . .

- thinking about what we could do running the truck full-time
- imagining what my ideal storefront would look like
- wondering where Lou was

- being annoyed that I was wondering where Lou was
- thinking about all the things I didn't know how to do, for the truck *or* a storefront
- listening to Ron play Wizard's Chess in my earbuds
- and unwelcome, intermittent snapshots from the Green Dream

. . . it was like ten stories all playing at once.

The fritters were delicious, at least.

But it was not the head-clearing process it normally would have been.

Farfar was on his laptop when I came in from school that afternoon, which was not the norm, either, his feet propped on the coffee table, a can of beer next to them, Koopa nesting on the top of the couch cushion behind his head—which *was* the norm.

"The Prius drive okay on its tiny wheel?" he asked, closing the laptop lid and reaching for his beer.

"It was fine. I felt like it was wobbly or something, but it was probably just in my head."

I dropped my bag behind the couch, gave Koopa a quick head scratch, and headed to the fridge for a drink of my own. Grape soda, obviously.

"So where do we go to get the tire patched?"

"Nowhere. Your tire is fine."

"What?"

"It just needs to be inflated. We can do that here."

"Wait. What? I thought—"

"Come on, Gubben," he said, getting to his feet and rubbing his hands together. "Let's go change your tire again."

Farfar had me pull the compressor out of the garage, explained how to fire it up, and let me reinflate the original, perfectly unpunctured tire, all while I was still struggling to figure out what the heck was going on.

"So, did you get up before five in the morning just to let the air out of my tire?" I asked while pulling the jack out of the trunk again.

"Of course not. I did it last night, after you were asleep."

"You were asleep before me, though."

"I am an old man, Gubben. I get up to pee at least three times every night."

"That's messed up."

"You had to learn someday, Gubben. Felt like the right time."

I *was* pretty happy at how quickly I got the tires switched the second time, though I wasn't about to tell him that.

"Can you *not* do this again tonight?" I said when I had the last nut tightened, the spare hanging from my hand.

"Come on, Gubben," he replied, clasping me on the shoulder and turning to head back upstairs. "Let's get cleaned up. You've earned yourself a Monster Thickburger."

That was the first lesson in Farfar's Business School—his unspoken apology/concession for our argument the week before. Though at the time, I thought he was just screwing with me.

Honestly, it was probably both.

## CHAPTER FOURTEEN

# I AM NO LONGER MAKING
# ANY DECISIONS FOR MYSELF

"O, LAST HOMECOMING, MAN. YOU'RE GOING TO THIS ONE, right?"

This from Jorge, a week later in speech while we were supposed to be practicing our recitation passages.

"Do you remember the last time I went to homecoming?" I said quietly, shaking my head.

Jorge started giggling, remembering, which mostly made my case for me.

I know the jerk told Farfar about the Cha-Cha Incident our freshman year. I was there, crying, when he showed Farfar the video in our living room. An undersized fourteen-year-old boy with a mop of dirty-blond hair, who'd somehow found the courage—after relentless pressure from his twin-brother friends—to step onto the dance floor for what they said was a dance you couldn't possibly mess up. *It spells out one-step directions,* they said. *Everyone does exactly the same thing, so you can't stand out,* they said. And I'd like to submit for the record that I did not mess up. I Cha-Cha Slid with focus and determination and *tenacity.* To the point that I had no sense of the fight brewing between two delinquent seniors behind me.

So, of course, when bystanders gleefully recorded the melee

on their phones, some of them caught this incredibly focused, determined, *tenacious* Cha-Cha Slider in the background, Cha-Cha Sliding, oblivious, for the duration of their stupid fight.

I can't say it technically went viral, but it definitely went local-viral. There were a couple of other a-hole seniors who called me Cha-Cha till winter break.

"We'll sit out the Cha-Cha Slide this time. Just in case," Jorge said, failing, badly, to not smile. "And Jesus and I can get you a female."

"I do not need you to get me a female. Now recite your stupid passage already."

Jorge glanced around, then leaned in, grinning. "I did hear you've already got yourself a female."

"What?"

"Don't be coy with me."

"What. On. Earth. Are you talking about?"

"Really, bro? Are you telling me she hasn't been showing up to your little cooking club every day?" Jorge nodded in Lou's direction. Lou, thank god, was focused on reciting her passage to Meredith.

"It's my *independent study,* ass. It's basically AP Culinary Arts. I'd like to see you try to—"

Jorge held up a hand, shaking his head and rolling his eyes. He'd heard my rant enough times to know the mille-feuille line.

"And what about Lou, Mr. Muffin Man?"

"Mr. Muffin Man?"

"Mr. Muffin Man," Mrs. Sommers chimed in—we hadn't noticed her circling over to our desks. "Who can't seem to focus with his partner on the task at hand."

"I'm sorry, Mrs. Sommers," Jorge said, smiling, knowing,

somehow, that we weren't really in trouble. I did not have that particular Spidey sense in the classroom. "That's my fault. But listen to this—Oscar here is planning to miss his last homecoming. Senior year. Isn't that terrible?"

She looked at me sympathetically. "Actually, that sounds like a fantastic idea. School dances are the work of a malevolent being, Oscar. You're wise to stay away."

"See?" I said.

"Now get back to your recitations."

Jorge continued to stare at me when Mrs. Sommers walked away, this stupid, expectant look on his face.

"She drops off all those stupid apples," I finally said, a little louder than I intended, but neither Lou nor Mrs. Sommers seemed to notice. Mrs. Sommers was already listening to part of Lou's recitation at her request for guidance—or, more likely, for free compliments.

"For forty-seven minutes, every day? What, is she dropping them off one at a time?"

"I don't know why she keeps showing up," I whispered, which was true. "I didn't ask her to. We don't even talk. She just sits there and does work while I cook."

"Hmm."

"What is *hmm*?"

"I don't know. *Hmm.* Interesting. Weird."

"Hmm."

"Either way, O. You're going to homecoming."

"Hmm."

———

"You should take her to homecoming," Terrance said another day, right as Lou had left the room after independent study and Terrance was coming in for voluntary lunch detention. I panicked for a second when he said it—Lou was barely out the door.

"I'm not taking her to homecoming," I said, putting my earbuds in to try to end the conversation. It didn't. He kept talking, before I could hit Play.

"My girlfriend's not allowed to come."

"They don't allow kids from other schools?"

"Not middle schools," he said sadly—even if I felt a tiny bit bad for him, I couldn't help thinking that was a pretty good rule. "But next year . . ." Terrance did some kind of silent, bottom-lip-biting dance, with his elbows out in front of him and an awful lot of pelvic movement.

"Terrance. What in god's name is that?" Mrs. Bixler said from the doorway, a Subway bag hanging from her hand.

"This is Oscar dancing with that girl that's always in here," he replied, still grinning silently.

"Lou?" she said, surprised, turning to me. "Lou, Oz? Really? Terrance, stop dancing. Eat your meatball," she said, holding the bag out for him once his pelvis returned to rest.

"No. Definitely no. That was just Terrance being creepy."

"Hey!"

"And I will definitely not be taking Lou to homecoming. Now, if you all don't mind, I've got apples to peel."

Mrs. Bixler looked back at Terrance, who raised his eyebrows through his first bite of meatball sub.

"She is in here an awful lot, just the two of them. Should I be leaving them alone?"

Terrance just lifted his eyebrows again a couple of quick times through another bite. Like a whole stupid pervball conversation with just his stupid eyebrows.

"Stop it. Both of you. Right now."

"I read enough romance to know how this works . . . the brooding, the tension. . . ."

At which point I left the room for a bathroom break, Mrs. Bixler's cackling carrying down the hallway behind me.

"Listen, I need you to do me a huge favor," Lou said on Friday, one week before the dance. Right as she wheeled in the next mother lode of apples, like always, without a hello—like we were midconversation and I wasn't in the middle of doing something.

I assumed it was something new with the apples, or another phase in her food-waste reduction mission, but it was not. It was definitely not.

"So, I'm sure you know I'm on the homecoming court, which I don't love, by the way—it's like we're in the 1950s still or something, voting for popular girls to wear sashes at the big football game. And that's not humble-bragging, either. I'm only there because the entire band voted for me."

She let out a deep breath and leaned forward with her elbows on the handlebar of the flatbed, pulled her long braid in front of her to wrangle with her hands.

"Do you know Kevin Huber?"

"I know who he is," I said. I knew he was in most of the honors/AP classes with Lou and Jorge and Jesus. I knew he was enormous, like a football lineman, but he didn't play sports that

I knew of. I knew he was in the band, and that he wore glasses, and that his voice was incredibly deep and incredibly loud. But I'd never talked directly to him, nor him to me.

"So . . . Kevin Huber has made it known throughout the band that he's planning to ask me to homecoming."

"Oh . . . okay."

"Kevin Huber has also made it known, at least according to Meredith, that he's planning an *epic hocoposal*." She put air quotes around *epic hocoposal*.

"I have no idea what that means," I said, though I could feel the panic start to creep in . . . like my subconscious was already splicing together the Green Dream and the Cha-Cha Slide.

"Like prom-posal, for homecoming. I know, it's all stupid. But Meredith warned me of a potential lower-brass flash mob early next week, possibly Monday during lunch, and that lower-brass flash mob could be playing 'Louie Louie.'"

"That's a really specific rumor," I said. "Does Kevin Huber play the tuba?" I was hoping he did, just for the almost-rhyme.

"Bari sax. And I'm guessing he can attach a handmade, puffy-painted sign to it."

"Hmm."

"Yeah . . . So listen," Lou said, standing up straight again. "I'd just say I'm not going or something, but I have to be there as student council president, and it'd look really bad if I skipped the court."

"So . . . am I making apple cider for the dance or something?"

"No . . . well, yes . . . but that's not the favor. I just need an escort. For the dumb ceremony part in the middle of the dance. And I need that escort to not be Kevin Huber."

"Oh, god."

"Yeah."

She completely misunderstood my *Oh, god.* Thank goodness. It wasn't meant to be out loud, and I know Farfar would be horrified at the thought. But she was so deep in her own panic, she was oblivious to mine.

"I don't know when he decided he had this . . . thing for me, but I've known him long enough to know that once he's decided on something, he's all in, a hundred and ten percent. Sorry, I hate the whole hundred and ten percent thing—it doesn't even make mathematical sense, but I'm a little frazzled here. So . . . can you help me? Please? We don't have to go to the dance together or anything. I just need an escort for when they announce the court. You can leave right after, if you want, I don't care."

"Umm . . ."

"I think if I say I'm just going with friends, and that I already have an escort, I should be okay. . . . I'll have Meredith say something to Bari Justin. . . ."

She was talking, as usual, as though the decision were already made and she just needed to fine-tune the details. My verbal compliance was not required.

"I probably need to avoid the cafeteria, though, right? Just in case he thinks his epic hocoposal is so good it'll woo me into changing my mind. . . . Do you think Mrs. Bixler would let me eat lunch in here fifth period? Aren't you already in here, too?"

It only got worse from there, in the week leading up to homecoming. Have I made it clear that I wanted zero part in all this? And yet there I was, days from Hocopocalypse (which would have been much better than *A Night Under the Stars*, by the way, but I'm clearly not in charge of making decisions), with Jorge whisper-singing next to me in speech—*"Everybody clap your hands. Clap clap clap clap clap clap clap clap . . ."*

"Why am I even friends with you?"

Jorge pretended to look hurt for a second, staring at me with sad eyes, before snaking his stupid neck to the side and whisper-singing, *"Sliiiiide to the left. . . . Sliiiiide to the right. . . ."*

"You know I'm only going for like five minutes, right? Just to walk out when Lou's name is called, and that's it."

"You know they start the next slow dance, right? All the homecoming court and their escorts? You'll be there for at least ten, O."

"Wait, what slow dance?"

Jorge's been a dependable friend over the years. Some would even say a safe space during some of those awful early years in elementary and middle school. And maybe one could argue that he was being that same support now. "Don't worry, O," he said. "I'll be out there with Ayanna." But then, one might miss the sheer *glee* on his face. Or hear the quiet, rhythmic clapping when I put my face on my desk.

"We should wear matching Chucks," Lou said on Tuesday, the second day she stayed in the culinary lab for lunch, eating the other half of Mrs. Bixler's foot-long turkey-bacon.

That's right. Not only was she allowed to stay through fifth period, she and Mrs. Bixler were *coordinating lunches*.

But Kevin Huber. I was acutely aware of his gargantuan frame, athletic or not, when he'd pass me in the hallway that week, glowering at me wordlessly, looking like he was either going to club me to death with his bari sax, or sit alone in a dark room playing one long, low, sad note over and over, like a foghorn from a whaling ship in the distance, somewhere in the misty harbor off the docks at the outskirts of my textile mill/bakery town, where the orchard goblins rustle in their beds but don't wake. . . .

"Matching Chucks," I repeated.

"I one thousand percent agree you should wear matching Chucks," Mrs. Bixler said in the silence, her half of her turkey-bacon hovering in her hands. She looked at Terrance, who nodded in agreement, chewing an enormous bite of meatball. The two of them sat at the table and watched us like a TV show, eating their stupid Subway subs.

You'll notice how Lou was just fine with *one thousand percent* when Mrs. Bixler was agreeing with her idea. Hmm.

"I don't own Chucks," I said.

Lou leaned back and peered under the table.

"You're wearing Chucks right now."

"I don't own any nice Chucks."

She looked again, assessing.

"Those are fine," she said. "We can just get some new laces. I can get black Chucks for me after school—I'll pick up the laces while I'm there."

So that decision was made, too.

Shopping with Jorge and Jesus (and Javy) and their mom after school on Thursday—they *also* decided we should match. I didn't understand all the matching. I really didn't. While Jorge and Jesus—even fifteen-year-old Javy, who was already as tall as the twins, just bonier, and with even more unruly hair—looked awesome in black pants and suspenders and bow ties, I looked, well . . .

Hmm.

Their mom took us to her sister's restaurant afterward, so at least I got a torta out of it. That was probably the highlight of the whole week.

## CHAPTER FIFTEEN

---

# EVERYBODY CLAP YOUR HANDS

I DIDN'T TELL FARFAR ABOUT HOMECOMING AHEAD OF TIME. I'D gotten plenty of input from everyone else, and I did not need him making a bigger deal out of it than it really was.

I mean, really, I bought some dorky clothes I would wear exactly once—ideally for half an hour, tops—and then donate to C of C, to walk across a dark gymnasium with someone as a favor, right? Nothing to make a huge deal out of.

We took the truck, just the two of us, to that microbrew in Franklin on Friday night. (I had no desire to go to the football game and parade festivities, either—the seniors won the float competition, like always, and like always, I did not care.) And again just the two of us on Saturday to the campus, since Lou had to set up the gym for our night under the dusty rafters, er, stars.

It wasn't until I got out of the shower after we got home that he had any idea.

"Do we have an iron?" I asked, standing in the hallway in my underwear, my gray dress shirt like an uncrumpled piece of paper in my hand.

How was I supposed to know cotton dress shirts come out of the wash as fabric raisins? None of my T-shirts did that.

Farfar stared at me blankly from the couch, his head craned around over the cushion, Koopa's equally confused face peeking over his shoulder.

"I have no idea, Gubben. Maybe? Why do you need an iron?" Then, "Do you know *how* to use an iron?"

"I washed this dress shirt, but now it's super wrinkly."

"I feel like maybe there are gaps in this story, Gubben." Koopa meowed in agreement. "Lilla sötnos missekissen is also confused."

I let out a long breath. "It's for homecoming. Tonight."

"Homecoming? That is like a dance, yes?"

"It is like a dance. Yes."

"Is this the same dance as the . . ." He clapped. Rhythmically. Jorge'd just *had* to show him the video.

"So do we have an iron?"

"Let me look," he said, uncurling himself from the couch and lumbering into his bedroom. "You didn't tell me you were going to the homecoming," he said from inside his closet.

"It's not a big deal," I said. "I didn't really want to. I got talked into it."

"Do you have a date for this homecoming?" he asked, coming back out with an old iron I'd never seen before and a small tabletop ironing board.

"No date. I'm just going alone. Jorge and Jesus will be there."

"You were just really in the mood to dance, then?"

Farfar set the ironing board up on the little kitchen table we never actually used and plugged in the iron, glancing up at me multiple times as he did it, expecting an answer. Obviously, no, I was not really in the mood to dance. As someone who chooses audiobooks and podcasts over music every single time, I was absolutely not just in the mood to dance—nor was I in the mood to tell him the truth.

But I did. Like an idiote.

"Lou just needed me to escort her tonight. That's all."

"Is *escorting her* somehow different from taking her to the dance, Gubben? Is this like *seeing someone* versus *going steady*?"

"She's on the homecoming court. They announce them again during the dance, and she just needs someone to escort her. I only have to be there for like ten minutes."

"Homecoming court? Is that like the queen?" His eyes lit up then, and he asked in an excited whisper, "Is Looo the homecoming queen, Gubben?"

He took the dress shirt from my hand then and spread it out over the ironing board.

"No, more like runners-up to the queen. Like the queen's ladies-in-waiting." (Do you know how dumb this whole thing sounds when you have to explain it out loud to someone who didn't grow up with the idea of a high school homecoming?) "Ayanna Powell got homecoming queen. Jorge's girlfriend."

"Must be a good-looking couple."

"Sickeningly so," I replied.

"And Looo wanted you to *escort* her?"

"Some guy she doesn't like was going to make a big show of asking her, in front of the whole school. I was just the emergency plan."

"That was nice of you, Gubben."

"Hmm."

He held the shirt up, crisp and smooth, and handed it back to me.

"So you are not going out to dinner together?"

"No, I'm not her date, Farfar. I'm just—"

"Her escort, yes, yes. . . . No corsage?"

"What? We're not—"

"It would have been nice to get just a few pictures, Gubben."

"It's not like that." I tried to explain again. "She had this idea to help herself out—like usual—and I went along with it—like usual."

"It sounded nicer before, Gubben."

"You can still take a picture of me in my dorky clothes before I go."

He let out another long breath.

"Someday, Gubben . . ." Then he seemed to change gears— I'm not sure where his *someday* was headed, but he seemed to think better of it. "Go get dressed." Farfar looked down at himself. "I will put pants on, too."


The parking lot was mostly full when I pulled up in the OG Prius, which was what I'd been hoping. I definitely didn't want to be there *before* everyone else. Invisible was my goal—minus the ten minutes walking across the floor with Lou and dancing awkwardly to a terrible slow song.

My first surprise of the night came when I walked in the door, though.

"Your grandfather texted me, Oz."

Mrs. Bixler stood with her arms crossed over her chest in front of the ticket table outside the gym.

"Lucky for you, I always have a couple of these on hand on these nights. Just for scallywags like you." She produced a clear clamshell container from the table behind her.

These were not dainty corsages, mind you. These were like small shrubs attached to a bracelet.

"I'm not her date," I tried, my eyes frozen on the corsago-saur in the package. "She just needed an escort."

"Oz, if I don't get a picture of the two of you, together, with *one* of you wearing this corsage, I'm failing you for independent study."

"What? You can't—"

"I want a picture, Oscar. End of story. Now go have fun."


The second surprise came when I found Lou, buzzing around the snack tables, even as Ms. Ross, the student council advisor, assured her everything was taken care of and she could go enjoy the dance.

Lou smiled when she looked up from the snack table and saw me standing there, and her smile pulled even wider when she looked down and saw my Chucks. And fine, for just a second or two there, I felt considerably less stupid, especially when she kicked one of her matching Chucks out in front of her.

"You look good," she said.

"You too. . . ." We matched way better than I'd expected—other than the Chucks, I'd really had no idea what she was wearing. But her dress, really simple, was nearly the same color as my dress shirt, with a black ribbon around the waist. While we weren't the most colorful couple there—even though we weren't a couple—we definitely . . . *fit*.

But her hair. I'd only ever seen it in her long braid. Ever. But that night, she had it all down, and it was smooth and stuff, but it had, like, doubled in volume. I thought it was a wig at first, which I know is just stupid. And I'm sure it objectively looked great, but I just kept thinking, *This part's wrong—I want it back in a braid*. Which was another weird, stupid, creepily controlling thought, and nothing I could (or should) ever say out loud, but that's what I kept thinking. No braid just didn't feel right.

Then I couldn't figure out why I even cared—why I would have any opinion at all about Lou's hair.

I pulled the corsage box from behind my back, stared down at its bright, full shrubbiness, and felt even dumber.

"Oh, wow. You didn't have to do that," Lou said, taking the box carefully from my hands. She looked up and smiled again, and I know, I should've told her that Mrs. Bixler gave it to me, that I was being forced—blackmailed, really—to present it to her.

But I didn't.

Lou said, "I didn't even think to get you a boutonniere."

And I just waved her off, took the credit I didn't really deserve, and said, "That's okay, I don't even know what a boutonniere is."

Lou took the corsage out of the box and slipped it over her wrist. And even though the enormous red rose took up half her forearm, she smiled at it, holding it out in front of her.

"I guess if we had to, we could split that thing in half," I said, my ears growing hot.

Lou giggled a little, a sprig of baby's breath nearly tickling the crook of her elbow. "It is kind of its own little woodland habitat, isn't it?"

"There was a family of beavers I had to kick out of the box earlier." And Lou's shoulders went up in this dorky laugh/snort. "I felt kinda bad—seemed to go against our mission a little bit."

"Well, if humans are already destroying the environment

anyway, at least I have this beautiful section of it preserved on my wrist."

"What time do we walk out?" I asked.

"Eight-thirty. We all meet here at eight-fifteen."

I checked my phone: 7:17. The gym doors swung open behind us, and a cluster of underclassmen, including Terrance, spilled out into the lobby, some rap song I didn't know blaring from inside the dark gym. I definitely could have waited awhile before driving over here.

Terrance slapped my back and nodded at both of us, approving, I guess, while his friends stuffed cookies in their mouths and filled cups with cold cider.

"Is this the Muffin Man, T-Dawg?" one of them asked after downing a plastic cup of cider.

"He makes the cider, too," Terrance said, his hand on my shoulder, smiling proudly at his buddies.

"Dude, seriously?" This from a taller one, his shirt halfway unbuttoned and his tie tied around his head.

"You should try his donuts," Lou said.

"Donuts?" Terrance backhanded my shoulder, like I'd been intentionally withholding from him. Lou grinned at me and winked, and I felt my ears go hot.

And with that, Lou called to Ms. Ross that she was going back to Mrs. Bixler's room for more cider.

"Lou, you don't have to do that," Ms. Ross replied, shaking her head. "I can take care of it." But Lou was already halfway down the hall. "That girl needs to be in charge of everything," Ms. Ross said next to me after Terrance gave me one last backslap and headed back into the gym with his crew. Honestly, I wasn't sure Ms. Ross even knew who I was.

"Hmm. Tell me about it."

Then she sighed, turning back to the table and the aftermath of the freshman boys.

"I don't know what I'm going to do without her."

Surprise number three—when I finally ventured inside the gym to find Jorge. I spotted him pretty quickly—on the dance floor, unfortunately—huddled with Ayanna and most of the soccer team.

He saw me at the exact moment the DJ switched to, you guessed it, the freaking Cha-Cha Slide.

Jorge raised both arms in the air and let out a triumphant yell, Jesus turning and recognizing the miracle, too, and joining in, followed naturally by half the soccer team.

I'd like to think Farfar would've been proud of me—at least for this one little part. While every bit of me wanted to turn and run out of the gym, out of the school, and head straight for the Prius, I pretended to laugh it off. Play along, as though I'd planned my entrance around that very song. That very stupid song.

So. Everybody clapped their hands.

Number four—when, two songs later, after I felt like maybe I could stand near Jorge and crew and bob a little bit and be okay (read: be invisible), the lighting from the DJ's booth changed, settling into a cool, steady purple show while he faded into the first slow song of the night, something I definitely didn't recognize, which was my cue to beeline for the sidelines.

I'd seen Lou a couple of times, in and out of the gym, not really seeming to accomplish much—more just verifying that everything she'd already accomplished was still in fact accomplished.

And okay, in my defense, I was required to be part of exactly one slow dance, and I was planning on only that one, period. I wasn't prepared for someone *else* to ask me.

Skylar Jarrett. She was a sophomore, an especially loud, popular one, and fine, she was definitely attractive. Her brother Caleb was a junior on the soccer team with Jorge and Jesus, though I think he was better friends with Javy. Skylar was in the same Foods I class as Terrance, where I was the teaching assistant.

"Oscar!" Skylar yelled, grabbing my wrist. She'd probably said my name more than once on my way past her and her friends, but my Cha-Cha-level laser focus was on getting to the lobby. "Do you wanna dance?"

I stared at her for a second, trying *not* to look down at her tight sequined dress like a pervball, and said, "Umm . . . sure."

And then there we were. Slow-dancing. Um, very closely. Skylar's arms were around my neck, her body right up against mine. And the slow-swaying circle began in earnest. And by *earnest,* I mean *without me breathing very much.*

I should've had nothing to feel guilty about. I was there to walk Lou out and, more importantly, serve my important role as not-Kevin-Huber, everything Lou asked me to do—like always. I had no idea Skylar Jarrett had a thing for me from Foods I— and apart from one obligatory song, no reason to have to say no. And honestly, I still don't know if Lou ever saw us—she was probably out in the lobby, monitoring the snack tables with the sudden influx of other non–slow dancers.

You make eye contact with an awful lot of people, though, when you slowly rotate in a crowded room. The first of whom was Kevin Huber, dancing with some underclassman band member I didn't know, staring at me over her head (really, his chest-up was visible over her head, nestled peacefully on his sternum) with that same look of bludgeoning me vs. long bari sax solo, but now with the look of a man who wanted to defend a young woman's honor.

I quickly looked away, next finding Bryce, Teegan plastered to him, both of them grinning at me, which felt gross.

Then to Jorge, looking confused, along with Ayanna, her neck craned around to give me the same look.

I looked down for a few moments, at Skylar's exposed shoulder, which she took as an invitation to dance even closer, which was . . . difficult.

When I looked up again, my brain basically short-circuited by that point, it was Meredith, Lou's best friend, dancing with Jesus. She looked like she'd been staring at me the whole time, waiting for me to see her, and she mouthed what looked like *You're a jerk.*

It could've been *Sure like your shirt,* too.

But I'm guessing no.

When the song finally ended, Skylar stepped back, her arms sliding off my shoulders, and said, "Thanks, Oscar," before retreating to her grinning friends.

"Um . . . sure" was all I managed (again) before restarting my beeline for the door.

I found Lou in Mrs. Bixler's room, in the storage room with the spare fridge, and I felt weirdly relieved. She had a cart with more apple cider loaded onto it, but she was still looking around for something else, like she wasn't in a homecoming dress . . . at her own senior-year homecoming.

"Oh, hey!" she said, smiling warmly when she saw me in the doorway. I noticed she still had the corsage on. "Can you give me a hand? People have torn through all the cookies, and I thought maybe you had some leftover muffins or fritters or something. . . . Maybe even apple pie and ice cream."

Even then, her ideas were spinning.

"Have you even been into the dance?" I asked, part of me hoping the answer was no.

"Did you know every single girl in student council left setup early to get their hair done? And then most of the guys left, too, because they're guys. I mean, I know as student council president, I have the greatest responsibility, but come on. Ms. Ross and I were the only ones left for the last two hours, making sure everything was ready."

I moved past her to the fridge, where I had multiple pies stashed away for the female faculty. (I mean, the male faculty could eat them, too, if they wanted—I'd just never had any of them gush over my baked goods to me.)

"There may still be a big bucket of ice cream in one of the freezers in the lab," I said, setting pies on the cart. "God, it's still hard to believe all this comes from those terrible school apples."

"I need to find out why we can't get better apples," Lou replied, and I could see the wheels turning for a new idea, a new cause. Better apples.

"It's a little after eight," I said, moving past her again to find the ice cream. "We should probably get back there, right?"

"Oh, yeah . . ."

I grabbed the utensils we'd need and threw it all on the cart with the cider and the pies, and we headed back toward the lobby.

"So, some girl asked me to slow-dance earlier," I blurted in the hallway, just as we passed a faded MAKE GOOD CHOICES poster.

"Oh. Okay. Did you?"

"Um. Yeah. She kinda surprised me."

"Cool. I mean, you're not worried about me, are you? We aren't here together. I just need you to escort me out there. You can dance with whoever you want." Then, a half beat later, "Do it up."

I'll be honest, I did not know what any of that meant, other than that I was relieved that I didn't seem to have done anything terrible in Lou's eyes. I mean, she'd tell me if I did.

"You two. Stop right there."

Mrs. Bixler stood at the end of the hallway in front of the lobby, holding her phone out in front of her.

We stopped, me pushing the cart, Lou walking next to me, and we instinctively leaned together and smiled.

"Perfect. Now stand over here." Mrs. Bixler pointed to a spot along the hall in front of a blank bulletin board. "I'm not trusting you to get pictures on your own, and I'm not letting Mr. Olsson down." Lou beamed at the mere mention of Farfar's name. "Or have you call my bluff about failing you, Oz. Put your arm around her."

I looked to Lou for confirmation, and she rolled her eyes and nodded.

"Good. Now, Lou, turn around. Oz, stand behind her, hands on her waist. We'll do this old-school homecoming photo style."

I saw them on Farfar's phone later, and those last two looked as painfully awkward as they felt, which, I don't know, was maybe Mrs. Bixler's goal—like an awkward-dance-photo rite of passage that we can look back on later and laugh at.

Honestly, that first picture wasn't bad, though.


Ms. Ross shook her head in disbelief when we showed up with the new dessert cart.

"Lou, you know how dances work, right? You do not have to be the mom of this party."

Lou just shrugged, scanning the snack table for any more areas of need. "I enjoy this way more than I enjoy doing the Cha-Cha Slide."

She didn't even look up when she said it, so I don't think it was any poke at me. I think it was just honesty. Honesty I totally agreed with, in fact.

Lou let out a sigh and looked up at me then.

"Okay. Guess it's time to do this. Ready?"

"Not even the tiniest bit."

"Me neither. Let's go."


I don't really even remember the walk into the gym after the DJ announced *Mary Louise Messinger, escorted by Oscar Olsson.* We were first in line, and the spotlight in the gym was blinding, and I knew we just had to make it to the designated spot in the middle of the gym without falling down, and then just stand there awkwardly, arm in arm, to wait for the rest of the court, and eventually Ayanna and Jorge.

And then, the slow dance Farfar claimed he would have sold the truck to see. Because sometimes he's a jerk.

Fortunately, I doubt we were much of a focus, even with only twelve of us dancing, besides maybe for Kevin Huber, entertaining thoughts both of killing me and of what could have been. Because Ayanna truly was the queen, her long braids woven into an intricate twist on top of her head. And Ayanna with Jorge—they were like a movie couple.

And dancing with Lou was like the polar opposite of dancing with Skylar. We must've looked like middle schoolers up there, my elbows locked and my hands straight at her sides, her hands resting on my shoulders, both of us teetering back and forth in a slow circle.

"People had better show up for the teardown tomorrow," Lou said, looking around the gym, not necessarily even talking to me. Because after another minute of silent teetering, she said, "It drives me nuts that we have to use Styrofoam plates for the pie."

"And plastic silverware," I (coolly) added.

"Right?" she said, her eyes looking into mine for the first time, just for a second. Her hands did lock behind my neck then, but I could see her brain continuing its mental checklist of things to do next.

When the song ended and the DJ invited everyone back onto the dance floor for another slow song, Lou dropped her arms to her sides and smiled at me. "Thanks, Oscar. Really . . . I need to go check on the lobby again." And she kind of waggled her fingers at her side a little bit as she turned to go, this tiny little wave, and I watched her head for the door. And fine, I can admit, I wouldn't have hated staying to dance the next song.

"Oscar." Skylar Jarrett was already at my side, a hand on my wrist. "You wanna dance again?"

I looked down for a second, at the blinding laces of my Chucks.

"Umm, I would . . . but I've gotta go scoop ice cream."

I think Farfar would've liked that part, at least. Because I know it got weird for a while after that.

I stayed long enough to serve all the pie and ice cream, which didn't last long, and we stood chatting with Mrs. Bixler and Ms. Ross for a while, about hating dances, about future plans (mostly Lou's), about whatever. I didn't go back inside the gym and I didn't stay until the end, and when I came into the apartment that night before ten, I kept my answers to some variation of *It was no big deal.*

## CHAPTER SIXTEEN

---

# STORY ENDINGS ARE HARD
# (THIS FRYER IS AWFULLY SMOKY TONIGHT)

LATE THE FOLLOWING WEEK WAS SENIOR NIGHT FOR THE TWINS. Thursday night, under the lights. Jorge and Jesus's final home game as Central Adams Hornets (*Fear the Buzz!*). Farfar had insisted we provide food for the reception afterward, since we'd been going to almost every one of their home games since our freshman year.

I think he'd hoped for a while that I'd stick with it, that I could be out there with them like I was through youth soccer in middle school. But, as I'm sure Farfar noticed from the bleachers, I am hopelessly uncompetitive. That junior high coach who screamed at me from the sideline after I messed up a breakaway to help a kid up from Franklin who'd tripped over my feet—that, I knew, was the end of it for me.

I loved watching Jorge and Jesus play, though—it's what I've always loved, watching people enjoy themselves—and we knew there were supposed to be scouts there that night to see them. Maybe even to see Javy, too. Kid's a beast in the goal. I guess if you'd been taking shots from Jesus in the backyard for the past ten years, stopping other people's shots would be no big deal.

And I loved sitting with their family, too, because, more often than not, it was the *whole* family. Grandparents and aunts and uncles, taking up a whole block of stands. Someone always had a cowbell, and I knew enough Spanish swear words from the twins to know that their grandfather was *really* into it. And Farfar and I, we were always right there next to them.

Senior Night was an event unparalleled. The whole giant crew of them—and the whole rest of the crowd, which fed off their fanaticism—going bananas when the twins walked across the track with their mom and dad, all four of them, for the senior recognition before the game.

I think Jesus secured his D1 scholarship dream in one night, too. Four goals. And another by Jorge on Jesus's assist. And with Javy amped up in the goal, they shut out a second-place Eastern team.

"Oh, there is Looo," Farfar said, a few minutes into the game, just before Jesus's first goal, pointing to the fence along the track where she stood, elbows over the rail, with Meredith.

"Cool," I said, and he shot me a look before standing to wave to her. And of course, when Lou saw him, her face lit up, too. It was ridiculous. She made her way up to us a little later, a few minutes before the half.

"Hej hej, Looo!" Farfar said when she sat down on the bleacher beside me.

"I thought I saw the truck out there. Are you guys working tonight or something?"

"We are serving goodies for the Senior Night," he explained. "We could use a little help, if you are interested."

Which I should've seen coming, honestly.

We went down halfway through the second half, Lou along with us now, to pull the truck in through the gate next to the concession stand, where some of the other parents were already setting up tables.

"Everything is free tonight, Looo, so you only have to take orders."

"Wow. Full menu?"

"Full menu. Special occasion." And I could see he was starting to get emotional.

But, man, that was nothing compared to the scene out there after the game was over and the team and the families were eating.

I don't think I'd seen Jorge or Jesus cry since elementary school, when their mom ripped them apart for daring Javy to poop in the recycling bin, which he did, and which took their mom all of thirty seconds to unravel.

But here they were, tears streaming down their faces while they ate carnitas from the trays their aunt had brought, while they hugged family members, while they hugged teammates, while they ordered munkar from Lou. Which meant Farfar couldn't peek out there without tearing up, which meant the smoke from my fryer kept getting into my eyes, too.

It was weird to think about. For me, this whole senior year has been about welcome ends, parts of my story I'd never want to extend or go back to. But for Jorge, for Jesus, these ends were big.

They still had a few playoff games left, but that was the last time they'd play on the same team on that field. An important part of their story—a part they loved—was on its last page.

I didn't have a whole lot of time to get wrapped up in the moment after that initial glimpse of tears, though. High levels of emotions mixed with hungry soccer players mixed with free donuts also equaled a lot of donuts. Lou just kept yelling out orders while Farfar leaned against the window next to her, chatting with Jorge's family members.

"You okay, Gubben? Need help?"

"I'm good," I called back, enjoying getting lost in the munkar zone for a while, like a mini–festival run. It was probably a good hour or more before Lou finally stopped calling out constant orders.

"That was insane," Lou said a little while later, right beside me, her hand on my shoulder.

I wiped my face on my sleeve and dropped a few last handfuls of munkhål into the fryer to share between us, and her hand slipped from my shoulder as she turned back to the window.

"Oscar?" she said a moment later. I turned and she stepped closer again, a different look on her face from just a second before. "There's a girl out there asking to talk to *you*."

I frowned and wiped my hands on a dish towel, stepping past her to the window.

Skylar Jarrett had her elbows on the window counter, grinning up at me, her blond hair in a messy bun.

"Hey, Oscar," she said, her grin creeping into a full smile. "I didn't know you work in a food truck, too."

"Yeah, I help Far—I help my grandfather run it. We've been doing this together for years."

I thought I heard Farfar hrumph a little bit as he turned away from the side of the window, but I couldn't be sure.

"Is that how you got so good at cooking?"

Her eye contact, man. It was intense.

"Probably. Yeah," I said, scratching the back of my head beneath my hat. Normally I'm such a brilliant conversationalist,

I know, but I had no idea what to say. I was pretty sure this was flirting and I had clear, visceral memories, suddenly, of our one slow dance, which wasn't helping. Skylar's group had needed a lot of "help" in Foods I since homecoming, calling me over to them daily for some inane question or request for another demo, and I generally obliged—I mean, I was the teaching assistant, after all.

"Is it too late to order your donuts? Or, what's it called? *Mun-cal*?"

"Munkhål," I said, smiling. "Baby donuts. They're the little ones. I can get you some."

Farfar had already taken them out of the fryer for me when I turned around. We both knew without a word that I totally would have let them burn if he hadn't—people don't usually ask to talk to me, thank god. Farfar handed them to me, probably an order and a half's worth stuffed into their usual paper cup. And just before I turned back around, I caught him and Lou rolling their eyes and smirking at each other, and, I don't know. It stung.

And yes, I realize now that I gave away the munkhål I'd intended to share with Lou.

"These are *amazing*," Skylar said after the first munkhål.

"They're really good right out of the fryer," I said, smiling stupidly at her. "They almost melt."

"I don't think I can eat any other donuts after this. You're going to have to be my personal donut chef from now on." She placed another in her mouth and gave a small wave. "See you tomorrow, Oscar," she said as she turned back to join her friends.

The two of them, Farfar and Lou, were popping the last few leftover munkhål into their mouths, pretending to be in midconversation, when I turned around. My stupid ears were bright red, and I couldn't really look at either one of them.

"You are a lifesaver, Looo. Thank you."

"Anytime. Seriously. I love doing this. I can see why you love this so much," she said, looking for a moment at me, a small smile on her face, before she turned back to Farfar. "I'd better get home, though. I've got an essay to finish."

She climbed out of the truck and waved back at us through the window before heading toward her car.

Farfar leaned back against my work space with his arms crossed, staring out the window at the dwindling soccer families. He raised an eyebrow at me.

"Hmm."

## CHAPTER SEVENTEEN

# MARY LOUISE MESSINGER V. CENTRAL ADAMS BOARD OF SCHOOL DIRECTORS

"I HAVE ANOTHER FAVOR TO ASK," LOU SAID TO ME EARLY THE following week, standing behind the first collection of apples. Her face was flushed, her glasses had slid low on her nose, and her braid had fallen in front of her black Adams County Jazz Festival T-shirt—I hadn't realized she was even part of the jazz band, if maybe that was where she stole Kevin Huber's heart, him staring at the back of her dark braid in the clarinet section.

"Do you play the clarinet?" I said suddenly, which, for once, derailed her.

"What? Um, yeah. First chair."

There we go.

I wiped my hands of the flour from the munkar dough I was pulling together for more fritters. Terrance had been relentless since Lou's mention of my donuts at homecoming, and I figured they would be nice alongside the grab-and-go muffins. The tall kid, Makai, had even started awkwardly reporting to me in the hallways whenever he'd had a muffin, which was basically every day. Like I was building an entourage of perpetually hungry freshman boys.

"What's the favor this time?" I asked, enjoying this rare, short-lived moment of controlling the conversation.

"I need you to come to the school board meeting with me. Tonight."

"For . . ."

"This apple solution is unsustainable."

"I thought it was going really well. . . ."

"No, it is. You're amazing." *Amazing*? Hmm. "But what happens when we graduate in a few months? Nobody's going to step in and take our place. Who even *could*? I mean, most people still don't even realize where all this stuff is coming from. In six months, all these apples . . ." Lou kicked the cart, the apples wobbling dangerously. "They're all in a landfill, along with tens of thousands more, pumping out methane."

I hadn't even thought about next year, honestly—at least not in terms of what would be happening *here*. I'd only thought or cared about what I'd be doing, and that it would never, ever involve setting foot in this place again.

"Okay," I said, holding both hands up to slow her rant. "I get it. We're a short-term fix. But why am I going to a school board meeting?"

"Since most people don't actually care about anything beyond themselves, the only solution is better apples or no apples."

"Is that your lead? I'm not sure you should lead with that."

Lou rolled her eyes at me, and as we both moved the apples to the storage fridge, she explained her new idea for a long-term schoople fix. Honestly, it was a great plan—I wasn't sure why it wasn't happening already.

"It's still not clear why you need me at the meeting."

She dropped her arms, exasperated with me (though, in fairness, she *hadn't* explained it).

"Look, can you just be there with me? Please? You don't

have to talk. Just stand there and look . . ." And she waved her hand at my body.

Honestly, I wanted to keep arguing—I did *not* want to attend a school board meeting. I had no idea what they even did at one, but I was fairly certain it was boring, and it sounded like more people making decisions on my behalf in a place I didn't want to be.

"Please," she said again. "I'm already on the agenda."

Finally, I rolled my eyes back at her and dropped my arms.

"Kevin Huber better not be there."

I found Lou in the front row in the school board room, ten minutes before the start of the meeting, looking over her notebook. She had on the same jazz band T-shirt and jeans from school that day, but she looked, I don't know, *formidable*, scanning through her notes.

"Nice Chucks," I whispered, tapping her foot with mine and easing into the folding chair next to her.

She looked up and smiled nervously—maybe feeling less formidable than I anticipated—and kicked me back.

The inside of the Central Adams school board room was not what I was expecting. In my head, it would be a mix of the high courts and a swanky, plush executive boardroom, full of dark, polished wood and leather and cigar smoke, nine impressive-looking old people behind a huge semicircular bench.

But really, we were in the first of three half-filled rows of folding chairs in a big open room with beige walls and blue carpeting. And in front of us were a bunch of folding tables arranged in a big U. The most official-looking things were the name placards in front of each seat and the gavel in front of the woman at the center of the U, the school board president. Apart from Dr. Caraballo, the superintendent, and a few other school officials in suits and dress clothes from the day, everyone else just looked like parents or grandparents.

"Did you put all those apples up there?" I asked, leaning in closer to hear—the room was so weirdly quiet for so many people. A single apple sat in front of each person at the tables. Some picked them up, looking at the apple, then at the person next to them, eyebrows raised. Otherwise, the apples sat unnoticed.

"I did."

"Wait," I said, and I dug my elbow into Lou's arm. "Is Kevin Huber's *dad* on the freaking school board?"

Lou's face broke into a wide smile, but she wouldn't look up from her notebook.

"Unbelievable."

I thought we'd have to sit through the whole thing, but they called our names—I had no idea Lou had put *my* name on the agenda, too—right after an awkward, all-adult rendition of the Pledge of Allegiance and a roll call.

My entire body went numb. It's not like standing inside the truck, talking to customers. Customers come to you, and ultimately you make them happy with delicious food that they've asked for. This was a bunch of school-related people, smiling politely, bored even, waiting to hear why two kids were there to slow down their very important meeting. About school.

*Come on,* Lou mouthed to me over her shoulder, her eyes wide, when she realized I hadn't stood up with her.

I followed her, finally, to the metal podium set up on the left side of the U, and I have never felt so exposed—like the Green Dream come to life, which was not an even remotely helpful thought in the moment.

"Ms. Messinger," Mrs. Landis, the school board president, began. "I believe you're here to tell us about your Girl Scout Gold Award, is that correct?"

"Yes, ma'am. Reporting on my progress and the effects of my service is part of the Gold Award requirements. Thank you for allowing me to be here tonight."

They all smiled warmly, and I could see it on their faces, that this was exactly what they wished for all teenage girls— I don't know if that was part of Lou's plan, or if that was just the effect she had on school adults.

"And are you responsible for these apples?" Mrs. Landis asked, and they each picked theirs up and smirked at each other, like they were nostalgic for better days in school, even though there's no way even a single one of them lived in a time when students gave their teachers apples as presents. (I mean, really, did that ever actually happen? Did Farfar do that in Åland? Is there a Swedish equivalent to this, like a bowl of lingonberries or something? A pickled herring for your teacher, perhaps?)

"Please," Lou said, nodding and smiling at them. "Take a bite. I promise they've all been washed thoroughly. They're the same apples that were served in our cafeteria today."

Their smirks disappeared as they suddenly looked at each other apprehensively, but Lou was so sincere, so perfect, so Girl Scouty, that they all eventually took a bite together.

I'll give them credit. They tried to keep smiling. They did. But they couldn't keep their nostrils from flaring or their neck muscles from clenching into cords while they chewed. A few shot panicked looks at each other as though they might have been poisoned by this so-called Girl Scout.

"As you can probably now imagine," Lou said, still smiling politely at them, "not many students *eat* the apples provided with their school lunch."

And with that, while some kept chewing the same bite and others looked suspiciously at their bitten apples for signs of foul play, Lou launched into the facts and statistics I'd heard dozens of times—the number of apples thrown away, untouched, each day; the number *that* number became over a week, a month, a school year; she even gave the estimated number over her entire school career, from the first day she got off the bus in kindergarten to today.

She even calculated into dollar amounts, based on average prices per pound for Red Delicious apples, wasted.

"My god, why are these so bad?" Mr. Huber finally cut in, still looking at his apple in dismay.

Lou continued, though, without addressing Mr. Huber's concern. She was still building up to that.

"My original Gold Award project wasn't necessarily about apples. My focus was on food-waste reduction in our school. After observing for a few days in the cafeteria, however, apples became the most obvious answer." And she went on to hit them with her facts about landfills, how our apples put out methane, twenty-eight times more potent than carbon dioxide, and all the resources wasted from seed to cafeteria trash can.

Most had set their apples back on the table by that point, as close to the edge as they could put them—except for Mr. Huber, who still just shook his head at the bitter little monster in his grasp.

"I'm happy to tell you that we've solved the problem—for this year." And this is where Lou looked at me for the first time. They glanced at me like they'd forgotten I was there—honestly, I kind of had, too. Lou had complete control of the room. She explained her procedures for collecting untouched apples in the cafeteria, and honest to god, every one of them leaned forward in their chairs, realizing, I think, for the first time, that they were dealing with way more than some precocious teenager. They were watching—*we* were watching—a world-changer.

"Every one of the apples we've collected this year has been repurposed, if you will, and distributed throughout the school and the wider community. Healthy apple muffins, offered to students and staff, anyone who needs a healthy pick-me-up for any reason; countless trays of homemade apple crisp, delivered to the Council of Churches for residents in need of a hot meal and Meals on Wheels, for many of the elderly in our community; homemade hot cider, sold by the Music Boosters at football games, the proceeds going back to our own award-winning music programs—"

"That's from you?" Mrs. Landis interrupted, a weird smirk on her face. She turned to Dr. Caraballo next to her. "That cider's *really* good."

"Actually," Lou said, "that's all him." And she turned to me, smiling. "This is Oscar Olsson, also a senior at Central Adams, and already a budding food truck entrepreneur. He's the mastermind behind the apple treats."

And all of a sudden, they were peppering me with food truck

questions (people really like talking about food trucks—and a few of them had experienced the rullekebab and/or munkar more than once) and about recipes and about handling that sheer, impossible number of apples on a weekly basis. And I will tell you, by that point, after Lou leveled the room, I was fine. More than fine, really—I can talk about our truck and our food all day. It was just like the Paper Bag Speech. They were rapt.

Finally, Mr. Huber cut back in, still looking exasperated. "I still don't understand what's wrong with these apples. Where are these things coming from?"

It was like Lou had been setting them up the whole time for that one question.

She paused, making sure they were all looking at her again, before leaning toward the microphone attached to the podium.

"Washington State."

All the board members sat back at once. Mr. Huber nearly pushed his chair to the wall, this look of disgust on his face, like the secret had finally been revealed and it was even more unconscionable than he'd feared.

"We live in the middle of *Adams County, Pennsylvania!*" he yelled, both arms in the air. "Two of the biggest applesauce factories in the country are ten minutes away!"

"And the Apple Harvest Festival," another board member chimed in.

"There's orchards all around my house," Mrs. Landis confirmed.

Lou let them go on like this for another minute, until their outrage started to die down, before she pulled them all back in.

"As I said before, Oscar and I have solved our apple crisis . . . for this year. But by this time next year, I'll be in college and Oscar will be in culinary school, if he's not already taken his food truck to the big city. And ten thousand apples will have already hit the landfill, with another thirty thousand by June.

"If we're committed to serving apples two to three times per week to our children—and like you said, Mr. Huber, we're in Adams County; I'm all for serving apples—then the only feasible long-term answer to this crisis is *better apples.*"

Lou didn't have to argue for the benefits of boosting the local economy, promoting local businesses, and reducing the environmental impact of long-distance shipping, even though I'm sure she had all that in her notes. The board got there on their own, over the next half hour, while Lou and I stood and watched. Half the board knew apple growers personally, and by the time they'd remembered we were still standing there, they'd even gone into discussions of locally sourced produce *beyond* apples. And they were probably more likely to act on it, too, if they thought it was their own idea. Lou wanted the *change* more than she wanted *credit* for the change.

They dismissed us before they continued with the rest of the meeting, thank goodness, but not before Mr. Huber came around the table to shake both our hands, which prompted two others to do the same. He looked even more like Kevin up close—just as enormous—but with a graying goatee and puffier hair. I couldn't help wondering if he had a bari sax of his own at home, and, if he had any idea of how I'd thwarted his son's dreams of wooing this amazing young woman next to me, if he'd also want to bludgeon me with it.

Lou was surprisingly calm in the parking lot afterward. I thought she'd be fist-pumping or karate-kicking the air or something, after completely owning a roomful of moderately powerful grown-ups like that, but she just smiled a little to herself, her notebook pressed against her chest.

"I'll get excited if they actually *do* something. Most people will agree with you to your face."

"Did you hear them? Mr. Huber's ready to deliver new apples himself."

"Maybe. We'll see—they could've just been patting our heads."

"You know I'm not going to culinary school, right?"

"It sounded good, though, didn't it?"

I dropped my head, nodding, trying to smile. I realized this was not the time to be all sensitive, to get offended by one line—which *did* sound really good—after what she'd just accomplished. I knew it was selfish.

But it was there. That tiny little sting of judgment. Even if she hadn't meant it that way.

"Thank you again," she said, kicking the toe of my Chuck with hers. "You were a huge help in there."

I nodded again. "Anytime."

"I'll see you tomorrow?" she asked. As though I'd had any say prior to this moment.

"I'll be there."


Quick point of fact, here: by the following Monday—Halloween Week—the cross-country schooples were gone. Replaced by Fujis from a local orchard, complete with promotional signage along the cafeteria line.

When Lou showed up with the cart on Tuesday, this goofy, disbelieving grin plastered on her face, there was barely a quarter of the usual amount.

She might annoy the hell out of me, but she just might change the world, too.

# CHAPTER EIGHTEEN

---

# FARFAR'S BUSINESS
# SCHOOL: SECOND LESSON

THAT SATURDAY MORNING, BEFORE LOU GOT THERE, FARFAR was showing me the bookkeeping software on the laptop, the next course in Farfar's Business School.

"I know this is not the sexiest part of running a food truck," he said, pulling up his expenses sheet from August, when we were hitting festivals regularly (versus September, when we, regrettably, slowed down).

"What's the sexiest part? The grease burns? The—"

He looked up from the laptop and waggled his eyebrows. "You are looking at the sexiest part, Gubben."

"Wow. How long have you been holding on to that one?"

"Three days. It was worth the wait."

I'd never really minded math that much, but this was really cool. This was numbers with a purpose. And honestly, sexy or not, it was fascinating how Farfar chose suppliers for meat cones, the local business he relied on to recycle our fryer oil, even where he went for the foil wrappers for rullekebab and cups and paper sleeves for munkar. And ultimately, how much we needed to sell to turn a profit, based on expenses that month.

"I have other income, Gubben. Social Security. Retirement from twenty years in Mariehamn. Investments. And mostly just rent to worry about for personal expenses. You will need to figure out how to bring in more than that someday, Gubben."

I leaned in close to the laptop screen while he pulled up more spreadsheets, his wire-rimmed glasses at the tip of his nose. He was in his usual spot on the couch, a pillow on his lap beneath the laptop, Koopa purring—somewhat begrudgingly, I think, with her spot taken—on top of the cushion behind his head.

"Everything's so . . . thorough. And organized," I said.

"I don't just sit and play *Mario Kart* all day, Gubben." Then, "I was always the organized one. I kept the books . . . Amir . . . he was the *ideas*."

I was about to ask him more—about Amir, about running the business together—when Lou showed up.

"Oh! I forgot to start the pancakes," Farfar said, hurrying to the stove while I opened the door.

Lou stood in the hallway, looking uncharacteristically nervous, holding a package covered in Snoopy wrapping paper.

"Hej hej, Looo!" Farfar called from the stove before she was even inside the door. "Chocolate chip or blueberry today?"

"Uh, chocolate chip, please."

"Good answer."

Lou stepped just inside the door, smiling down at Koopa, who had come to figure-eight between Lou's feet in greeting.

I slid onto my stool at the counter and looked back at her, raising my eyebrows.

"Are you coming in?"

Finally, she stepped forward, and said in a rush, "I got you something, but it's kind of stupid. It's just . . . a thank-you . . .

for your help at the school board meeting . . . and all the home-coming stuff. . . ."

"You got me a present? For walking you thirty feet across a dark gym?"

"It's a really weird present," Lou said, pulling at the end of her braid with her free hand. "It's actually probably not even much of a thank-you."

"I like the Snoopies," Farfar said, grinning from the stove. "Open it, Gubben. I want to see this weird, stupid gift."

Lou shoved the shoebox-shaped package at me and slid onto the stool next to me, looking down like she was embarrassed by the whole thing. I tore the first bit of Snoopy paper before she jumped in again. "I was going to get you a Metallica CD," she blurted, which stopped both of us from what we were doing to stare at her. "But I didn't know what ones you might have, or if you even have a way to *listen* to CDs. And I didn't know if you were really into vinyl, so . . ."

"Metallica?" Farfar said, spatula frozen in midair.

"It's what he listens to while he cooks at school," Lou explained.

"Gubben, I thought you were listening to Harry Potter again?"

"Harry Potter?" Lou asked, now looking just as confused as Farfar.

I nodded, my face suddenly hot. ". . . *Chamber of Secrets* . . ."

"Do you even *listen* to Metallica?"

"God no," I said, trying not to look at Farfar's face at all. "I don't really listen to music very often. Just books. Sometimes podcasts."

"Why did you tell me you were listening to Metallica?"

She still looked more confused than hurt, really. Like my lie was too stupid to even be mad at. Which it was. I know.

"Just . . . joking, I guess." Because I couldn't say, *Because you were already invading every part of my life, and I wanted to keep control over some little piece of it.*

"Well, I'm glad I took the vinyl remastered box set out of the cart."

I started tearing the paper again, just to hopefully get beyond any more Metallica discussion, and I will say, she was right. It was a weird thank-you gift.

"It's a French fry cutter," Lou said, her face blushing now, as though I'd miss where it said COMMERCIAL GRADE FRENCH FRY CUTTER in big letters on the side of the box, alongside a photo of a French fry cutter and a plate of freshly cut fries.

"It *is* a French fry cutter," I confirmed, looking from the box to her red face, grinning. "Thank you."

I kept looking at the box then, while Farfar plated up pancakes and said something about loving French fries—which, duh—knowing that if I waited, Lou would give her full explanation. Which she did.

"I had two ideas, really. . . ." The arms were out in front of her all of a sudden, presentation mode, over top of her pancakes. "First, I thought it might be good—profitable—to offer French fries on the truck. I mean, I've even had a few people ask at the college if we offered them with rullekebab. So . . . I don't know, maybe it's something to consider trying. This guy's got suction cup feet," she added, shaking the box a little on the counter, "so I think it's designed to work either on a countertop or attached to the wall."

It wasn't a terrible idea. Obviously. I just didn't expect her thank-you gift to come with suggestions, or Lou to improve our business. I mean, I don't know *why* I didn't expect it.

"And second: I've heard you gush about this goat cheese poutine stuff. And I looked it up, along with classic poutine recipes, and there's no way you can't re-create the same thing yourself."

"I'm not going to steal their idea for our truck."

"No no, I just meant for you. Personally. To indulge yourself. You can make pretty much anything—I know you could do it."

"Oh."

"Gubben. I want you to make us goat cheese poutine," Far-far said through a bite of chocolate chip pancake. "Today."

"You already have the fryers going," Lou said. "Maybe you could try it out today on the truck."

"Hmm. What do you think—college-kid taste test, Gubben?"

Lou looked sheepish, tugging at her braid again and glancing up at me over her glasses. "I've got three bags of russets in the car."


I'd read all kinds of fry prep recommendations on my phone on the ride to school and to C of C (for what would be our last megadelivery of crisp, though we didn't know it then). By the time we were parked at one of our usual spots on the Gettysburg campus, we'd decided that if this was something that was going to work on the truck, it had to just be *cutter* straight to *fryer*. We wouldn't have time or space to mess with soaking and patting them dry or any nonsense.

Turns out cutter-to-fryer works just fine.

"Gubben. Why have we not done French fries?"

I shoved another handful in my mouth and said, "I'm pretty sure I asked you that, like, five years ago."

He reached for a few more from the pile we'd dumped onto a foil wrapper on my worktop. "I have no recollection of this."

Lou took the last three, just beaming at the two of us. There was nothing for her like her ideas working out.

"Okay. Okay. The next batch has got to be for taste tests."

Shocking news: college kids like French fries, too.

We did a double shift that day, stopping briefly at the apartment (with a quick stop for a few more bags of potatoes) before heading up the road to Franklin to set up outside one of the new microbrews. Rogue's Roost. They didn't have a kitchen yet, and it worked out perfectly for us—they'd take orders inside the bar and send runners out to deliver food. They'd even snap a picture of our chalkboard menu and display it on one of the flat-screens inside the bar. Honestly, it was one of the coolest arrangements Farfar had made for business, and we still got a fair amount of walk-ups from folks strolling around downtown.

I'm not sure how much Lou had explained to her parents at that point about her now nearly weekly part-time job on a food truck, but it had only been Saturday afternoons to that point, merged into time she'd planned to fulfill Gold Award hours. This was different. This was likely a late-late night outside a bar in another town. This took some convincing.

"Mom, I've told you about this," she said into her phone,

sitting in the passenger seat in the parking lot. "I've been help-ing out my friend's grandfather . . . with his food truck business, yes. You had one of the donuts last week. . . . Yes, that's where it came from. . . . Why do you have to put Da— Hi, Dad."

She had to start over again, Farfar grinning at her from the driver's seat.

"Yes, he's paying me . . . way too much," she said, shooting a glance back at Farfar. "I take orders at the window and handle the money . . . Franklin . . . Railroad Street, a parking lot just off the square . . .

"Behind the old bank?" she whispered to Farfar. He nodded. "Yeah," she said back into the phone. "Really late . . . the brew-ery doesn't close until midnight. . . ."

She listened for a while then, her eyes rolled up to the ceiling.

"*Employment* can't hurt my résumé, Dad. . . . Are you seri-ous? I can't ask that—it's a *job*. . . ."

Lou listened again, then let out a long sigh.

"Will you guys be okay if my dad picks me up at ten?" she asked Farfar, looking deeply frustrated and deeply apologetic. *Defeated* was not usually a way I could've described Lou, but . . .

"Of course, Looo. You don't have to go along if it is a prob-lem. We'll be fine. We just like your help. Some people are good at ideas, right, Gubben?"

He looked at me with the tiniest smile, his eyes suddenly shiny. I nodded.

Lou glanced back at me, then turned back to her phone.

"Ten o'clock is fine. But don't expect a free donut."

Lou huffed and dropped her phone into her lap after a *Thank you* that did not sound terribly sincere.

"Sorry," she said to Farfar.

162

Farfar just chuckled, though. "It's okay, Looo. Parents worry. *Good* parents worry. We are just glad you are joining us."

And he was right. I *was* glad, honestly. So much of being around Lou was listening to her talk about herself, it seemed, but for the full twenty-five-minute ride into Franklin, we talked potatoes.

Where we might be able to store them on the truck. How many we might need on a normal day, on a festival day. What to charge. If it should be a combo option with rullekebab and if we'd need to order baskets. If the potatoes would need any kind of prep at home before the truck. If the two fryers were enough to handle both munkar and fries when things got crazy and what it would take to add a third.

It was all just potatoes. But it was a real-world business discussion—creativity and feasibility and costs and logistics, all at once. I loved it.

"You could totally do goat cheese poutine," Lou said, leaning against the window counter right after the Rogue's Roost runner left with another pile of finished orders.

The sun had already set, and the lights strung above the alley along the back entrance to the brewery cast an inviting glow. It was warm for October, and we'd actually gotten more foot traffic than we'd expected. Between the campus and the brewery, we were on pace for a decent festival day of sales—at least a smaller one.

"For me or for the truck?" I said, stretching and taking a much-needed break from the fryer.

"I don't know. Both?"

"It doesn't feel right," I said, taking off my O's cap and swiping my forehead with my sleeve. Farfar was leaning against his workstation, his arms folded, just letting the discussion play out, I guess.

"Where's their actual café again?"

"Uh, somewhere in Delaware. . . ."

"I think you're probably safe."

"Probably," I conceded, realizing as I said it that I was inexplicably arguing *against* goat cheese poutine. "But I don't think we have the space to add any more stuff, do you?" I said, pulling Farfar into the discussion instead of leaving him to stand there, grinning at us.

"The gravy would be the biggest problem," he said, dunking the last fry from our latest pile into kebab sauce. "Isn't that what Carl and Cathy usually run out of?"

"Wait," Lou said, throwing her hands up in front of her right before Farfar's fry hit his mouth. Kebab sauce dripped onto his shirt. "Drop another basket of fries."

"We've already eaten four of them," I said.

"I've got an idea . . . *loaded kebab fries*!"

"Loaded kebab fries," I repeated, saying it more to myself. Letting it roll around in my mouth. I glanced up at Farfar.

"Gubben. Drop more fries."


It was a freaking masterpiece. Fresh-cut fries. Two slices of kebab meat, chopped. A crosshatch of red and white kebab sauces. Crumbled feta. Diced jalapeños and tomatoes. Beautiful.

"When festival season starts, Gubben . . ."

"I think we have a new menu item," I finished.

Farfar gave Lou a high five while she beamed nearly to bursting, and I did the same, and I'm pretty sure our hands stayed locked just a second past normal.

And that's when Lou's family showed up.

"What are you guys doing here?" Lou yelled, startled, dropping my hand and leaning past me out the window. "It's only nine o'clock."

"Geez Louise," her dad said, holding his hands up. "Just thought we'd come check it out. Maybe try a bite to eat. Is that okay?"

I remember thinking her dad looked just like her—tall, thin, dark hair thick like Lou's, cut short—until I looked at Lou's mom standing behind him and saw Lou's exact face in thirty years, staring back at me.

Lou turned around to roll her eyes at us, but Farfar was already out of the truck, circling around the front to introduce himself.

They were charmed almost immediately. Lou and I stood together and watched as the three of them chatted easily—about where Farfar was originally from, about why kebab is a big thing in Finland and Sweden, about how wonderful Lou was—while the guy with them, an older brother I didn't know Lou even had, glanced back at us, looking bored, fidgety. I couldn't figure out why he'd even come along—he was clearly a grown adult, probably in his early twenties, but he hung behind like a cranky teenager, stuck there with all of us.

Lou stayed silent the whole time, until the food runner from Rogue's Roost came out with another round of orders and Farfar had to climb back inside the truck.

Lou's parents looked over the menu, even more intrigued now after talking to Farfar, while he and I started on the orders.

"I can take your orders when you're ready," Lou said out the window, businesslike. Begrudging, but businesslike.

"I gotta try the Hej Hej! Special Rullekebab," her dad said, unable to say it without smiling. "Sweetie, you know what you want?"

"Mmm, can I just have a bite of yours if I get the Äpple Munk? Did I say that right?"

I looked back from the fryer and saw them bump hips, like they were totally still in love with each other—a lot like Jorge and Jesus's parents, actually—and I couldn't understand why Lou seemed so annoyed with them.

"JJ? Anything for you?" Lou's dad asked, but her brother just shook his head and mumbled something about not feeling great.

Lou started to total it up, but Farfar called out, "It's on the house! I'm so glad I got to meet you!"

Her parents put up a cursory argument, but they were too overcharmed to resist.

"You're allowed to take your food inside Rogue's Roost and sit down," Farfar said. "They have very good beer."

I caught her mom and dad glancing at each other quickly before her dad smiled and said, "That's all right. It's a beautiful night out here."

It was only nine-thirty by the time they'd eaten and raved to us how good it all was, and how they'd have to find us in Gettysburg more often, but Lou turned back to us, suddenly looking exhausted, all the loaded-kebab-fry magic drained out of her.

"Will you guys be okay if I go now?"

"Yes! Of course! Go ahead," Farfar replied quickly. "Thank you so much for all your help, Looo. Kebab fries for life!" he said like a giant dork while Lou stared at the floor, and when she looked up, Farfar winked at her. She gave a small smile, and he pulled out a wad of folded bills for her. "Hopefully at least another book or two," he said.

It was well after midnight when we made it home, and we definitely could've used Lou's help when the postbar rush stumbled up to our window. A dinner rush at midnight, after we'd been in the truck nearly twelve hours already, was almost more than I could handle. Luckily (I guess), it was mostly donuts, and Farfar had prewrapped a bunch of rullekebabs ahead of time in anticipation of the rush, so he stayed at the window. He was way better with the drunks than I was, like he could flip a switch and match their booming, messy laughter as though he'd been drinking right alongside them all night.

I needed to just fry things in relative silence by then, and I barely kept my eyes open on the drive home, Farfar's station a little louder than normal and the windows open to help him stay awake, too.

"I had no idea she even had a brother," I said as we rumbled out of Franklin into pitch-black farmland.

"He did not look so hot, did he?"

And that was the last he said the rest of the way home.

# CHAPTER NINETEEN

## THINGS WERE GOOD

FUJIS. FRENCH FRIES. LOU EVEN JOINED US ON HALLOWEEN, when we set up the truck downtown like we always do to hand out hot chocolate to trick-or-treaters and their parents—even though she talked about her UPenn application nonstop the entire night. I mean, it was annoying, but it wasn't *terrible*, you know?

By the first week of November, I could get all the collected apples—the new, local Fujis—prepped in one period, especially with most of them going straight into pots for the ongoing demand for cider. Though sometimes I'd hold off, just so poor Terrance could have a reason for showing up for lunch detentions.

But the following Tuesday, within the first fifteen minutes in the culinary lab, while I quartered Fujis, Lou had already gone back and forth a dozen times on whether she'd get in or not. And whatever she was supposed to be working on in front of her—AP whatever—wasn't getting done.

Finally, she dropped her pencil onto her notebook and sat back in her chair.

"I mean, it's fine if I don't get into Penn, right?"

"It's fine by me," I replied, dumping a pile of apple quarters into a stockpot.

"That's not helpful."

I wasn't trying to be dismissive. I just thought it was an easy question. An easy question that she kept asking over and over.

"Yes. It is fine if you don't get into Penn," I said, looking directly at her while I said it, trying to give her the serious tone she was looking for. "It's not like you aren't going to get into a bunch of other schools."

She dropped her forehead to her hand, her eyes scanning her open math book. "I've worked so hard. . . ."

"For what? For some fancy school—for someone sitting in an office at an *Ivy League* school—to look at your stupid transcripts and tell you you're good enough? God, Lou, who cares?"

"*I* care," she shot back, defensive. "Just because it's not important to you, doesn't—"

"Lou, what is it that's important to you? Don't you want to be a doctor or a researcher or something? Isn't that what you told Farfar?"

Lou frowned at me but didn't respond right away.

"I mean, do you want to be a doctor to help people, or do you just want to be able to tell people you're an Ivy League doctor?"

"That's a really shitty thing to say."

"I'm arguing on *your* behalf!" I dropped the knife I'd just picked up back onto the cutting board. "*It is fine if you don't get into Penn.* Do only Penn grads go to medical school? Are all the doctors you know Penn grads? Are any of them? There are so many ways to get to what you want, all this stress seems completely pointless."

"It opens up more opportunities," Lou finally said, clearly redeveloping her argument on the fly, which was infuriating—because, again, *I was arguing on her behalf.* "You don't understand."

She wouldn't look at me when she said that last part, which made me think she was *trying* to piss me off. Which pissed me off.

"Whoa," Mrs. Bixler said, standing in the doorway with her coffee mug, looking back and forth between the two of us. "I could hear you guys from the hallway. Oz, do I have to ask you to put the knife away?"

She laughed to herself and set her mug on her desk. "Seriously, you guys okay in here?"

I just raised my eyebrows and shook my head, trying to get back to my apples.

Lou finally said, "I'm just stressed. College apps and stuff."

Mrs. Bixler walked over behind her and squeezed her shoulders. "You're gonna be fine, Lou. Don't let it overwhelm you."

I'd like to point out here that Mrs. Bixler went on to make essentially my exact argument, and Lou did not fight back or tell her she didn't understand. She just spent the rest of the period working in silence, and I happily did the same. (Harry was getting good—I loved *Azkaban*.)


Lou didn't show up to school on Wednesday—I figured she'd stressed herself into the stomach flu or something. I know that doesn't make sense. I'm not trying to get into med school.


So it was Thursday.

Lou was back. Other than a weak hello with the new cart of apples, she didn't say much of anything the whole period. She asked if I needed a hand, which was weird—not that she wasn't helpful, that was just not how it normally went fourth period. I worked on my thing, she worked on hers.

I told her I was fine, and that was it. Quiet, productive work for both of us for the next forty-five minutes.

At the end of the period, after Mrs. Bixler had come in and noticed the quiet with raised eyebrows but relative quiet of her own, I left for a few minutes to hit the bathroom.

And when I came back, I could hear the two of them talking, and for some reason, I slowed up outside the door.

"I just hate him sometimes . . . so frustrating . . . like he doesn't care about his future at all—or anyone else's. . . ."

My stomach sank. I circled right back to the bathroom.

I know, I don't know how many times I'd made it clear to Farfar that I couldn't stand her. I get that there's a pathetic double standard here, and I'm too sensitive, and all that. I know. But I was just not prepared to hear that from Lou. Not after, you know, we'd become kind of friends.

I know. I know. Stop being an idiote, Gubben.

We weren't *kind of* friends. We were friends. With Jorge still in soccer season, I was spending way more time with Lou than anybody else in my life, besides Farfar. And even those numbers were probably pretty close.

And I know I'm more of a cranky old man than Farfar most of the time, but, yeah, I liked her being around—way more than I was willing to admit.

I liked that she showed up every day.

I liked that she was more comfortable in a room with me, working away in the kitchen, than in the commons with all the other seniors lounging around during privs.

I liked how she worked on the truck after that first time or two. And I liked listening to the two of them talk, she and Farfar, almost constantly if we weren't busy with orders.

I even kind of liked the stupid apples. I wouldn't have guessed I'd be able to handle a job of that magnitude, mostly on my own, even after years on the truck with Farfar.

So I was stung when I heard what Lou said to Mrs. Bixler. Stung that she'd say it to *Mrs. Bixler,* of all people.

Lou was gone to lunch when I came back the second time. With most of the apples already prepped or in stockpots, I spent the whole next period making batches and batches of pastry dough to stock up in the fridge—lots of pies coming— arguments swirling in my head the entire time. Arguments I'd formed a billion times before—arguments I'd made to Farfar a billion times, too.

*. . . like he doesn't care about his future at all . . .*

**CHAPTER TWENTY**

---

# FARFAR'S BUSINESS
# SCHOOL: THIRD LESSON

WE TOOK THE TRUCK TO DISTRICTS THAT FRIDAY, EVEN THOUGH it was ridiculous to take the truck to a soccer game over an hour away when we weren't selling any food. But that was the next lesson in Farfar's Business School—driving the truck on the highway. And Gettysburg to Hersheypark Stadium was all manner of highway.

Lou wasn't at the game, which was just fine with me.

But Skylar Jarrett was there.

She came up to sit next to me as soon as she saw me in the stands, held her arms out for a hug, as though that were our normal way of greeting each other. I introduced Farfar as my grandfather, and he smiled, not insincerely. He was polite.

"I love your accent!" Skylar said, leaning into my shoulder to talk across to him. "Where are you from?"

"Finland," he said. "You would think I would be used to this cold." He rubbed his hands together and blew on them, smiled again, and turned back to the game. Skylar kept her shoulder pressed to mine.

Skylar talked to me then for a while, about things going on with her friends I didn't totally understand—partly because I couldn't pin faces to any of the names she was saying.

"Are you a senior as well?" Farfar asked a little while later, in a lull in conversation coinciding with a corner setup.

"No, I'm a sophomore. My brother plays," she said, pointing at the cluster in front of the goal. "Caleb. Number fifteen."

Farfar nodded, looking out at the field as play resumed. "Your brother is a very good defender." Which was true. Javy was a beast in the goal, but Caleb was an equally huge part of their ridiculous point differential this year.

"Thank you," she replied, beaming. "I can't imagine this team without the twins next year, though." Farfar perked up a little bit, at least, realizing she knew about soccer and knew our boys. "Did you hear Jesus is going to play Division One next year?"

"Loyola?"

Skylar nodded excitedly. "They offered a full scholarship. I think he's already committed."

Farfar smiled wide then, genuine—one of his boys achieving his dream. He might even have been getting a little dewy-eyed, too, but I noticed he turned his attention back to the game right then, rubbing his hands together and cupping them around his mouth to yell *"Go Hornets!"*—which I'd never seen him do even once. He loved watching their games, but he definitely wasn't a yeller.

And fine, I yelled then, too. My voice only cracked a little.

Farfar went to find Jorge and Jesus's parents at halftime, and Skylar immediately put her arm through mine.

"A bunch of us are going to Red Robin after the game—you should come."

174

I didn't know if she meant a bunch of the families or a bunch of the high schoolers who'd traveled here for the game. Maybe both.

"Uh . . . I don't think we can." I could feel the heat of her arm on my arm, my side, through our sweatshirts. "We drove the truck."

"The food truck? Here? Are you selling food after the game or something?"

"No. Just practice."

"*You* drove the food truck here?" she said, grinning up at me. (Lou's shoulder, I'd noticed, was square with mine. With her lanky frame, she was probably a good five inches taller than Skylar, who looked up at me while she leaned into my shoulder.)

I couldn't help smiling, and for some dumb reason, I could feel my ears go hot, too. "I mean, if I'm going to run the truck on my own someday, I'm going to have to know how to take it on the highway."

"Oh my god!" she said, and she had that aggressive eye contact thing going again. "The picture of you behind the wheel of the food truck is *adorable*!"

She squeezed my arm with hers, even pulled me down a little while she said it.

She wasn't subtle. But it really wasn't the worst thing in the world, to have someone attractive—I'll say it: Skylar was hot—that obviously into you.

I'm sure Farfar had to have experienced it a few times, too—Mr. Cool-Guy Ponytail. There had to be someone outside of Farmor and Amir. Hell, maybe it *was* Amir—he'd never told me how any of that actually started.

Anyway, Skylar's arm was still attached to mine when Farfar

175

came back. I saw him look twice when he stepped past us to his seat. And she kept it there the rest of the game—the whole second half—even as the rain started to fall and she pulled up her hood and rested her head on my shoulder. Even as the game ended on penalties, and Jorge and Jesus and the rest of the team huddled around a crying Javy after giving up the last goal and Cocalico (wherever the heck that was) stormed the field to mob their striker/champion/hero.

"If you come to States next week," Skylar said, her head finally lifting from my shoulder but her arm tugging mine down a little bit, "maybe leave the truck at home. You could hang out with us after the game."

I smiled and nodded. Farfar stood to stretch and fold the towel he'd brought to sit on, and when I looked back at Skylar on my arm, she gave me this ridiculously cheesy smile. There were drops of rain in her eyelashes and her cheeks were flushed from the chill, and I will tell you, it felt okay. Definitely better than *I just hate him sometimes* and *doesn't care about his future at all.*

"I should probably get back to my parents," she said, and she pulled me into a long hug. "Be careful driving home in that food truck, mister."

Then she said a quick goodbye to Farfar and headed down the steps to find her family. Farfar was staring at me, nostrils flared, when I turned around.

"What?"

"What?"

"You're looking at me weird."

"I am waiting for you to go down the steps so I can get out of this rain . . . *mister.*"

"This Sky-lar seems to like you an awful lot," Farfar said from the passenger seat on the ride home.

I nodded, blushing, hoping it was dark enough that he couldn't see it.

"Yeah . . ."

"Do you like this Sky-lar an awful lot?"

"I don't know yet."

"Just be careful, Gubben. Relationships can be tricky, especially if you're not sure of things."

"I know, I know. . . ."

"Do you know, Gubben? Hmm. How many relationships have you been in?"

"I've stopped counting."

"Did you *start* counting, Gubben?"

"Hey. Hey. The muscles just came in this year, okay?"

"All those push-ups for the online gym, yes?" he said, reaching over to poke the rippling bicep of my outstretched arm, holding the steering wheel.

"No poking the driver. Safety first."

## CHAPTER TWENTY-ONE

# WHERE I WANT
# THE STORY TO GO

IT RAINED THE WHOLE WEEKEND. SO NO TRUCK. NO LOU. JUST *Mario Kart,* a trip to Golden Dragon for the buffet, and a steady stream of Instagram DMs from Skylar until I gave her my number and we switched to texting.

"Gubben, you will never beat me if you keep looking at your phone."

"You're walking right into my trap, old man."

I didn't win a single race that weekend.

There was still a good chance of rain on Tuesday, even in Philly, where our first-round matchup was for States. As the second seed out of District Three, we were paired up with the winners of District Twelve, which was basically Philadelphia. (Jorge explained all this to me, obviously—it all sounded very *Hunger Games*y to me.)

Farfar wasn't willing to make the trip on a Tuesday night to potentially sit in the rain again, but the school offered a bus for students to go, leaving right at the end of the school day. Lou, again, was absent—she'd remained mostly silent the past two days in the culinary lab. I was shocked she showed up at all, after declaring her hatred for me to Mrs. Bixler.

Skylar was there, in seat eighteen, right over the wheel well, saving a spot for me. We rode together with our knees propped up on the seat back in front of us for the full two and a half hours to the South Philly Supersite, which, despite its arena-sounding name, looked pretty much like any other high school stadium.

Just like at the Districts game, Skylar sat attached to me the entire time. The entire 5–2 loss, her arm in mine. And then the quiet two-and-a-half-hour bus ride back in the dark, just the soft glow from people's phones going on and off throughout the bus around us, like we were inside a jar of lightning bugs in summer.

I leaned my shoulder against the window, and Skylar fell asleep with her head on my other shoulder, both of our knees propped up on the seat in front of us again.

My mind swirled most of the ride back. For some reason, everything just felt . . . *surreal.* That really was the last game Jorge and Jesus would play together. Yeah, Jesus was going to keep going, move on and keep playing at Loyola in less than a year, with new goals and new dreams, I guessed. But everything the two of them had worked toward together, the fantasies they'd mapped out as kids at the playground—that was now officially over, a weirdly anticlimactic end on a strange field on a rainy Tuesday night, hours away from home.

Granted, they'd made it farther than any team in school history, and what they'd accomplished was incredible, but it was surreal to be just a few minutes on the other side of it. That story was over, and it was like we still had our hands on the back cover of the book.

And at the same time was this new thing happening with Skylar. I mean, it felt good to have this girl like me so much, to want to fall asleep on my shoulder, to flirt with me unabashedly on a daily basis at school. That was not the norm for me.

But Farfar's words in the truck on the way home from Hershey kept repeating in my head: *Relationships can be tricky, especially if you're not sure of things.* All of this felt so different, and honestly, I wasn't totally sure of things—whether this was where I wanted the next part of my story to go.

And for some stupid reason, I kept thinking about how annoying Lou was, and how wrong she was, and Skylar would shift a little bit on my shoulder and put a hand on my leg, and I'd be like, *Idiote, why is this even in your brain right now?*

When the bus finally got off on the Gettysburg exit, a little after midnight, Skylar pulled in a deep breath and lifted her head off my shoulder. I turned my head to look at her, and she was smiling up at me a few inches away, and as we rumbled into the familiar streets in town toward school, she pulled me closer and kissed me.

And while the major part of my brain was like, *Wow, Oscar, I really enjoy this fascinating new sensation,* there was this other nagging part, this annoyingly analytical part, that was like . . . *Hmm. This kinda tastes like . . .* celery?

Is that right?

That can't be right.

## CHAPTER TWENTY-TWO

# VERY REAL TALK

"HAVE WE DISCUSSED THE BIRDS AND THE BEES, GUBBEN?" FAR-far said, just as we started our third lap on Wario's Gold Mine, the one track I hated almost as much as Rainbow Road.

"Uh . . . I'm pretty sure that was covered in online health."

I launched my red shell, which he deftly blocked with the banana peel he'd been holding on to.

I finished fourth after getting hit by a stupid ricocheting green shell, Farfar's Yoshi already halfway through its victory lap. I tossed my remote on the coffee table, picked up my melting bowl of mint chocolate chip, flopped back into the cushion in disgust, and took a huge spoonful.

"Do you know how a condom works?"

I'd like to point out here that mint fumes make choking even worse.

"It is time for *real talk*, Gubben," he said, swapping his empty bowl for his beer and a scratch behind Koopa's ears on the cushion behind him. "I truly hope to be a gammelfarfar, but I am not sure now is the best time."

I stared at him, momentarily frozen, while he raised his eyebrows over a sip of beer.

"Um . . . are you under the impression that I've been trying to impregnate someone?"

Fact check: I was not.

"Gubben, this Sky-lar has been to our apartment. Things seem to be getting hot and heavy rather quickly."

"Please do not say *hot and heavy*."

"Gubben. Do you know how a condom works?" he asked again.

"Oh my god, can you—"

"Ohh, lilla missekissen Koopa-poopa . . . Gubbe-Gubbe does not want to tell us if he knows how a condom works."

"Stop talking to the cat about condoms and . . . *me*. That is, like, not even in the realm of possibility right now. . . ."

When I said it, it felt true. Yeah, there had been a lot of kissing in the week since the bus ride to States. A *lot*. And a fair amount of wandering hands—though nothing infiltrating any undergarments and nothing into anyone's nether regions. Honest.

I mean, I'd obviously thought about sex before—I'm not trying to say I hadn't (regardless of how badly I'd prefer to be not saying any of this). But it had always been in more . . . abstract terms.

*I do not understand what abstract sex is, Gubben,* I could hear Farfar saying, which is why I did not say that out loud at the time.

Even if I liked all the . . . *stuff* we were doing, I still wasn't totally sure about things, which maybe sounds terrible.

If there's one thing I've learned from Farfar about relationships, it's that it *matters* that you're sure about things—even before he ever said those words to me. That there are serious consequences if you're not, if you just go along with what you think you're supposed to do.

And after one week, I just wasn't sure about things.

And okay, maybe this is more than you need to hear, but I was still really thrown by the taste thing, sticking in the back of my head. Even after we'd both chewed gum, after donuts, after I had a grape soda and she had a Sprite . . . it was still there. I even asked what her favorite vegetable was—in the middle of a movie we were barely watching—under the guise that I was just generally curious about all things food-related.

"Uhh . . . I guess broccoli?" she said.

"How do you feel about celery?"

She looked at me, rightfully, like I was an idiote.

"Um, I liked when my mom made me ants-on-a-log when I was a kid? Otherwise, I'm not a fan. . . . You're really weird, by the way."

And she went right back to kissing me, which only made it more impossible to expel from my head.

All this to say that I stand by what I said to Farfar next.

"Fine. Yes. I know how condoms work. Me and Jorge and Jesus bought some from the vending machine in the bowling alley bathroom a few years ago."

"And you . . ." Farfar started to straighten his index finger and approach it with his other index finger and thumb.

"Yes! Yes. Please stop."

Thankfully, he put his hands back down and reached for his beer again.

"I am telling you, Farfar. Honestly. I do not think I will need to . . . *use* that bit of information anytime soon."

"I would suggest you not use those particular condoms, either."

"Yeah, I didn't think they looked terribly trustworthy."

He got up to go to the kitchen and tousled my hair, which seemed like an odd gesture for the conversation, and came back with another beer.

"I am proud of you for being honest, Gubben," he said, settling back into the couch and picking the next track—Mushroom Gorge, his token of appreciation. "Not just with me, but with yourself."

He let the course overview play through and turned to face me.

"I know you know to have consent, Gubben. That you would never pressure anybody. But remember, if *you* are unsure, it is okay for you to say no, too."

Farfar looked at me for another moment, his face serious, sincere, before settling back in to start the race.

"Hmm. That went much smoother than the last time I had to give this talk. . . ."

## CHAPTER TWENTY-THREE

# ENTER PUMPAMUNK

IT PROBABLY SHOULD'VE BEEN A SIGN, HOW RELIEVED I WAS that Skylar and her family traveled to Ohio every year for Thanksgiving.

But honestly, after the year I'd had to that point, I was relieved to get back to a routine that was just *ours*. Thanksgiving doesn't really exist in Finland or Sweden (duh), and with just the two of us here, we'd always kind of done our own thing. Even Maggie and Juliet leave town for the day to go to Juliet's sister's house out in western PA somewhere. Lillajul was our day, anyway.

So we spent most of the day with Rhonda at the Council of Churches, preparing Thanksgiving meals for an alarming number of folks in need, along with to-go meals for families who applied for help. I'm still blown away that Rhonda's family—her husband and two grown sons and their wives and even a young, big-headed grandchild toddling around—give up their whole Thanksgiving Day to be there with her, too.

"Mike'll smoke me a turkey tomorrow while I'm shopping with my sisters," Rhonda told us with a tired, happy smile.

We stuck to our usual, having one modest plate of food each around lunchtime, the rest of the day devoted to cooking and serving. Well, *I* stuck to our usual—*Farfar* gulped down a second plate of mashed potatoes and stuffing when he thought I wouldn't see him, then smiled at me guiltily when I did. Not his best moment.

And when we'd helped clean up after the serving line closed at five, we headed out for our own annual Thanksgiving feast. Golden Dragon Buffet.

We sat at our usual table in the mostly deserted restaurant, beneath the enormous painting of rainbow koi I've loved since I was a kid, and toasted our crab Rangoon.

"I'm thankful I've only got six months left before I'm finished with school forever."

Farfar rolled his eyes and shook his head.

"I am thankful for the new friends we have made."

"Lou," I said, rolling my eyes and shaking my head back at him.

"I was going to say Sky-lar, but yes, definitely Looo . . . since that's what you were thinking."

Dirty trick.

"And I am thankful for the impressive young man you have become, Gubben. And I am thankful that you have still not found a way to beat me at Rainbow Road . . . or any other track." He thought for a moment while I flared my nostrils at him, our Rangoons still hovering over the bowl of duck sauce. "Yes. The end."

"Everyone knows Yoshi cheats."

And, as per tradition, we tapped Rangoons, plunged them into the duck sauce, and shoved the whole things into our mouths in one bite.

And then we went to refill our plates.

We got run out of the outlets the year before on Black Friday, even though we'd coordinated the location with the Magic Bean—they'd send early shoppers to us for donuts (or a.m. rullekebab—no judgment here), we'd send them to the Bean for coffee. It was working really well before Security told us we had to leave a little after nine.

So this year, we decided to just sleep in on Black Friday. (Well, I slept in; Farfar was probably still up at old-guy o'clock.) And after a lazy morning, we had all afternoon to prep for the Tree Lighting downtown.

"Is Looo still in town, Gubben?" he asked when we finally rolled off the couch around lunchtime.

"Why?"

I knew why.

"Tree Lighting will be busy," he said, stretching his arms above his head, his belly enjoying a little time in the light. "I would appreciate the help."

"What about Jorge?" I tried. "Soccer's over. . . ."

"Gubben. Jorge has never once *asked* to help on the truck. Have you noticed this? He will always help if we ask, because he is a good friend and a good person, but I don't think he really *wants* to be there. He is not *hoping* that we ask him. I think maybe sometimes he was hoping we would not ask."

I knew this was true. Jorge *would* say yes, like he'd said yes to the different festivals the summers before. And he worked hard and was great with customers. But if he could, he'd meet us there at go time and drive home at festival's end. He definitely didn't *love* it like I did.

And Lou . . . Lou had become just as good as Jorge at running the window and coordinating orders for us. *And* she liked being there to help set up, to debrief as we cleaned up, to chatter endlessly with Farfar all the while.

I knew all this.

I just wasn't really looking to give up any of my newly free Thanksgiving/Little Christmas break to someone who *hated me sometimes.* Someone who could spend all this time with me in our truck, in my culinary lab, and still think I didn't care about my future just because it didn't line up with *her* idea of success.

"And I just like Looo, Gubben," Farfar said, and I knew I couldn't tell him any of it just then.

"You two are in charge of the menu this evening," he said, laying the chalkboard across the counter in front of us. He'd just brought it up from the truck in the garage, and Koopa was already curled up in Lou's lap on the stool, and I could hear her whispering "Lilla missekissen" while stroking Koopa's back.

This, naturally, caused Farfar to go into a fit of Swedish baby talk. Koopa then tried to roll onto her back in Lou's lap, yowling feverishly, and ended up rolling right onto the floor.

"Uh . . . that may have been too much for her," Farfar said, coming around the counter and scooping her up in his arms. "It is up to you," he continued, talking to us but nose to sötnos with Koopa, "if you want to add fries, and what kinds, and anything else. You call tonight."

"I don't have any russets in my car this time," Lou said, smiling.

"I can run to the store—I took care of all my veggie prep this morning while Gubben was still snoozing."

"Sleepy sleepy Gubben," Lou said, grinning at me, which threw me off completely—it was strange to hear *Gubben* out of anybody else's mouth, much less Lou's, and I didn't understand how she suddenly could be teasing me after what she'd confided to Mrs. Bixler. She didn't *sound* like Presentation Lou.

"You should probably start the munkar dough, Gubben. Figure out the menu, and I'll pick up whatever else we need."

Thankfully, my dough-making routine gave my brain something else to think about, and we ended up having a great discussion on fry options and pricing for the evening. It was actually kind of exciting, this chance to test out the fries for real before taking them to festivals in the spring.

"Planning for the future on the truck," I said, staring at Lou's head while she wrote the menu heading along the top of the chalkboard. "My favorite thing."

She didn't even look up. Like it didn't even register—which made it feel even dumber, since it didn't sound at all natural to begin with.

"We should've started planning earlier," she said. "We totally could've done poutine tonight."

Like it was scripted, we got flurries that night. How perfect was that? Lincoln Square was a mob scene—a festive mob scene that was *really* into our offerings.

We kept the normal kebab menu in full, since that was Farfar's jam, plus they're handheld and wrapped in foil—perfect for standing around with cold hands.

We decided to try fries for real, along with loaded-kebab-fry baskets, which I thought would take a while to figure out the workflow for, since this was the first item we'd ever made that crossed from my station to Farfar's. But it really just amounted to me (or Lou) sliding a fry basket over to his station to finish off. And we sold quite a few.

We stuck with the traditional Äpple Munk and the favorite munkhål, but we also added a seasonal one I'd been working on in Mrs. Bixler's room during this dramatic lull in school-apple leftovers. I'd perfected a pumpkin cream cheese filling to go with a cinnamon sugar coating. It was like if pumpkin pie and donuts had a baby, and that baby turned out to be the Chosen One from the prophecy. *Pumpa*munk.

And lastly, hot chocolate. Lou was there at Halloween and had pushed hard to add it for the Tree Lighting crowd.

"I can handle all that at the window," she'd said, already excitedly adding it to the menu board earlier that day. "You two won't have to deal with it at all."

Farfar shot me a look with Koopa still in his arms, and I rolled my eyes and shook my head. But I knew he was right.

*Everything* sold well. In just a two-hour window.

The three of us sat on the back bumper of the truck at the end of the night, after most people had left, sipping hot chocolates of our own, watching flurries fall against the warm backdrop of Christmas lights in the circle.

"How *is* the pumpkin cream cheese hot chocolate?" I asked Lou, who was sitting between us.

"It's a bit much," she admitted, forcing down another sip. "I got a little overzealous, I think."

"Happens to the best of us," Farfar said, chuckling. Then, "Has Oscar told you about Lillajul?"

I knew it was coming.

Everything felt like a jumbled mess in my mind. The fact that I didn't miss Skylar. The fact that I couldn't shake the sting of Lou's words to Mrs. Bixler. What the juxtaposition of those two thoughts even meant.

I just knew, watching Lou nearly gag on the last glop of melted pumpkin cream cheese hot chocolate gloop, that I wasn't upset that he'd told her.

## CHAPTER TWENTY-FOUR

# A CHRISTMAS APPETIZER

I'D SAY WE BOTH CRUSHED LITTLE CHRISTMAS, FARFAR AND I.

Lou was there early, like it was any other Saturday, like she was there to help on the truck, her long braid hanging from beneath a white knit cap and over the shoulder of a striped red sweater with little tiny skiers woven into the design.

"My grandma got it for me a few years ago," she said. "It's kind of ridiculous, but it makes me smile."

Farfar still made chocolate chip pancakes, even though we had a full day of cooking and eating ahead of us, and the three of us slid stools up to the island counter so he could lay out the plan for the day. And give Lou the full explanation of what Lillajul really was for us.

"They do not do this across Sweden or Finland," he explained. "This is a tradition only in Åland. It is celebrated on the Saturday before the first Sunday of Advent, the kickoff to the Christmas season to come. A *Christmas appetizer*," he said, grinning at me. "One small gift."

And, like always, the two of them went back and forth, Lou asking endless questions about the history and traditions and what he did as a kid back in Åland, and Farfar reveling in the chance to explain it all in detail. I, like usual, was happy to listen.

Farfar had even prepared a Lillajul Itinerary, I think solely for Lou's benefit—he'd never written one out before that I could remember.

I started on the dough for saffron buns after breakfast, to give them the hours they needed to rise. Farfar brought the decorations up from the garage, along with the small potted Christmas tree he'd picked up early that morning, maybe three feet tall with the pot. I think folks in Åland probably get a full-sized tree, as well, in the following week or so, but with just the two of us, in a second-floor walk-up apartment, our tiny tree was all we needed. And it looks nice from outside, sitting on the end table in the front window.

Our tree only takes one string of lights, plus our tomte tree-topper, our collection of Moomin character ornaments, and, one of my favorite of our unique, nothing-to-do-with-Åland-or-anything-else-but-our-apartment traditions, the little origami ornaments we make new each year after everyone's eaten, just before our one-present opening. I think Farfar came up with it in our first years together, as a way to draw out our little two-person celebration a bit more.

While I stepped in to help with the tree with Lou, Farfar started on the glögg. Two large potfuls—one traditional alcoholic, made with an alarming number of bottles, one non-alcoholic for me and the rest of the children (even if I *was* about to become a legal adult).

By the time the dough was ready to be rolled out into scrolly-S-shaped buns, the apartment smelled like unrefined holiday cheer. And once they were in the oven? Jösses. If you could be hugged by a smell, walking into our apartment at 3:00 p.m. on Little Christmas would be like a two-armed bear hug into Mrs. Claus's bosom.

"So, julbord," Lou said, looking down at the itinerary again, after the last of the Moomin ornaments—Fillyjonk—was on the tree.

"You know smörgåsbord, yes?"

"Hmm, I never realized that was a Swedish word."

"Ja. *Julbord* means 'Christmas table.'"

Which tended to include a lot of pickled herring and beets and some other things that might not thrill a non-Swedish crowd. Or me. And since we'd made our own version of Little Christmas all these years, we'd made our own version of a julbord, too—the non-traditional holdovers from Farfar's years with Amir, the traditional returnees for Maggie and Juliet, and the second round of non-traditional that we'd introduced together—like a timeline of our overlapping lives. It had turned into a kind of potluck now, with Jorge and Jesus usually bringing tamales and some other goodies from their aunt's restaurant, and Maggie and Juliet adding a few dishes of their own.

"Are homemade pizzas usually part of a julbord? I was going to guess ham or something."

And then, Farfar just started talking. About Amir. About leaving. Like Lou already knew.

"We could do whatever we wanted," he said. "We were maybe a little giddy, a little childish. But it was our first Lillajul together, just the two of us. And we were both still raw, still guilt-ridden at what we'd left behind. Me more than Amir," he admitted, dropping his head.

Farfar *never* talked about this. *Never* shared this part of his story. But with Lou, I don't know, it just came out of him— these things I'd wondered about for years. She sat silent on her stool, her chin resting in her hand, eyes locked on him like she was soaking in everything she could.

"That first year," he continued, smiling again, his voice thick, "Amir said no meatballs, no salmon—nothing I had been eating at the holidays for the previous forty-five years."

"Pizzas," I said.

"Homemade pizzas." He nodded and glanced at me for just a second. "We didn't even do the saffron buns and the glögg the first few years, even though they were my favorites. Just pizzas and a present. Not until we started inviting Maggie and Juliet and they started asking questions about traditions, and I wanted to give it a try again." Farfar looked at me again while I pulled the clean mixing bowls from the drying rack. "It is exciting through someone else's eyes, yes?" And when I smiled and nodded, he added, "Amir thought so, too."

It was an interesting way to come out—to just pretend as though you're already out (which, outside of Lou, I guess he was) and wait for the person to catch up.

With someone like Lou, well, she had no problem catching up. And I wondered how many other people he'd done that with—if there was only a certain kind of person you could do that with, or if a person had to somehow prove themselves to you in some way without them knowing. Or maybe Lou was just different, and Farfar knew it.

But Lou didn't blink. Just leaned in and absorbed his story like every other one he told.

"So," she finally said, glancing around the apartment, "is Amir . . ."

"Yes, he passed away," Farfar said. "Fifteen years. Not long before I got Gubben, here."

Lou looked at me, spooning flour into a measuring cup for pizza dough, and back to Farfar, but she didn't interrupt, and I knew, just by the look on his face—like he was breathing in the first breath of cold air when you step outside from the warmth of the apartment in the morning—that this was it. Lou was about to get our whole story. Things I didn't even fully know.

"Amir had an accident. It all happened very quick."

"Like, a car accident?"

He nodded. "Not a big one. We thought he was okay. He *seemed* okay at first. But . . . the internal bleeding, it was much worse than they realized. We both went to bed that night, fell asleep beside each other. But Amir didn't wake up. Sometime while I was snoring, he stopped." Farfar paused, somehow managed a smile, and looked at Lou with shiny eyes. "He always claimed I snored worse than him, but that was a lie—he was like sleeping next to manufacturing equipment." He shook his head and looked down again. "An aneurysm in his sleep. And he was gone."

"Oh my god. I'm so sorry." Lou looked genuinely heart-broken for him. "So, you didn't get to say goodbye. . . ."

Farfar shook his head again, just barely.

"Just good night."

We were all quiet then for a moment.

"So, you and Amir, you lived here? In Gettysburg?"

"In this apartment, yes."

Lou looked back at me; I could see pieces fitting together in her brain.

"But you didn't live here yet," she said to me.

I shook my head. My voice wasn't working at the moment. Luckily, Farfar filled in.

"Gubben was still in Åland. In Mariehamn with his grand-mother. Farmor. And his parents sometimes."

Lou looked nervous to ask the next question, but I think she could tell Farfar was ready for it—that we'd follow this natural back-and-forth as long as she wanted, as much as she wanted to know.

"And Farmor—*Dad's mom*, right? Farmor is . . ."

"She is still alive," he replied. "Still in Mariehamn."

"And she was your . . ."

"My wife. Yes. Twenty-four years. Before I left. . . ."

And that was where I could see the guilt painted rose at the outer edges of his cheeks, his ears, like mine. Trying to be honest. To fill in the factual details of the story. He was married twenty-four years. Had one child, a son. A son who later fell into drugs, battled addiction. And after he thought his son had won the battle, Farfar dropped a bomb on it all and left. I could've filled those pieces in for him, tag in and finish the story, but my voice was still on lockdown, and Lou had all the patience in the world to hear it from Farfar's mouth.

She could listen to him all day, right?

"That's when you came here? With Amir? To Gettysburg?"

He nodded. "That is when we came here. Amir first. He had an uncle who was a visiting professor at the college. I had already . . . things had already fallen apart with Linnéa—Oscar's farmor—and I missed my friend." He shook his head the tiniest bit, erasing the half-truth that must've been automatic for so long. "I missed Amir."

"I wasn't even born yet," I said, finally finding my voice, thick as it was. Farfar smiled at me, his eyes wet, and I wasn't sure if it was because it was easier to tell the story with help, or if he was just thankful for a moment to take a breath, or both.

"So, how long did you live here . . . before Amir . . ."

"Ten years," he said. "Ten very good years."

"And that's when you started the food truck? Here in Gettysburg?" He nodded again. "Were there even a lot of food trucks around then? I thought the big boom was just a few years ago with that Korean barbecue truck in LA."

Lou researches everything. Farfar smiled.

"Amir's family ran a popular kebab shop in Mariehamn. It was a pretty easy transition for him—at least as far as the actual work. Me, not so much. I could cook a little bit, but I had never made munkar before in my life. They just made me happy, and I knew that is what I wanted to offer, as strange a combination as it is."

"I don't know," Lou said. "If you ever go to the Gyro Fest at the big Greek Orthodox church in York, people eat a huge gyro, then go back for honey puffs. Doesn't seem like that much of a stretch."

"Looo, this is why you are my favorite person."

Lou's hands, which had been playing with the end of her braid, fell to her side, like she was melting. I watched her and, honestly, despite the hurt I was still holding on to, I melted a little, too.

"It took a bit of time to figure out how to make them. But it was a *good* time. This kitchen was very messy, let me tell you, for many months. But it was a new life. We felt like we could do anything. . . ."

"Like make pizzas for Lillajul," Lou added, and Farfar chuckled.

"And I didn't want to sit in an office ever again."

"Hmm. I know what you mean," I said.

He rolled his eyes. Lou, too.

"You get to spend half your day in Mrs. Bixler's room," Lou said. "How bad could your day possibly be?"

"Hey, I work my butt off in there."

"Yeah, but you *love* it." She shook her head at me, and I couldn't help thinking about what she'd said in the hall, and it stung all over again, even if I didn't want it to.

"So just like that," Lou said, turning back to Farfar, "you went from engineer to donut—munkar—maker?"

"I still got to show off my engineering skills with the truck. Our first one was an old bread truck. Pepperidge Farm."

Farfar had this big, goofy grin on his face, and his eyes were still wet, his ears still pink.

He described the modifications to that first truck in loving, painstaking detail while we continued preparing for the rest of the night, chatty with emotions and embarrassment. Lou even more encouraging in response. All easy parts of the story, now, weaving through the early years, the two of them—Farfar and Amir—hustling their way into regular stops at the college, outside office buildings, construction sites. Even a regular, loyal base of Battlefield Park rangers. Eventually upgrading to a new(er) truck—the one Lou'd been trundling around in with us for the past two and a half months.

Farfar had had his first test mug of glögg, smacking his lips like he does every year, and I had pizza dough proofing and half the saffron buns scrolled into shape on trays, by the time he had talked his way back to the end of his days with Amir. The beginning of his days with me.

"So, can I ask," Lou said as Farfar ladled a second test mug for himself, "how you got here? From Mariehamn?" She was looking at me when I turned around from sliding the first two trays of saffron buns into the oven, and I instinctively looked at Farfar.

He downed the rest of the tiny mug and took a deep breath, leaning back against the sink.

"Gubben was four years old when I met him for the first time. Back in Mariehamn. I did not know he even existed before then."

He paused, and Lou was silent again, waiting.

"A few months after I lost Amir, I received a phone call from Linnéa—we never spoke after I moved here—that I needed to come back to Åland. Immediately."

I could see him starting to falter again, looking down at the floor. He mumbled "Sorry" and bent down to scoop up Koopa, who'd just stalked in from her nap on the windowsill, and rumbled something quietly into her ear while she meowed. Then he set her back down on the floor again.

"It's when my dad died," I said.

"Oh, god." Lou held a hand to her mouth, then instinctively to the end of her braid, pulled in front of her. "Right after Amir?"

Farfar nodded, frowning, pulling at the end of his ponytail—something I'd never seen him do before. But he managed the same line he'd told me for years.

"I lost a son and gained a grandson in the same trip."

"What happened to your dad?" She looked back at Farfar. "Your son? Not another accident."

"Filip had some problems when he was your age. Drugs. But I thought he'd moved past them by the time I left. I thought he was better. He *was*."

"He overdosed," I filled in. "I was four. I don't really remember any of it."

I couldn't read the look Lou gave me. It wasn't just sympathy, though. And she stared at me for what felt like a long time, before I finally said, "Could've used you there," thinking of her demo speech a few months before.

She tried to smile, but she had the same look Farfar had earlier—like she was taking in that first breath of frigid air.

I still couldn't figure it out, but she didn't ask any more questions for a while.

Luckily, Farfar kept filling in the story without her prompting, but I noticed her sudden silence. How she kept staring at me while Farfar talked, like she was analyzing me and not really even seeing me at the same time. Her last few saffron bun attempts were a total disaster.

"It was all too much loss for Linnéa. Too much to ask of her, to continue raising Oscar on her own. At the time, it was too much. I took custody, even though I'd only known Gubben for a few days. Even though I was terrified it would be a disaster."

"It was probably a little bit of a disaster," I said, smiling, my nose burning.

"Little bit," he conceded, smiling back. "But we did okay, eh, Gubben?"

I nodded. "We did okay."

And we did. We did okay.

## CHAPTER TWENTY-FIVE

# BETTER THAN
# THE DELUXE EDITION

MAGGIE AND JULIET SHOWED UP AS THE LAST TRAY OF SAFFRON buns came out of the oven—right after Jorge and Jesus had arrived. The twins didn't bat an eye at Lou being there.

They did, however, bat a few eyes when Maggie grinned at Farfar and said, "Is this the girlfriend?"

Lou was actually the first one to speak, somehow, Jorge and Jesus trying not to elbow each other and laugh, Farfar's ears turning pink to match his increasing glögg flush, my eyes and mouth frozen open.

"No, that's Skylar. I'm Lou," she said, extending her hand. "I just like to help on the truck."

"Looo is our good friend," Farfar said, recovering, resting an arm over her shoulder. "*And* an indispensable employee of Hej Hej! Incorporated."

It was a cheesy line. Seriously. But it fit in the moment, cutting some of the awkwardness. That is, until he dialed it back up again.

"She was Jorge's replacement," he said, squeezing Lou's shoulder and winking at Jorge. "It was time to upgrade the eye candy."

"He *is* the ugly one," Jesus quipped.

Farfar took the small Crock-Pot of Lit'l Smokies from Juliet, who had a panting, straining Winston in her other arm, and the attention turned mercifully to food—to the julbord now nearly complete with steaming saffron buns, tamales, homemade salsa and guac, and now Juliet's repulsive-sounding but highly addictive chili-sauce-and-grape-jelly-glazed Smokies.

Honestly, I hadn't been sure Lou even knew I had a girlfriend, which I know is stupid.

Everyone settled into spots on the couch while Farfar ladled mugs of glögg for himself and Maggie and Juliet (his fourth or so by that point), then little ones—our old Moomin mugs—for the "kids." That was when Koopa, looking for refuge from Winston, leapt into Lou's lap.

"Hej hej, lilla missekissen," Lou said, lowering her head and burying her hands in Koopa's flanks. "Mina lilla sötnos."

"Uhhh . . . ," Jesus said, grinning from the other end of the sectional. "What was that?"

Lou blushed, still scratching under Koopa's neck while she purred like a minibike, and Farfar swooped in with a tray of glögg, beaming at his *two* precious preciouses together. He set the tray on the coffee table and unleashed his most impressive string of Swedish baby talk to date.

"Wait," Lou said, eyes wide. "What was that last part? *Lilla pussgurka?*"

Farfar nodded. *"Pussgurka."* He couldn't hold back his ridiculous smile, the old goober. "'Kiss pickle.'"

"Kiss pickle?" Jorge said. "What kind of name is *kiss pickle*?" He put a hand over Jesus's face without looking, Jesus's grinning mouth already open. "Do not call me your kiss pickle, burbujita."

"Really, conejito?" Jesus said, shoving Jorge's hand away and flicking his ear.

"Translation, please," Farfar said, grinning at them both. It was hard to imagine sometimes that these two were at the top of our class.

"Our aunt," Jorge explained. He pointed a thumb at Jesus: "'Little Bubble.'" And then at himself: "'Little Bunny.' Jesus was on the chunky side as a little kid—her chubby little bubble."

"And Jorge left little turds all over the house."

"My grandma always called me Schnickelfritz," Maggie said, smiling and sipping her glögg. "I always thought it was just a nonsense word, but it actually means 'troublemaker.'"

Then Juliet chimed in with a whole string of names she was called by her family: Pumpkin, Turkey-butt, Tooter-pop.

"How the hell would you even translate that?" Maggie managed between laughs, leaning into Juliet next to her on the couch.

And I will say, I could listen to Farfar wrestle with *Tooter-pop* all day.

And then, after our lengthy, enlightening discussion on terms of endearment, from pets to people, Maggie was thoughtful enough to bring it all back to the awkward.

"So, where is this girlfriend?"


"Gubben, you did not have to get me a Lillajul gift," Farfar said after I dropped the gnome-paper-wrapped box in his lap, long after we'd started eating and laughing and making our annual mini-origami ornaments for our quarter-sized tree. Even though the origami had started as a way to draw out the day when it was just the two of us, it had become the prerequisite for the gift exchange. Everyone in the apartment had to make at least one origami ornament for the tree. We never kept them, so we never have an excuse to not do it the next year.

Jesus stepped up his game with that origami Christmas T. rex.

But Farfar said it every year—*Gubben, you did not have to get me a Lillajul gift*—even though I've never not gotten him one, at least not since Maggie and Juliet started joining us and Maggie started sneaking me out of the apartment to go shopping with her.

"I wasn't going to," I replied. "But I thought it'd be awkward to open up the keys to my new car and then have nothing for you."

"How did you know I had a spare key cut for the Prius? You ruin the surprise!"

Everyone's attention was on Farfar then, each of their single presents from him now opened: Maggie's bottle of local wine and Juliet's growler of beer from Rogue's Roost next to Juliet's leg where she sat on the floor, leaning against the couch next to Maggie's feet. Winston sprawled out next to her, finally ignoring Koopa in favor of his new rawhide bone. Jesus sat in the corner of the sectional, his feet buried beneath him in between cushions like a little kid, Jorge lying on his side on the floor beneath the TV, Lou on a stool at the counter, looking in.

"What is the *Wii U*, Gubben?" Farfar said, unable to keep the grin off his face as he balled the wrapping paper in his hands and stared at the box in his lap. "Don't we already have a Wii?" Then, more concerned, "How much did you spend on this?"

"Not too much," I said, grinning back. "It's refurbished."

"And old," Jorge added helpfully.

"And old. Nintendo's already moved on to newer systems. Plus," I said, tossing a second present onto Farfar's lap and picking up his blue Wii remote from the coffee table, strumming the rubber bands holding the battery cover in place with my thumb. "This system's backward compatible."

I watched Farfar peel back the paper on his unauthorized second present and nod to himself. He let out a sound like a deeply satisfied bear.

"Oh, god," Maggie said, laughing.

"Let's hook it up, Gubben."


"They released a deluxe edition for the newer system," I explained, leading to our lengthy, highly technical discussion of *Mario Kart 8* for Wii U vs. *8 Deluxe* for the Switch, while I hooked up the new system to the TV and Farfar refilled glöggs. Lou snacked on another saffron bun, watching quietly from her stool.

I honestly thought I'd finally gotten him—that my brilliant gift for Farfar had reached a new level, where we exchanged gifts as equals. But then he paused the game a few rounds in, after unlocking our second new kart, and said, "I still need to give you your gift, Gubben," and left the room. There was still an unopened box beneath our little tree, but he came back from his room with a yellow envelope.

"God Lillajul, Gubben." He handed the envelope to me and smiled, sheepish. "Och gratis på födelsedagen. You really are an old man now, eh?"

"Doesn't feel like keys," I said, shaking the envelope and squeezing all around the edges.

"No, Gubben . . . not keys."

I looked up at him, confused, then lifted the flap and pulled the sheaf of papers from inside. Another itinerary.

"Time to go back, Gubben. See where you are from."

Two weeks in Åland. After graduation.

I looked through the printed-out pictures, read the dates and times, the little bits I could decipher in Swedish, while Farfar explained it all—the plan to hit Mariehamn a lot, but staying in a little cottage, where we could still cook together, in Kvarnbo, near where he grew up.

"Time to go back to where I'm from, too, Gubben."

## CHAPTER TWENTY-SIX

# THE END OF
# CELERY SEASON

I KNEW FOR WEEKS THAT IT NEEDED TO HAPPEN. ENDING IT with Skylar. Honestly, she was a lovely girlfriend. Easygoing, loved hanging out with me, took my hand or my arm everywhere we went. Hot. She was definitely hot. It should've been easy.

But every time we'd be making out, which was happening with greater frequency and intensity since she'd gotten back from Ohio that Monday after Thanksgiving, two days after Lillajul— that nagging part of my brain kept pointing out the *taste*. That damn *celery*, like, hovering over the back of my tongue.

I mean, is it possible that maybe some people just *match*, chemically? Is there, like, actual *chemistry* behind people having chemistry? Do some of us just *align*, taste-budularly? Is that the scientific explanation for soul mates?

This probably wouldn't be a Farfar's Business School lesson or anything—and I can just see him howling at Farfar's Intimate Relationship Clinic. (We'd need to come up with a better name for that one, too.)

But every time, noticing and trying really hard not to notice the celery, I'd hear his voice from that ride home from Districts: *Just be careful, Gubben. Relationships can be tricky, especially if you're not sure of things.*

(FIRC lesson number two—How to not hear your grandfather's voice in your head while you're making out . . .)

For weeks, I'd think it, notice it, try to ignore both and be a better boyfriend. Because I really did want to be a good boyfriend. But it just wasn't there, no matter how much I wanted it to be—how much *easier* it would be.

I'm pretty sure Farfar would know exactly what I mean. Times a billion.

It's hard to fathom just how excruciating that must've been, to have to tell Farmor, after twenty-four years.

She was at my locker, waiting for me at the end of the day, a Friday, well into December. She was grinning at me, like she knew something I didn't, and planted a long kiss on me when I slid my book bag off my arm. Still noticed it.

"Do you have to work this weekend?"

"No big events or anything, but probably some."

"Me and my mom are going shopping."

"Nice."

"She told my dad we were Christmas shopping, but we're really going shopping for prom dresses."

God, the look on her face. This sly smile, and bright eyes, taking my arm and leaning closer, and I felt like complete shit.

"Wow," I managed. "It's really early for prom dresses, isn't it? Isn't prom . . ."

She took my panic for something else, and with the hallways mostly empty, she leaned in and kissed me again, and my brain couldn't mask it at all. And I actually thought, how does the chemistry only work on one side? What do I taste like to her?

I told her in the car. The Prius. Still sitting in the school parking lot.

I'd been giving her rides home each day, even though her brother was going to the same house now that soccer was over.

I didn't have any good reasons—no explanation to offer that would make any sense (celery?)—so I just blurted it out, right before pressing the starter button. *I think we need to break up.*

She just looked at me, stunned for a moment, her eyes wide, her mouth hanging open, whatever she was about to say dissolved in her throat.

"Okay."

That's all she said. *Okay.*

She blinked a few times, squeezed the straps of her book bag, then just got out of the car, walked from the senior lot to the student lot—I'm assuming to her brother's car before he left. And that was it.

From *together* to *not-together* in a matter of seconds.


That weekend felt strange—it rained nonstop, the temperature hovering in the forties, so it remained consistently miserable. Farfar had gotten us hooked up with a dying mall in Franklin that wanted us to set up outside the main doors in the parking lot of a JCPenney to welcome/warm up holiday shoppers.

We sold mostly hot chocolate, an occasional munkhål or fry, while most shoppers hustled by us in the rain, looking utterly devoid of holiday cheer. It was a pretty big letdown after Lillajul—like that day wasn't just the kickoff to the season, but the main event itself, and we'd fast-forwarded into the slog of January.

Our trip to Åland was still months away, and Lou was

obsessed with her UPenn app, which she was expecting to hear back from that week. So that was basically all the two of them talked about the entire time in the truck, an endless cycle of panic and stress and reassurances and college plans and back to panic. Again and again. Farfar didn't seem to mind—god, he seemed to enjoy it, even.

No messages from Skylar, and I felt simultaneously empty and relieved and guilt-ridden, so I was left to listen to Farfar and Lou all day.

What else was I supposed to do? It felt stupid to chime in with my problems—breaking up with my sophomore girlfriend of less than a month who tasted oddly of celery—compared to Lou's worries of planning out her entire perfect Ivy League future.

I wanted to, though.


"You are more focused than usual, Gubben," Farfar said on Sunday afternoon, after our combined efforts had gotten us Lakitu, our last unlockable character. "Where is your phone?"

"Charging in my room."

He just stared at me, eyebrows raised, until he finally looked down at Koopa in his lap.

"I feel like there is more to this story, lilla pussgurka."

"I broke up with Skylar."

"Hmm."

"What, *hmm*?"

"Nothing, *hmm*. Are you okay?"

"Yeah, I think so. It sucked—I still feel terrible. But . . . *relieved*. She wanted to shop for prom dresses this weekend."

"Isn't prom in . . ."

"Not winter."

"Hmm. This Sky-lar really liked you."

I nodded again, staring at the menu screen.

"I am sorry, Gubben. I know it does not feel good. I think it is harder to do the breaking than to . . . be broken up *with*, yes?"

"There's no guilt in being dumped."

"That is an ugly expression, Gubben. *Dumped.*"

"It *feels* ugly. She didn't do anything wrong."

"No. She didn't do anything wrong," he replied, his voice trailing into a low rumble. He let out a long, slow breath, one I knew preceded a beer. "But you cannot always help how you feel for someone, Gubben. It would have only gotten harder later. You did the right thing."

Farfar had never once asked how I felt about her. He just knew.

"Does this mean you will be staying home with me all evening, Gubben?"

"I think it does. Two eligible bachelors, a cat, and *Mario Kart*."

"Hmm."

"*Hmm,* what?"

He stood and placed a yowling Koopa on the floor.

"Let's go. Time for Monster Thickburgers. We have serious work to do tonight."


We had a good talk that night, through Monster Thickburgers and countless rounds of *Mario Kart* on the "new" system. Like always, he somehow knew exactly what I needed, and we spent the night hashing out *my* plans for the future. *Real talk.* The costs of opening a brick-and-mortar café versus maintaining the truck. The probability of running both and how much help that would require, and how many more hours we could squeeze into twenty-four to make it happen.

It all seemed so impossible and so impossibly perfect, if that makes sense. I could imagine the path through it all, Farfar and me together. I could see myself taking on a larger role, making decisions, being the one up before dawn in my own kitchen and being there to shut the lights off at night. Being so exhausted and overworked and *satisfied*, because it was finally working toward what *I* wanted.

We unlocked a lot of crap that night, too.

# CHAPTER TWENTY-SEVEN

## OUTRIGHT REJECTION

LOU LOOKED LIKE HELL WHEN SHE CAME INTO THE CULINARY lab the week before winter break. I was working on some different cupcake ideas, some things I hoped to include on our café menu someday. She had on old gray sweatpants I'd never seen her wear before and a faded, oversized Ravenclaw sweatshirt. Which by itself wasn't a big thing—it's not like I'm ever dressed to impress anyone—but she moved slower than normal, sliding into her usual chair like she'd been working out for hours the day before. Her skin looked pale, her mouth turned down—honestly, I thought maybe she had the flu.

"You okay?" I asked, my measuring cup paused in midair.

Lou didn't say anything at first—didn't even move. Just stared at her book bag on the otherwise empty table. She looked like she was about to cry.

"I didn't get in," she finally said to her book bag, pulling her braid in front of her.

"To Penn?"

She nodded just once, almost imperceptibly, the corners of her mouth dipping even further.

"At all."

"What does that mean, *didn't get in at all*?"

"They don't want me at all. Not even as a general applicant. Just . . . no."

"Oh."

I dumped my sugar and started whisking, trying to think of the right thing to say next.

I *wanted* to say the right things to her.

"Wasn't it, like, a crazy long shot to begin with? What'd you tell Farfar, like, less than five percent of applicants or something get accepted?"

"I know," she said, rubbing her face in her hands. "I know. I just thought I'd at least get wait-listed. What's wrong with me that they decided I'm not even good enough to go in with the rest of the general applicants?"

"Lou, stop being stupid. Nothing's wrong with you."

She put her head down on her arms on top of her book bag, ignoring me, apparently. I'd listened to her and Farfar go through her chances of getting in all day on Saturday, and yeah, I felt bad for her, but it was getting old.

"Weren't you already prepared for this anyway? You've got a whole list of schools you love, ready to go. What about Buckminster . . ."

"Bucknell," she said into her arms.

". . . and Swarthington . . ."

"Swarthmore."

". . . and Frankfurter and Maple?"

She looked up finally, her lips pressed and her nostrils flared. "Is that one supposed to be Franklin and Marshall?"

"I like mine better." (See? I was trying.) "Do you even have to redo any applications or essays or anything? Aren't they all the same? Just hit Send on the next round and move on."

Lou shook her head, then pulled the zipper open on her book bag. "You're not getting it."

Which pissed me off a little, but I still held it together. Gave myself a moment while I poured batter into cups.

"These schools are all really hard—almost as hard as Penn. If I can't even get wait-listed at Penn, how am I going to get accepted at Swarthmore?"

"So, what, you're not sending applications to any of them now?"

She tossed a heavy binder onto the table and huffed. "I already sent them."

"So what's the problem?"

"What if I don't get into any of them?"

"Go somewhere else." She rolled her eyes like I was an idiot, and I could feel myself starting to unravel. "And maybe get over yourself. You're still going to get into a good school, work your ass off, and have the career you really want. It's really not that big of a deal, Lou."

She shook her head without even looking at me—again, *while* I was trying to help her see the bigger picture, *on her side*— and flipped her binder open, leaned over her work like she was dismissing me.

"You don't have to worry about any of this."

I slid two pans into the wall oven and closed the door harder than necessary. "Yeah. I get it. I don't care about my future."

Lou finally looked up from her stupid binder.

"I didn't say—"

"Lou! I fucking *heard* you!"

She stared at me like I was crazy, which just made me feel crazier.

"In the hall! With Mrs. Bixler the other week! I was *there*, Lou. Outside the room. I *heard* you."

She just kept staring at me, wide-eyed, before shaking her head again and looking down.

"Look, I've had a really bad day. I have no idea what you're—"

I slammed my fist on the counter, sending the spent mixing bowl clanging to the floor, the spatula leaving a trail of batter smeared across the floor tiles. Fully unraveled.

"Why do you still even show up here every day, then? If you can't stand me, what the fuck are you even *doing* here?"

I'm not sure I could even describe the look on her face at that point, but she definitely wasn't looking down anymore. She was looking at me. And I was gone. I planted both hands on the edge of the counter and squeezed until my fingernails dug into the particleboard underneath.

"You force your way into every part of my life. In school. At home. At work. *All* of it, you're there. You've become besties with *my* grandfather, you tell *my* teacher—*my* teacher—that you hate me, that I don't care about *my* future. So then why are you still here? Why did you pick *my* life to so thoroughly fuck?"

Lou stood, blinked fast—a lot like Skylar in the car, actually—and started to pack up again. I saw the first tear hit the closed cover of her binder before she shoved it back into her bag.

"So I'm guessing you dumped Skylar," Terrance said loudly, thumbing into his phone as he walked through the door without looking up.

He stood staring then, his phone still in both hands, looking from Lou to me, back to Lou. "I wasn't . . . uh . . ."

Lou threw her bag over one shoulder and rushed past Terrance, tears falling openly. I released my grip on the countertop, my fingertips numb, my shoulders slumping.

If I felt empty after breaking up with Skylar, now I felt like I might collapse in on myself.

"I was not expecting that," Terrance finally said, more to himself than me.

Mrs. Bixler came in then, too, coffee cup in one hand, a stack of papers tucked under her other arm, assessing the awkwardness.

"Why was Lou crying? I just passed her in the hallway."

I ran a hand over my face, and Terrance let out another helpful *uh*. Mrs. Bixler set her stuff down on the counter, taking in the bowl and the dirty spatula on the floor.

"Did something happen with her brother again?"

"What?"

She shook her head then, leaned over to pick up the bowl, and stood back up with a sigh.

"Never mind."

Finally I said, "College crap—the only thing she even cares about."

Mrs. Bixler frowned at me, shaking her head. "Wow, Oscar. I love you, but you really have no idea what you're talking about."


And I didn't.

Lou didn't show up those last two days before break, never once looked at me during speech—the one class we were actually scheduled for together. I think even stupid Bryce noticed it, glancing back at me when Lou would bolt from the room at the bell without a word.

I went into break one hundred percent ready for a break. From all of it.

The closest I'd ever been to any kind of social life in school had ended in complete disaster—left me feeling guilt-ridden and shitty and still with the same stupid hoops to jump through to get to the finish line. It made me, more than ever before, ready to focus one hundred percent on the work I wanted to do—making great food that made people smile, planning out how to have a career on the truck, whether I could make it with a café—and leave all the rest behind. Never look back.

Which obviously didn't happen.

# CHAPTER TWENTY-EIGHT

## MORE THAN FRIES

I SPENT THAT FIRST NIGHT OF BREAK AT THE TWINS' HOUSE. JOSIE was home from college.

Their mom and aunt and abuela would be cooking for most of break, so that night was just a pizza feast. Besides, of course, the fresh-baked Christmas cookies their abuela kept pulling from the oven, insisting they were no big deal, smiling proudly in a new, oversized Loyola sweatshirt. Their abuelo had one, too, identical, and the two of them were almost sickeningly adorable, both of them a little hunched over with age, one never too far away from the other.

He goosed her once, in the kitchen, while she looked in on the cookies in the oven. She swatted him with the pot holder in her hand, then goosed him back. He jumped a little and giggled. No one else was in the kitchen to see it. I just happened to have a sight line from the couch, the only witness.

I thought of us—of Farfar. Would I ever have witnessed something like that, if I'd ever met Amir? Would that part of Farfar's life have had little snapshots that were just as sickeningly adorable? Two doting, doddering old men, shuffling around inside a food truck, still stupid for each other?

Would he have let me see it?

———

"So, Jorge and Jesus say you've had *two* girls attached to you this year?" Josie said, laying down a trio of jacks and a six to play off my only piddly set. "I'm out, by the way."

I managed an *uhh* while staring at the incalculable mass of cards still in my hand.

"I'm away at college and you turn into some kind of player?"

My face and ears burned crimson.

We sat at their huge dining room table, after too much pizza and even more Christmas cookies: Jorge, Jesus, and me. Javy and Josie.

And Ayo. Whatever childhood crush I might have clung to quickly vanished in the shadow of Ayo, Josie's six-foot-five soccer-player boyfriend from Arcadia. He was nice, and funny, and headed to law school in the fall after graduation. And I was acutely aware of my status as a disgruntled, marginally success- ful high schooler who was good at making things out of apples. Nobody did anything to make me feel that way—like with Lou, it was just hard sometimes to be around so many people who were so good at school.

"Negative eighty-five," I replied, flipping my stack to the middle of the table. "And I would say I have zero girls currently attached to me."

Jorge laughed to himself, but Jesus chimed in. "Dude, Caleb wanted to kick your ass—" Jesus's eyes went wide for a second, and he quickly glanced around to make sure his mom or his abuela hadn't heard him. "But I talked him down," he finished, quieter.

"That's kind of you, Jesus. Thank you."

Josie needed every painful detail, of course. Which Jorge and Jesus and even Javy relished as well, because they're apparently all sick, despite how nice they may seem on the surface.

"I don't know where you keep getting *two* girls," I said to Jesus, shaking my head. "I had one girlfriend for barely a month."

"O, I don't know what you wanna call it, but when someone spends *periods* with you, every single day, by choice . . ." Jorge raised his eyebrows, taking his time shuffling the deck for the next hand.

"I don't know what you'd call it either. I can't st—"

"Yeah yeah, you can't stand her. We've heard all this. And yet there she is, every day, watching you bake cupcakes."

"O does have mad cupcake game," Jesus added, grinning and swiping the deck from Jorge's hands to start dealing. Thankfully.

"Wait, who are we talking about here?" Josie said, leaning in.

"Lou Messinger," Jorge said. "She's crazy smart, in charge of everything, all that stuff." Which was interesting, coming from Jorge—the one person sitting ahead of her in class rank. "And spends every waking moment with our boy here."

"I'm telling you," I said, feeling my ears go pink all over again. "I don't know why she keeps—kept—showing up. She doesn't like me, either. She's closer to Farfar, honestly."

"Yeah, I saw she was back in the commons the last few days," Jesus said. "Did you dump her, too?"

"Stop—I did not—"

"Does she have an older brother?" Josie interrupted, looking down at her phone.

"What?"

"You said Messinger? I wonder if she's related to JJ."

"Yeah," I said, remembering. "I think that's his name. He was there with their parents one night, in Franklin, when Lou was working on the truck with us. He looked rough."

"Wow, that's him," she said, still frowning into her phone.

"You know Lou's brother?" Jorge asked.

Josie sat back in her chair and nodded. "He was a couple of years ahead of me. He was a lot like how you described Lou. I remember he was the salutatorian that year, crazy-high SAT scores, involved in everything. He got into an Ivy League school."

"Whoa—which one?" Jorge asked.

UPenn. Lou's brother went to UPenn.

"What's he do now?" Ayo asked, peering over Josie's shoulder to see her phone.

Josie looked up at me, and I couldn't read her face at first. Concern, maybe.

"I guess he's at home. He dropped out. Apparently he joined a frat his first year, fell into life hard, you know? Into drinking, into drugs, and he was done. Back home . . ."

She was quiet for a moment—we were all quiet. Then Josie continued. "He's been in and out of rehab. I heard he OD'd again just a few weeks ago. At home."

"Seriously?" Jesus asked. "At home, like, with Lou there?"

Josie shrugged. "I think it was a few weeks before Thanksgiving. I don't know if he's still home now or what."

It was a slow click, picturing the fidgety ghost of a guy in the Rogue's Roost parking lot.

Lou's Narcan speech—so close to me but like she wasn't even seeing me, her response to Bryce's ignorant comments afterward.

A few weeks before Thanksgiving.

Lou missing a rare day of school, and when she came back . . .

*I just hate him sometimes . . . like he doesn't care about his future at all . . .*

And then, her reaction to Farfar's story about my dad.

"Oh, god," I said to myself, staring at my new hand of cards, unable to make sense of them.

"That bad, O?"

"She was talking about her brother."

"What?"

"I gotta go."


This should be the part where I rush over to find Lou. Apologize. Explain. Apologize again. All that.

But it wasn't that simple. There was a lot I needed to sort out myself.

So, after I gave all my hugs and forced down a few more cookies and said my goodbyes to the whole family, I drove around town in the Prius, coasted through the Battlefield until the inside was finally warm, and ended up at the campus, where we often parked on weekends. The campus was deserted, all the college kids home for break, and I stared off at one of the old main buildings, the silhouette of its cupola slightly darker than the ambient light of the night sky. The heat blasted at my feet and filled the car with warmth from the bottom up, and I tucked my earbuds in and pressed Play on the latest chapter of Harry. The Yule Ball, believe it or not.

I know the fact that Lou wasn't talking about me that day shouldn't have been the most important revelation from that night. But that's where my brain stayed.

Because what did it change?

If, in all that time we'd spent together over the past three months—the hours and hours together in the culinary lab, the hours wading through shitty apples, making deliveries, the days spent with me and Farfar, on the truck, in the apartment, offering ideas and making plans, blending seamlessly into our routines . . . in all that time, if she was never thinking that she hated me, or judging me, or my plans for the future . . . then what?

And how did it change how *I* felt? Almost every moment spent with Lou—even if I somehow let myself enjoy it—was colored by how I thought *she* felt. What I assumed she told herself about me. Poor poor me.

Jösses, if only Farfar had told me, right?

If I replayed all those moments, all those hours together, but removed that toxic filter, the whole story looked different.

Just a girl who, for whatever reason, liked being with me . . . liked being with me doing the things I really loved.


New Year's was a mess, too.

Lou's family was out of town. I didn't know how to explain it all to Farfar—how I'd flipped out on her on one of her worst days, because I was convinced she lived in constant judgment of *me*. How my relief that that wasn't the case was coupled with the realization that her family had also been ripped apart by drugs. And that, honestly, she'd witnessed it more closely and intimately than *either* of us had.

From what I could guess, she'd brought her brother back from the dead, *at least* once. Maybe more than that.

I know Farfar could've helped me through it. I could've asked.

I still didn't really want to believe that Jorge was kind of over helping on the truck, either. But it was impossible to deny it after New Year's Eve in Lincoln Square.

The setup was just like the Tree Lighting after Thanksgiving, only with way more people. So even with Lou at the window, it would have been hectic. But Jorge wasn't Lou. He hadn't worked the truck since the summer.

"O, man, I gotta jet by nine. Ayanna's big on New Year's—her whole family is—and she'll kill me if I don't get there before ten."

And by 8:20, he was checking his phone every thirty seconds, poking his head out the window, commenting on all the families that were packing up and heading out after the early kids' ball drop at eight.

"It was nice to have you back," Farfar said, patting his shoulder and handing him a fold of bills. "It has not been easy to carry the eye-candy burden alone."

He sighed when Jorge walked away, back to his car to enjoy the rest of his night with Ayanna. "I really wish Looo were here, Gubben."

"Yeah. Me too."

Not just because we got slammed from nine till well after midnight—just the two of us—Farfar manning the window and the rullekebab station, me utterly swamped at the fryer, all of Adams County, it seemed, demanding to ring in the new year with fresh donuts.

My mind wandered during that chaos of fries and munkar, my body purely on autopilot, running on fumes. Picturing Lou, thinking about what to say, what could happen next, what *would* happen next.

The look on her face when she rushed out of the culinary lab.

Her face, leaning over mine during her Narcan speech.

The school board meeting.

Leaning over her binders while I worked, and *green*.

I thought about where we all were last year, when Jorge was enough to help on the truck, when there was no hot chocolate, no loaded kebab fries. And thinking ahead, I knew I didn't want to go back.

And when I crawled into bed that night, nearly two hours into the new year, I knew it was about more than fries.

## CHAPTER TWENTY-NINE

# NO ONE SAID THE GUY WHO MAKES DONUTS HAD TO BE SUAVE

"I DON'T GET WHY YOU'RE SUCH AN ASSHOLE TO ME."

Those were her first words—the first thing Lou said to me since she'd rushed out of the room before break, over two weeks before.

She didn't look angry, standing in the doorway of the culinary lab, ten minutes into fourth period, her hands gripped around the handle of the apple cart.

Really, she looked more hurt. Confused.

And maybe it's kind of crappy of me, but can I tell you that I was relieved—that she'd clearly been thinking about it all break, too?

But I'd imagined going to find her in the commons—whenever I'd worked out the details and built up the courage—where I assumed she'd been spending her fourth periods again. And I'd ask her for her help, or say I needed a favor, and then I'd lay out what I needed to tell her, and it would all be fine. That's what my brain was trying to work out when she walked in, and I definitely did *not* have it worked out yet.

So my response of "Uhhh . . . yeah. I'm sorry" didn't really cut it.

"No, I'm serious," Lou said, pulling the classroom door closed and stepping around the cart. The cart was stacked full of sealed cups of what the cafeteria deemed *assorted fruit*—juice cups, partially frozen strawberries and peaches, applesauce, all things she'd never brought here before—along with a few boxes of Fujis. She moved in front of the counter across from me, her hands squeezing at her pant legs at her sides. "I don't understand why you hate me so much."

I was silent for a moment, frozen, because the truth was, I *did* say how much I couldn't stand her, all the time. But now, I really didn't.

"Lou," I said, after a pause that was way too long, judging by the wetness in Lou's eyes. "I don't hate you. I . . ."

I wiped my hands on a dish towel and ran a hand back and forth through my hair. "I thought you were talking about me."

"What?"

"In the hallway. When I heard you complain to Mrs. Bixler . . . *I just hate him sometimes. It's like he doesn't care about his future at all.* I thought you were talking about me. I didn't . . . I didn't know about your brother. . . ."

Lou looked down, dabbed at her eye, the corners of her mouth trembling. She shook her head and looked up again.

"Why would you even think I'd say that about you?" she said, not engaging in any talk about her brother. She held her hands out and looked around the room. "You're right, I show up here every day. I have a *scheduled class* this period, but I work ahead, just to show up here."

I felt my shoulders drop, blinked a few times.

"You're right, again—and I'm sorry—I have pushed my way

into your life. I . . . I *love* being part of your life. Part of Farfar's. And I'm sorry I've done that. . . . I'm sorry I forced that on you." She looked down at her shoes.

Lou looked up then, a tear slipping out. "I still don't understand, after I've gone to such lengths to be around you—why would I even *think* that about you?"

Now it was my turn to stare at my shoes.

"I . . . I'm just . . ."

"Why do you hate me?"

"Lou, I don't hate you. . . ."

"All my best days from this year—from all of *high school*, Oscar—they've all been with you."

I nodded, my eyes still locked on the floor. I wanted to say *me too*, because, really, it was true. But I couldn't get my voice to work.

"So what is it? What is it about me . . . what I *do* . . . that makes you—"

"Lou . . . you don't understand. It's not you." I took a shaky breath, forcing myself to continue. "I'm not smart. I hate school. I don't want to go to college. And you . . ." When I looked up, I knew I had tears in my eyes, too—I couldn't will them away no matter how hard I tried, no matter how stupid I felt—but Lou was right there, a step closer. A step away. "Everything about you makes me feel bad about *me*."

And then she kissed me.

Her cold hands on my face. And when she stepped closer, into me, it was like I couldn't get my arms around her enough.

Like my muscles were all twisted, coiled tight, from my jaws to my arms, through my legs—but like my whole body was sinking into her at the same time. I squeezed my eyes tight, squeezed her long braid in my hand, and melted.

When we finally pulled apart, I said, "Okay. That doesn't make me feel bad." Both of us a mess now with laughter and tears.

"Oh my god, now you're *both* crying?" said Mrs. Bixler, frozen in her doorway.


So, crying through a first kiss is probably not the most suave way to go about things, I know.

But it definitely did *not* taste like celery.

## CHAPTER THIRTY

# LOU UNLEASHED

GOD, THE LOOK ON FARFAR'S FACE WHEN WE CAME THROUGH the door that afternoon holding hands.

"It is about time, Gubben," he whispered to me, wiping a ridiculous happy tear from the corner of his eye while Lou fussed with Koopa.

"You don't know what you're talking about," I replied, shoving him away, but Lou stood up with Koopa in her arms, beaming at both of us like she knew, too.

And she's basically lived at our apartment since.

Through January, when—with my oversensitive brood-fests out of the way and the three of us now working wholeheartedly together—the full capacity of Lou's powers was unleashed.

"She reminds me of Amir," Farfar said to me one night after Lou got up from her stool at the counter to call her parents. "Bursting with ideas and energy."

"And I think she beats your organization, too," I said, looking at her open notebook.

"Hmm. A little intimidating, I think, yes?"

"I think, yes."

We were deep into discussions about how to winterize the truck—ways to continue a flow of income during the cold months without festivals or community-gathering holidays or even enough people walking around outside to make any parking spot a lucrative venture. We talked about catering opportunities and optimizing social media (beyond my basic Instagram skills). We even started building a mock-up website for the business, which Lou was, unsurprisingly, really good at.

"My eighth-grade ELA teacher did this big project where we designed our own candy companies," Lou said later, grinning into Farfar's laptop. "My company was voted Best Overall Website."

"Of course it was," I said, leaning into her shoulder and tossing her braid into her face. "My eighth-grade teacher made us take reading quizzes after every single chapter of *The Outsiders* and *The Giver.*"

"I loved *The Giver!*"

"Just stop."


Through February, when we started talking about the possibility of a brick-and-mortar café someday—something I was a little scared to say out loud but that Lou got behind full Lou-force. Maggie and Juliet were there that night, too, invited down for some mid-February glögg to weather the fourth consecutive day of record lows. Maggie *loved* the idea—loved the menu we'd cooked up—and talked about real estate downtown. She owned more than just the art gallery, apparently.

"You and Amir talked about this *years* ago, Erik. Remember? Just before the accident."

Farfar nodded once, a smile pulling at the corner of his mouth.

"Didn't we even look at that awful old schoolhouse with the fire damage?" Juliet chimed in from the far edge of the couch, Winston asleep on her lap. "Amir was in love with that dump."

"It *was* a dump," Farfar said, quiet, getting up to refill his glögg. "Needed a lot of money. A lot of work."

"You didn't want to do it?" Lou asked.

He took a long sip from his mug. "I like the freedom of the truck."

"You would've done it," Maggie said, smiling. "You always did *anything* he was excited about."

Farfar nodded again, looking up at me, at Lou squeezing my hand, and let out one quiet laugh.


When Lou talked about her brother for the first time, a month or so after he'd completed his latest stint in a rehab facility. What it was like to *find* him, to be the one who had to do something to save him. To see it happen all over again and feel like there was nothing she could do to stop it, to fix it for him.

"I'm pretty sure he's lying about what time he gets off work," Lou said, head back on the couch, Koopa tucked in next to her leg. "But he says all the right things to my parents. It kills me, because it makes me question if he was really the kind of brother I thought he was when I was a kid." Her voice caught. She continued, still staring up at the ceiling, "And I know that's not fair."

Farfar told her—told both of us—what it was like to watch it happen as a father. About the guilt of *not* being there when it happened all over again.

We talked a lot about guilt.

234

And when, a few weeks later, Lou got rejected by every single elite private school on her list and broke down in our apartment. I thought she might murder Farfar at first, in a tear-and-snot-smeared rage, when he tried to explain to her that she wasn't special.

"That is not what I mean, Looo," he said, a hand on her shoulder. "You are incredible, and you will do—*already* do—amazing things."

Lou stared at the carpet in front of our couch, her chest heaving.

"But there are more than thirty thousand high schools in this country alone. More than thirty thousand valedictorians—more than *three hundred thousand* top tens. Just this year. There were more than three hundred thousand last year, and there will be another three hundred thousand next year, too. Every school has a Looo."

"What kind of pep talk is this?" Lou said, still looking at the floor. "Is this some kind of weird Swedish wisdom that's not translating?"

"He's the worst at this," I confirmed.

"It is *liberating*, no? *You are not special.* No one is just waiting for you to show up. No expectations. You are free to figure out what you love and . . . *fling* yourself at it."

Lou stared at him then, glaring, clearly not feeling liberated, and he let out a long sigh.

"You got into Pittsburgh, yes? Their Honors College?"

Lou nodded.

"The same University of Pittsburgh with the world-class hospital system and medical school?"

Lou nodded again.

"Then stop being an idiote." Lou's eyes went wide, like she'd been stung. "Go to school and figure out how to save people's lives."

She showed up the following week with Pitt sweatshirts for each of us.


At our annual March Madness *Mario Kart* Tournament—along with the twins and Javy, Maggie and Juliet—when Lou's Toadette nearly upset the top-seeded Yoshi in the second round but got blasted by a blue shell right before the finish line, and Lou started swearing and couldn't stop. Farfar couldn't stop grinning, his hands folded behind his head, the rest of us crying from laughter.

(I was in seventh grade when I realized March Madness had anything to do with basketball.)


When, in the Prius the one night in early April—during a fit of pathetic self-doubt after bombing one of my final essays for senior English—I asked Lou how she even started liking me.

"Well, I didn't at first," she said, which, I'll be honest, stung a bit. "Not that I *didn't* like you. I've always liked looking at your face."

"What?"

"What, you have a nice face. I could curl up inside those dimples."

Pretty nice recovery on her part.

"And don't get me started on when your ears turn pink like that." She reached over and squeezed my earlobe, hot to the touch. "But then I loved how confident and competent you were in the kitchen, with all those apples. I don't know, it's like you're always so sure of what you want, and you work hard and take it seriously and, I don't know, I liked being around it."

She shook her head and looked out the front windshield, her hand dropping to my leg.

"And then when we went to the Council of Churches that first time . . ."

"What?"

"Oscar, seriously, do you not know this?" She looked back at me again. "Kindness is *hot*."

"Hmm. Okay. Good to know."

"I'm not sure I even want to ask when you started liking me."

I thought about the Green Dream, that first time, and felt my ears go pink again.

"Yeah. Probably best that you don't."

I eventually told her anyway.


And when springtime hit for real, and festival season was finally approaching, which meant school was almost ending—for good. We talked graduation, and our trip to Åland, and our future-but-soon-to-be-present from there, and, despite the last few hoops to jump through in all my other classes, everything felt perfect. Like everything I ever wanted was about to become *real*.

Like my *real* life was about to start.

And it started with the festival in Smithsboro.

## CHAPTER THIRTY-ONE

# SMITHSBORO

"I HAVE A PRESENT FOR YOU, LOOO," FARFAR SAID IN THE kitchen that morning—that first Saturday in May—just before we headed downstairs to the truck. "For your first festival."

I'd never seen someone tear up over a pair of canary-yellow Crocs before. But she put them right on and gave Farfar a long hug. And I don't know what she whispered to him in Swedish, but suddenly his eyes were wet, too.

"All right, all right. We should probably go before you're both a puddle. We've got a lot of hours ahead of us."

"Awww, Gubben, we have enough time for a hug," he said, pulling me in with one arm, still squeezing Lou in the other, Koopa yowling jealously at his feet.

And we did. We did still have time for a hug.

"Wow, it's getting hot already," Lou said, her yellow Crocs on the dash as we rumbled down 15 toward the Maryland line.

"Close to record highs today," Farfar said. "Over ninety. Ready to sweat, Gubben?"

"Already am."

But the drive was beautiful. We'd never done this festival

before—had never been to Smithsboro—but when we got off 15 for winding two-lanes through state parkland, the morning sun low and bright, I swear, the greens were neon.

Farfar had found this festival a few months before, in an article in the *Gettysburg Times*. Regional enough to make our small-town news. He'd told Lou and me about new members of their town council, and their plans to change a street name in conjunction with the festival in May.

It didn't seem like a big deal at the time—a tiny town changing the name of one of its downtown streets—but Lou was pumped as soon as Farfar told us. Garland Avenue—named for a Confederate general who'd died in battle somewhere nearby—being renamed Unity Avenue.

He'd even pulled out old pictures to show Lou, fueled by her enthusiasm, of the Millennium March, almost twenty years before, the four of them—Maggie and Juliet, Farfar and Amir—beaming in front of the Washington Monument. And I still had the two of us in my phone, in our pink crocheted hats, standing in almost the exact same spot.

And Farfar was right. Pulling up to the curb along the perimeter of Leiter Park—a beautiful expanse on the edge of downtown Smithsboro, stretching to the base of the Appalachians—seeing all the other food trucks and the array of vendors setting up in the grass, the makeshift stage being assembled in the middle, it all felt perfect.

It was going to be a great day.


"Damn, it's got to be ninety degrees already," Lou said, leaning out the window for air.

There was still an hour before the start of the festival, but trays of dough were already resting in racks, potatoes washed and ready to go through the slicer, a huge batch already shoestringed in a bin next to the fryers. The spit was radiating heat from the corner while Farfar finished prepping veggies for rullekebab.

Lou's swearing had picked up considerably since *Mario Kart* March Madness—and with Lou, it had now somehow become endearing. Farfar never found it quite so endearing with me. Hmm.

"We need ice cream," Lou said, leaning back against the window counter, her face flushed.

"We don't sell ice cream."

"I know we don't sell ice cream," Lou replied, rolling her eyes. "That's why I'm suggesting we sell ice cream. It's only May, and look at us. Imagine it's late July, in a crowded park like this with no shade, and we're parked inside Satan's ass crack here."

Farfar giggled to himself at his kebab station, his rolled-up bandana already soaked through, his wire-rimmed glasses pushed up on top of his head while he worked. Lou looked like she could've smiled, if she weren't so flushed and uncomfortable. She rocked it in the cold, but it seemed the heat got to her pretty quickly.

"I don't have to imagine it. We do it every summer. You're gonna, too, if you don't wimp out on us before June."

"I'm just saying you could sell a fuck-ton of ice cream out here."

I was still thrown every time I heard her do it—this student council president, first-chair clarinetist, double-math-taking wunderkind, swearing like a dive-bar line cook after a string of picky customers. Honestly, I think *Mario Kart* broke her.

"Maybe she is right, Gubben. Maybe we could sell a fuck-ton of ice cream."

My head whipped around to Farfar—he was barely able to keep the smirk on his face from exploding. I'd never heard him swear *at all*, much less drop an F-bomb. But then I saw him wink at Lou.

God, if *Mario Kart* broke Lou, honestly, I think Lou broke Farfar.

"You already sell a fuck-ton of munkar, Gubben. Why not—"

"Munkar ice cream sandwich!" Lou cut in, literally jumping and clapping her hands.

They were both grinning at me then, the Brooding Baker scowling over his soon-to-be deep-fried delicacies, and I finally caved.

"That would totally work," I conceded.

"Right? Like those homemade-waffle ice cream sandwiches, but *better*, because fucking *donuts*, right?"

She had her arms out to the side, leaning forward a little, her face flushed with more than heat now.

"You know, you've been swearing an awful lot," I said. "You do realize this is my grandfather, right? That you're repeatedly dropping F-bombs in front of my grandfather?"

Lou looked a little taken aback, maybe more at herself than at me, but Farfar just smiled again and waved me off, mumbling what I'm fairly certain were some serious Swedish swear words under his breath.

"We're soon ready, Gubben," he said, facing his station again. "Why don't you take your lap of the grounds?"

I took my lap with Lou, hand in sweaty hand. I pointed out trucks I recognized from other festivals, and we stopped at each of the others for a quick menu read, most of them coming out of DC or Baltimore or northern Virginia. For a small town in rural western Maryland, the diversity was impressive, as were the growing crowds.

We swung through the vendors' tents, where most were putting the finishing touches on their display tables—from original oil paintings to jewelry to decorative gourds to corn-straw brooms.

"I really want the fairy gourd house back there," Lou said, squeezing my arm as we stepped back out into the sun.

"Graduation gift, maybe."

"Oh my god, I would love you forever."

I glanced at her, feeling my ears turn on me. Lou was watching for them, too, a huge, goofy grin on her face, and then she kissed me.

"Is that Bryce?" she said, after pulling away.

"Wow, that's the worst follow-up ever."

But then I tracked her eyes to the far end of the park, behind the low chain-link fence at the edge of an empty baseball field.

I don't know where they came from. Where they parked. Families and festival-goers had been setting up camp chairs and blankets for the past half hour—you could already tell it was going to be packed—and I hadn't seen any of them come from that direction. One group, all men, none of whom looked to be scoping out the food options.

242

I know that worthless coward saw us.

I know it.

We could see his stupid red hat before he ducked into the cluster of men.

"Why would *he* be here?" Lou said.

"Doesn't really seem like his crowd, does it? Maybe he's really into decorative gourds, too."

But we didn't think much more of it at the time. We didn't have time to.

We got back to the truck, I started dropping the first batches of munkar, and that was the last I could really think about *anything* for the next couple of hours. If this really was the kickoff into my adult life, things were going to be okay.


We were *on* Garland Avenue.

I hadn't realized it when we'd parked—hadn't noticed the street signs.

Garland Avenue bordered the park, a few blocks off Main Street at the edge of the town. Our window faced out over the park, so the street signs were behind us. We never saw the crowds gathering.

Only on TV screens later.

"What is going on out there?" Lou asked, sometime after noon, leaning out of the window. We both turned around from our stations then, both saw the never-ending line of customers looking in the same direction as Lou, some pointing somewhere past the back of the truck.

"What are they even protesting?" I heard Lou say to a

customer, still standing by the window with a loaded kebab fry in one hand and a cup of munkhål in the other.

There was no possible way to hear them. Not inside the truck. But the newsclips later, taken from people's phones primarily, showed that first group of "demonstrators"—the group that included Bryce and his dad, maybe more—circling the old street sign at the corner of the sidewalk at Locust Street and Garland Avenue. Soon-to-be Unity Avenue.

I don't know if Farfar would even remember them—some of them holding a giant Confederate flag like a banner, like they were protecting the sad little street sign, chanting "Heritage! Not Hate!" over and over.

Sons of Confederate Veterans, I'd heard later on the news. But that was just the start. Because I don't think people thought that much of it, to be honest. A bunch of idiots chanting around a street sign; the police were sure to break that up eventually. It was unfortunate and embarrassing, but there were still bands performing seventies covers on the stage and tons of great food to eat and crafted gourds to purchase.

I could see some of the people in line shouting back and flipping them off, but, I mean, they stayed in line, because they still wanted their loaded kebab fries and munkhål, too.

"They have the right to protest, Gubben," Farfar said. "Even if they are idiotes."

"Fucking assholes," I heard Lou say, and I saw Farfar chuckle again. And then it was back to work.

But an hour later, the police still hadn't intervened, and it was crazy hot, and everything felt . . . unsettled—like oil shimmering in the fryer right before the basket drops.

"They said the street sign change is supposed to happen at three," Lou said, when we finally had a slow moment after the lunch rush. "But they're still out there. God, those dipshits have to be dying out there in the sun."

"Is Bryce really out there with them?" I said. "I hope he dies of a heatstroke."

"Gubben." Farfar shot me a (wholly undeserved) look. "He is still a kid."

"I can't see them from here," Lou said. "But I bet he is. . . . Heatstroke really wouldn't be the worst."

I raised my eyebrows at Farfar—even his precious Lou knew it was true.

"Whoa," Lou said then, standing back from the window.

They just looked like festival-goers who'd had enough. Honestly, they may have been. From our tiny window out to the park, we had no way of knowing what was building around us. No way to follow what was spreading on social media. We still just had people lined up for rullekebab and munkar, and that was really all we had time for.

But when Lou stepped back, a group emerged through the crowd, screaming down the "demonstrators" around the street sign, some of the folks in our line looking frozen, hoping the tide would stream around them, others jumping into the melee, yelling and crowding toward the street.

"Stay here, Gubben."

Lou and I both stood silent—something I think we'd both go back and change if we could, and something that revealed us both as the kids we still were, too.

Farfar squeezed my shoulder and climbed up front and

out the passenger side to the sidewalk. Through the window, I could see it all breaking down—the music had stopped, replaced completely now by the shouts of each group. Families and friends were packing up their camp chairs and blankets and heading in the opposite direction through the park, while others joined in the yelling. No one ordered any more food.

Lou squeezed my hand when I stepped up to the window beside her. Fear lodged in my throat—I'm not sure I was able to breathe, much less speak. Farfar glanced back at us just once, raised his hand to remind us to stay where we were, and stepped toward the craziness out on the street.

Lou and I, we could see the epicenter if we leaned out the window to look beyond the back of the truck, less than a block to the corner of Locust and Garland. Locust and *Unity*.

Many of the original protestors—the Sons of Confederate Veterans crew—were gone, replaced by members of uglier groups that had come to take up the fight. KKK. Proud Boys. Some *American Identity Movement*. They were all listed on the news later. Small groups of hate-mongers—the very worst of humanity—no more than twenty of them now, shouted down and pushed back by counterprotestors and pissed-off festivalgoers.

But Bryce was still there, frozen in the middle of it all.

"Jesus, it's like a mini-Char—"

Lou never finished, cut short by the terrified screams on the street.

In my head, the screams lasted for ages—just endless cries of terror in the hot afternoon sun—but really, it was barely a few seconds.

The crowds scattered, I caught a glimpse of Bryce still

standing in the street, turning back to see the oncoming car, and Farfar lunging to shove him out of the way.

And I stood there, feet frozen to the sticky floor of the truck, and watched Farfar fly through the air like a child's stuffed animal turned superhero, like a limp teddy bear strangled by a makeshift cape.

## CHAPTER THIRTY-TWO

# REWIND. REPLAY.

AARON CRUE.

That's the guy's name who hit him.

Twenty-four. Local community college student. Criminal justice, I think, though I don't believe he was very far along in his coursework.

We didn't know any of that at the time. We didn't know that he'd stormed off from his waning group of "demonstrators" moments before, yelling back at the counterprotestors that they'd all be sorry. We didn't know that a few of the counterprotestors followed him up Locust Street to his car, still shouting, some even laughing and heckling. We didn't know that they weren't even official counterprotestors—just pissed-off festival-goers who had no tolerance for this guy's bigotry. Or that they threw food at his car when he first pulled out from the curb.

Farfar may have witnessed some of this. I don't know. I only know that he saw Aaron Crue's car—an old Malibu, a lot like Lou's, only maroon—flying toward the intersection in reverse. That he saw most people scatter, but Bryce, for some reason, still standing oblivious in the street, facing the park, frozen amid the chaos. *Still a kid.*

Farfar saved him.

I can't believe he saved him.


The day after we rumbled out of Gettysburg and navigated the truck through the winding country roads of western Maryland, I stood alone at the edge of the parking lot of this nameless hospital, apparently in Hagerstown, staring out at the green-on-green patchwork of the Appalachians, trying to erase that last impossible image of Farfar from my mind.

I remember this one time years ago, driving back from Caledonia, when a deer jumped out onto the road, and the minivan coming the other way tried to stop, and it was like it hit the deer in slow motion. And I remember how the deer still launched off the bumper, its body sideways, parallel to the road, spinning across the surface like a top, until it came to rest in the grass a few feet off the shoulder.

(And how we both cried when we got home a few minutes later.)

That's the best way to describe how Farfar looked, flying off the rear bumper of Aaron Crue's red Malibu.

Standing at the edge of that parking lot, I tried to recall moments on the couch together, yelling at *Mario Kart* on the big screen, or Farfar's rumbling voice, spewing ridiculous Swedish baby talk to a madly purring Koopa in his arms, or the feel of his rough hands on top of mine, teaching me the proper way to knead dough when I was just a kid.

But I couldn't.

All I could see, over and over, like some terrible internet

and barrel back to PA, back to before that ever-loving shit-show of a weekend.

"Oscar, can you come inside with me for a moment?" Her hand slid down my shoulder, and it hit me that I didn't even know where the truck *was*.

She guided me across the parking lot, and I could see through the emergency room windows into the overcrowded waiting room. The TV on the wall was on CNN, replaying the scene from the park, just like in my head, over and over, and I looked away right before the red Malibu showed up on the screen and erased Farfar from it.

More phone footage. From somewhere near the truck.

I shook my head. I couldn't go back in there yet.

The officer looked where I was looking and she must've understood, because she hesitated and said, "How about we have a seat on the curb over here?"

I nodded, still shaking, and let her guide me along the sidewalk away from the sliding entrance doors. I sat on the smooth cement curb, my back against a brick pillar so I didn't have to see the waiting room TV, or the group of people huddled around it, some crying, some pointing, some on their phones with their eyes still fixed on the screen.

Rewind. Replay.

It was hard to look away.


I don't remember most of what the officer asked me, and I didn't have much in the way of answers beyond who we were and why we were there at the festival. We knew nothing about the rest of it.

When she was finished, she looked back through the doors into the ER waiting room, then back at me.

"Come on," she said. "We'll go in through a different entrance."

When we made it back up to the fourth floor, Lou was there, in the small waiting room outside the ICU.

I couldn't have smelled the best at that point, still in the same clothes, the same sticky Crocs from the festival the day before, but Lou didn't shy away from my embrace. She stayed in my arms for a long time.

Her parents had driven down the night before to take her home. She fought them at first, demanding to stay with me in the room with Farfar, all three of them in tears. But she wasn't family, and she eventually had to relent, on condition that she come back the next day and that I call with any updates.

"How is he?" she finally said now, leaning back from me.

I held on to her braid like a lifeline, my other hand clinging to the end of her Girl Scout summer camp T-shirt, and told her the little bit that I knew—mostly that he still wasn't responsive, even after they'd drained the excess fluid from his brain overnight.

It was still less than twenty-four hours since the accident and there seemed to be some small sense of relief from the nurses that he was stable. But stable still meant he was breathing with a ventilator and he had yet to wake up. Stable meant they'd cleaned up the lacerations he'd sustained from bouncing along the asphalt and were keeping a close eye on any internal bleeding.

Stable meant they couldn't tell me for sure if he was ever going to wake up.

After Dr. Chadry came through with his third non-update,

he stopped and looked at me and Lou, sitting on either side of Farfar, each one of us holding his hands.

"It's okay if you need to go home for a bit."

I just shook my head, had to look away.

"I think he's stable for now. . . ."

Stable.

"And we'll call you right away if anything changes." He hung at the door another moment. "And you said there's no other fam—"

"It's just me," I said, staring hard at Farfar's chest, mechanically rising and falling beneath the thin sheet. "Just me."

"He won't mind," Lou said a few minutes later. "If you go home for a bit."

"My phone's dead. . . ."

Lou got up and came over to my side of the bed, wrapping her arms around me from behind the chair.

"I already gave the nurse my number, Oscar. I'll stay with you. But you need to pack some things if you're going to stay." She kissed the top of my head, tears pooling in my eyes again. "And you smell terrible."

I choked out a laugh and squeezed her arms to my chest.

*A toothbrush wouldn't hurt either, Gubben,* I could hear him say in my head, and it killed me that I couldn't hear it for real.

Lou drove us back home to Gettysburg. We didn't go through Smithsboro, didn't take the same roads, but they were the same kind of rolling country two-lanes we'd taken the day before.

And it's a route I know now by heart.

It must have rained while we were in the ICU with Farfar, but the sun fought through a mess of low, heavy clouds, making parts of the drive nearly blinding with green and glare.

"What am I going to do?"

Lou turned her music down and glanced over at me, shaking again in the passenger seat.

"Well, first, you're going to take a shower."

"No, I mean—"

"I know. Let's start with a shower. We'll pack a bag for you. Get some food. And we'll come back. That's enough for right now."

I closed my eyes against a sudden beam of sunshine. "Where's the truck? I don't even know where the truck is. . . ."

And just like that, all the *stuff* from our life—the everyday routines and responsibilities—came rushing back, like they'd disappeared for the past twenty hours.

"Impound lot. It's fine, I already called this morning. Let's just get cleaned up and get back to Farfar, okay?"

I turned and watched her, eyes locked on the road, hands gripping the wheel at ten and two.

"How are you . . . *doing* things?"

She glanced over at me for a second, then back to the glare of the road.

"I don't know what else to do."

Koopa was yowling like crazy inside the door when she heard my key in the lock, just like I'd pictured. It sounds stupid, but I almost didn't want to face her. To have to tell her—the cat—the news.

Luckily, Lou slid past me and went in first, immediately scooping up Koopa in her arms.

"Min lilla kattkatt, lilla missekissen," I could hear her murmuring softly into Koopa's ear, and I felt a fresh wave of tears coming on again.

It didn't seem possible for everything to be exactly the same inside the apartment, but there it was. Exactly as we'd left it. We'd forgotten to put the syrup away, and the griddle was still plugged in over top of the stove, our plates still sitting sticky in the sink. Just waiting for us to get home and tidy up. Twenty-four hours, and it felt like archaeologists coming across some ancient homestead scene, petrified beneath the ashes.

"Hey," Lou said, catching me frozen, staring at the kitchen. "Koopa says you need a shower, too." And on cue, Koopa let out another yowl from Lou's arms. "Now go."

So I plugged in my phone on the kitchen counter without waiting for it to power on and hit the bathroom. Part of me felt guilty for taking so long then, but I stood under the showerhead until the water went cold.

*Stay here, Gubben.* Those were the last words he'd said, before . . . And I just kept seeing that moment, over and over, rewind and replay. And I kept thinking, *Is that it? Are those really the last words I'll ever hear him say? Stay here, Gubben?*

I'm still waiting for the answer.

Please tell me there's more.

And with those images running on a loop in my head, I had to start asking the next big question. *Now what?*

What if I was all alone now? I mean, I was eighteen. An adult. No one was required to take care of me, make sure I was okay. Tend to my dreams or pump the brakes on my eagerness to get started.

*Someday, Gubben.*

This was what I'd been begging for for years. To be done with all the bullshit and get on with my life. But Farfar was always in that picture.

My partner. My mentor. My everything.

Was this really my *someday*?

*Is* it?

What lessons in Farfar's Business School hadn't we gotten to?

When I stepped out of the shower, the bathroom a solid wall of steam, I had more questions than when I stepped in. I smelled better, granted, but I felt more lost than before—like the shock was wearing off and reality was even worse.

Maggie was at the counter with Lou when I finally came out in clean clothes, and she immediately attacked me with hugs.

"Oh my god, I saw the TV coverage and tried calling and calling, and texting and texting, and nothing," she said through tears. Lou was crying, too, having been the one to have to fill her in on everything that had happened. Lou leaned against the sink, now full of suds. The griddle was gone, too.

"I'm sorry," I said. "My phone was dead. I didn't think to check." And my words caught again; I was struck by how child-like they sounded. That I didn't know *how* to be an adult.

But Maggie just squeezed me tighter and shushed me, a hand on top of my head, like a mother consoling a child—which wasn't quite right, but was close.

I checked my phone then, wiping my eyes on my clean shirt-sleeves. A string of voice mails and texts from Maggie, just like she said, and in the past few hours, a bunch from numbers I didn't recognize.

"Reporters, I'm guessing," Maggie said, looking over my shoulder at my phone plugged in on the counter. "Just ignore them for now. We can worry about those later—*I'll* worry about those later. You just get your bag packed."

It was basically the same advice Lou had given me. I watched Lou nod to herself and sniff, wiping down the counter.

I packed in a daze. My brain unable to comprehend the addition of *reporters* to this equation.

"Toothbrush?" Lou said from my doorway a few minutes later, dishcloth in hand.

"I already brushed."

She looked at me, her eyes soft, a small smile.

"You may want to do it again tomorrow, too."

"Right."


With my duffel stuffed full of random clothes and toiletries, we made plans to leave, having to drive separately from this point. Lou's parents, understandably, wanted her home after such a terrifying experience, and likewise wanted her back in school the next day. Back to her normal life, as much as possible. The thought of *school* the next day, though, seemed absurd.

"Do you have an extra key?" Lou said. "I'll take care of Koopa if you're not here."

She scooped the cat up again, and I could see, despite her calm, her uncanny sense of responsibility, that she was barely holding it together, too. She just knew how to take care of things.

"I love you."

She just nodded and smiled into Koopa's fur.

I'm not sure what made me think of it, or why it felt necessary, but before we left the apartment, I went back to Farfar's room, carefully pulled the picture of Amir from the side of his dresser, and slid it into my bag. I don't even know how long that one donut of Scotch tape had been holding it in place, but it pulled a layer of finish from the side of the dresser, the shape of Ohio.

*Hope he doesn't mind.*


It's crazy how normal everything was when we left. A bright, gorgeous Sunday in May. People out walking. Tourists exploring. The kind of day where we'd make a killing on the campus, parked out all afternoon.

Smithsboro was a national news story. *Farfar* was a national news story. But for everybody else, national news stories only existed on TV or in phones. Inside screens. Behind glass.

Like if I just decided to drive over to the campus right then, I'd find Farfar there wondering where I'd been all morning, a line of customers growing impatient—or as impatient as you can get on a gorgeous spring day waiting for fresh donuts. Not unconscious in a hospital bed, in a hospital whose name I still didn't know, in a town I'd never been to before yesterday.

"Are you two both okay to drive?" Maggie asked us on the sidewalk, Lou's and my hands locked together. We both nodded, and Maggie said she'd follow us to the hospital. She'd never been there before, either.

That same gorgeous, torturous drive, and a little less than three hours after we'd left him, we stepped back into the fourth-floor ICU, back into the nightmare behind everyone else's screens.

I'd been holding out hope that we'd walk in and he'd be awake—that the hospital just got too busy to call when he came to—but there he was, just as we'd left him.

His chest moving up and down to the rhythm of the respirator. His head wrapped in bandages, covering the hole they'd drilled into his skull last night to drain fluids and reduce swelling. *Ventriculostomy.*

His eyes still definitely closed.

Stable.

"Oh, Erik," Maggie said, rushing to his side, and Lou and I stood back, hands locked again, and let Maggie take in this first crushing sight of her friend.


Lou had to go home later that day, and at some point Maggie did, too, not technically being family, but I didn't leave again for the next three days.

They put another hole in him, this time into his throat. Tracheotomy, the nurse explained. More relief for his mouth and his throat, now that he was . . . wait for it . . . *stable.* But if I'm being honest, as horrible a thought as it was, having them cut a hole into Farfar's windpipe, it was nice to see his mouth again.

After four days, that was the best I could get.

Bryce's name was never released. Since I guess he hadn't turned eighteen yet, he was just mentioned as "the minor" the victim saved. *Still a kid.* But they definitely released the fact that "the minor" was part of the protest against the street name change—incorporated, whether he wanted to believe it or not, with the different hate groups there that day.

Farfar was kind of a national hero, though.

Maggie released his photo—with my permission, legally—along with the fact that he was a gay man. Beyond the endless footage of the incident itself, some outlets were piecing together bios—some even with photos I'd never seen before, of a younger Farfar at different rallies, Amir by his side. *A seventy-five-year-old gay immigrant who sacrificed his life to save the life of a young man who may very well have hated him, just for being the beautiful man he is.* That's how one article put it.

It could be Bryce on a ventilator right now, knocked out by an uglier, more demented version of himself.

Aaron Crue is the villain in this story, though. The mug shot that will pop up whenever anyone Googles *Smithsboro* for the next decade.

But Bryce should be there, too. Maybe Farfar would've done what he did for anyone left standing in the street. Maybe that was just his natural reaction. But I know he knew Bryce was over there, knew he was a classmate, even if one I couldn't stand. Still just a kid, in his eyes. And a big part of me blames Farfar, too.

Why'd he even have to get out of the truck?

We could be on Rainbow Road right now.

We're supposed to be getting ready to go back to Åland. Far-far and me, back to where it started.

*In a scene eerily reminiscent of Charlottesville . . .*

I remember the line from the news that night, after Lou and Maggie had both driven back home to Gettysburg. The reporter, standing at the edge of the park in Smithsboro, near where our truck should've still been sitting if it hadn't already been towed.

*When the evil shows up, which it does far too often, heroes emerge. . . .*

But he shouldn't have had to be a hero that day.

He was already my hero.

And I just want him back.

## CHAPTER THIRTY-THREE

# EFFORTLESS

FARFAR'S ROOM WAS AN EXPLOSION OF FLOWERS AND CARDS from people all across the country, none of whom I'd ever met. His hospital bills were covered. According to Lou, Mrs. Bixler started a GoFundMe page, which blew up quickly, until Mrs. Bixler received personal messages from a few different donors that made it clear that I—we—would never see a medical bill, no matter the cost.

With AP tests starting that week, Lou had no choice but to go back to school. I wouldn't have let her skip, even if her parents somehow allowed her to, and I knew Farfar would say the same thing. She'd worked too hard. Plus, sitting and staring and hoping—what made up most of those first days—I didn't want her to have to endure that, too. So she drove down a couple of nights, and FaceTimed every day for non-updates, but her primary job was Koopa and APs.

And it may have been a dirty move, but I told her that when he woke up, he was going to ask about how she did, and she was going to want to have only one possible answer. So I didn't know yet for certain, but I was pretty sure Lou broke the AP tests over those two weeks.

So, you know, it goes both ways here.

It was only fair that I let her tell him, right?

Jorge and Jesus visited regularly, too, but they were in the same AP boat as Lou—these last hoops they'd worked so hard to reach. The whole family had come by the hospital a couple of times, and even though it initially felt good to see them all, to be on the receiving end of all their hugs and kindnesses, it too quickly became the same sitting and staring and hoping, too many of us waiting for any sign of change—minute by endless minute—that didn't come.

Stable.

But it was Maggie and Juliet who'd been here the most. Juliet was out of town that weekend of the festival, hadn't been paying attention to the news on her drive back from her sister's.

A few nights after everything went down, the three of us in various states of quiet discomfort around Farfar's room, Maggie noticed the picture of Amir I'd taped near his bed.

"Oh my goodness, Oscar. Did you put that there?"

I nodded, and Maggie put her cool hand on top of mine, our chairs pulled side by side, a few feet away from Farfar.

"You got to see them together."

It wasn't really a question, but I was hoping she'd take it as one.

"Oh, Oscar . . ." She already had tears in her eyes, remembering. "It's hard to believe that was almost thirty years ago."

"When they first moved here?"

Then she told me the line about not believing in soul mates. About how effortless they made it look, Farfar and Amir, being together. But it was by no means *effortless.*

She told me that, with Amir set to leave Åland, to move to America and start over (even with a more open-minded society, Amir's family wouldn't accept it, and Mariehamn wasn't a very big place), Farfar realized he'd either have to start over, too, or be buried alive by his own life. To continue on for however many decades he might be lucky enough to have left . . . *pretending.* And I guess he just couldn't.

I thought of the Mii characters from a few months ago, after Race Night, hidden away at the end of the parade.

"I think sometimes," I said, scared I was betraying him by saying it out loud, "part of him wishes he could have kept pretending." I wasn't sure he could even hear us—I kept looking for any little sign of change, but it was just the same mechanical rise and fall of his chest, his head still on the pillow—and I kept thinking about his words that night: *I wasn't sure about anything. . . . I'm still not. . . .*

"I can't imagine what the moment must have been like for him," Maggie said, staring sadly at him. "To come home one day and know you have to shatter your wife's entire world, after more than twenty years, whether she was blissfully happy or not."

We were both quiet then, watching him breathe, these emotions swirling from all different pieces of his life.

"Do you remember much about her? Your farmor?" Maggie asked, squeezing my hand again.

"Not much," I said, shaking my head. "A few fuzzy images,

you know? Her house. The kitchen. Her sitting at the table. But nothing particularly warm."

Maggie nodded, but part of me felt this new wave of guilt, wondered what kind of regret *she'd* lived with all these years, moving on to a new life of her own.

"It's not that she was mean or anything," I added. "Not that I remember, anyway. Just that I can't say, *Oh, we used to laugh all the time,* or *We used to cook together* or *She used to read me stories every night.*"

I took a deep breath.

"That was him."

Maggie told me stories of their years together, in the apartment, the four of them like a newly formed family. Of helping with the truck in its first days. Of dinners and day trips. Rallies and demonstrations. Amir's endless ideas for their future. Juliet nodded and smiled at parts, in her chair across the room, adding little bits of her dry commentary throughout, and I just listened.

Maggie pieced together other parts for me, too. More of how *I* got here.

A lot like Farfar's telling to Lou at Lillajul, the stories circled back on themselves, heart-swell and heartbreak on overlapping timelines.

"He'd gone back for Filip's funeral," she said. "The first time he'd made the daylong trip since he left. More than ten years."

She said my dad, seemingly on the upswing, was out of school when Farfar left. Had a job. Two, in fact: one at a small grocery store, which he'd gotten because the owner was a

GIF, was his body, at that moment of impact, flying impossibly fast and impossibly far, from the back bumper of the red Malibu, body horizontal, parallel to the street, spinning like the blades of a helicopter before rolling to a stop in the grass at the edge of the park.

Over and over.

Rewind. Replay.

God, Farfar.


I'm not sure how long I was standing there when the officer came up behind me and put a hand on my shoulder. But that was the moment I realized how badly I was shaking. It was the first time I'd stepped outside since getting to the hospital the day before, and this morning was nothing like that one—overcast, humid but chilly, the air thick with mist.

"Oscar, right?"

I nodded without looking at her, but just hearing my name made the tears come again.

"I'm so sorry for what's happened, Oscar," she said, and even though I knew it was just an intro line to get to what she really needed, it felt sincere. She was the same officer who drove Lou and me to the hospital, trailing the ambulance with sirens blaring.

"I need to talk about a few things with you. Before you go home."

At the mention of home, I could see Koopa, meowing at the apartment door through the night, wondering why no one had shown up for her yet, and the thought of her panic made me break even more, and all I wanted to do was jump in the truck childhood friend of Farmor's; the second at a small commercial bakery, which, Farfar said, he'd gotten on his own, after doing well at the grocery store—and, if I'm being honest, I kind of loved, even if he played no part in raising me, and even if he wasn't technically a baker. He hadn't even met my mother yet, at least not that Farfar knew of.

Lots of things happened in the years Farfar was gone. Here. During those stories of him and Amir. The addiction taking over, hooking up with my mother at some point—not a terribly romantic story—being taken in by Farmor when neither parent could, or was willing to, do the job.

"When he got the call," Maggie said, "he didn't even know you existed. Had no idea that he was officially a grandfather, even if divided by an ocean. He said he lost a life and gained one in the same phone call." A variation of the line Farfar had told me for years.

Maggie said he hadn't spoken to Farmor in nearly ten years on the day she called to tell him. Farfar's leaving hadn't gone over too well with her, understandably, and trying to talk to him—to maintain an amicable relationship, to remain friends, as he'd hoped—just wasn't possible for her.

"He broke her heart, Oscar," Maggie said quietly, like she didn't want Farfar to hear, and squeezed my hand. "He said at the time it was the worst day of his life—knowing he was delivering the worst day of *her* life.

"She could understand it. Maybe. But she couldn't be any part of him. Not if she wasn't his wife."

I couldn't even wrap my brain around it. That kind of pain. Thinking you're spending your entire life with one person—*your* one person—only to find out one day out of the blue that it just couldn't be anymore. That, really, it hadn't been for a long time. Maybe, I'm sure she thought, *ever.*

And to know you're the one causing that. God. Farfar. I didn't know how he'd lived with it—how he lived with it *before,* knowing all those years. If every bit of joy was clouded by it.

It's such a strange, unsettling thought—like he has these distinct *chapters* in his life. His childhood, which I know very little about. College, which I learned about through him and Lou. His first adult life, with Farmor, with my dad—his traditional family life that ended so badly on so many levels. His second adult life, moving here with Amir. His third adult life—me.

I've only had one chapter of my life; I only know one part. And I've never imagined I could end up with so many more, like him. I've always just thought *childhood, adulthood, done.* Or *school, out of school.*

I'm scared to death that I'm facing the end of chapter one. That it's time to neatly pack away the remains of this first part. Chapter two should be *done with school.* Period. Starting adulthood on the truck, with Farfar. Maybe, though I haven't said it to her, my chapter two starts with Lou, the way his later chapter started with Amir.

But god, chapter two can't be my life without Farfar. Not yet. That chapter has to come later, right?

## CHAPTER THIRTY-FOUR

# THE TRUCK

"LISTEN. WHEN HE COMES HOME, YOU'RE GOING TO HAVE TO be the one to do these things for a while."

I watched Lou unload a plastic grocery bag onto the counter—pancake mix, milk, syrup, chocolate chips, eggs. It was the first night since the accident that I'd slept in my own bed, and while I did so with an incredible sense of guilt, as soon as I slid under the covers, I was out, ten straight dreamless hours. And then, bright and early, here was Lou, a look of hope and determination on her face to go with the groceries, and I had no choice, like always, but to go along with it.

"Lou. I know how to make pancakes." Then, "We don't use mix."

"Then why don't I see any pancakes? It's Saturday, isn't it? I'm not early."

I ran a hand through my hair, letting out a long breath.

"I love you."

Once it had come out that first time, it was hard to turn it off.

"You know what I love?" Lou asked, pulling me in for a kiss. "Pancakes. Let's go." And she smacked me on the butt with a spatula she'd pulled from the crock behind me. Because that was apparently who she was now.

So we made pancakes. I didn't use the mix. And it was the first thing that even felt halfway right in the week since the festival.

"Do you really think he's going to wake up and come home?" I asked from the passenger seat of Lou's car as we wound along the familiar path back into Maryland to the hospital, the morning sky a blanket of gray, a steady light rain falling.

Lou was quiet at first, concentrating on the brake lights in front of her. She glanced at me, then said, "I do. I really do."

And I don't know why, but it seemed like it had to be true, coming from Lou.

"But if—*when*—he does, it's going to be different. We don't know the extent of the injuries yet . . . how long-term some of them might be."

I'd thought about all this already, what the possibilities might be.

What if he woke up and, like in some kind of soap opera, he had amnesia and didn't know who I was?

What if he was paralyzed?

What if he couldn't speak? Couldn't eat? Couldn't take care of himself at all on his own?

What were the *actual* chances that I'd just simply *have him back*?

And like she was reading my mind, Lou said, "So we may have to plan as though he won't be able to do any of the things he could do before."

I nodded, unable to keep the tears from spilling again while I watched out the window, wondering how the same drive could look so different over the course of a week, things growing and changing all the time.

"When we pick up the truck today, Oscar, it may really be *your* truck from here on out." I could see tears spilling off her chin, too, even while her words were so measured, and I put my hand on her leg while she drove. "We should really prepare for you to do this—if you *want* to still do this—on your own."

It was the first time I'd really had to even consider the question—even if I wasn't ready to answer it. If I couldn't have Farfar beside me—if he was *gone*—was this still the life I would want? Was it still the dream—god, worse, was it *only* a dream— if it was just me on the truck?

Just me.

I pulled my hand back from Lou's leg, staring out the side window into the passing trees.

I thought about having to find someone. Someone new to help. There was no way I could run it alone, I realized. *That is one of the first things you will learn, Gubben . . . how hard it is to find good help.* And I pictured Lou at school, in a dorm room with bright, cheap furniture and a new roommate, working hard, studying away, her plans unchanged. Her path clear.

"Do you think I should've had a backup plan?" I turned to look at her again, clutching the wheel, and it was like the old filter clicked back into place for a second. "College?"

She shot me a quick glance, confused, then looked back at the road.

"How are *we* supposed to prepare for this, Lou?"

We reached the first scattering of businesses on the outskirts of Hagerstown, places I only knew in passing, in reference to this disaster. I could feel the squeeze in my chest, like

I'd been following this path that had disappeared beneath my feet and, when I looked back, realized there was nothing behind me, either. Just me. No clear direction to go. I couldn't see beyond graduation in a few weeks, other than what now *wouldn't* happen—*couldn't* happen—anymore.

Lou turned to face me at the first stoplight, still confused, but her eyes immediately softened as she realized what I was really saying. Her face and shoulders fell, and the look she gave me broke my heart.

After all this time, after being so sure, maybe I *was* lost.

I knew what I wanted. And I had no way of getting there.

We stopped to see Farfar first, the nurses cleaning him, moving his limbs when we came in, and I thought for the briefest moment that something had changed. But the two nurses just smiled at us sweetly, sadly, almost apologetic, as they explained to us the dangers of bedsores.

And again when Lou kissed his forehead before we left, I thought for sure I saw him stir, just the tiniest bit, but it was just my imagination. Like little heartbreaks, over and over again.

We found the impound lot, part of a towing company in Hagerstown, and though the rain had stopped, the blanket of gray remained.

"I hope he's okay" was all the man in the small office said when I slid the unintelligible paperwork back to him. He slid the truck key to me, and Lou and I went back outside.

My knees went weak as soon as I saw it, parked in a long row of vans and small work trucks along a high chain-link fence. Like a part of me clicked back into place and caught in my chest. Like even if I couldn't see the path, I at least recognized where I was.

And then I opened the driver's-side door.

The stench was unbearable—like stumbling upon a crime scene, which it kind of was.

Lou and I both recoiled, Lou stepping away with an arm over her face, me hunched over behind the open door.

One week.

It'd been one week since we'd been in the truck. One week since that moment, frozen to the floor . . . watching him . . . and everything was exactly as we'd left it. Kebab meat still on the spit. Munkar dough still prepped on racks. Potatoes still sliced in the bin, raw fries waiting to be dropped.

The only difference was seven days of sweltering heat, and the fact that the truck had been towed, a good ten to twenty miles, with the front end lifted a few feet off the ground.

Oil from the fryers covered my workstation and the floor beneath, all the way to the back of the truck, where kebab grease from the spit spilled over and pooled with it along the back wall in a mottled, putrid mess.

It was all ruined. Just like that, the little bit of dream I'd been clinging to, that little bit of path, gone. How was I supposed to do this without him?

"Oh, god."

Lou stood behind me and squeezed my arm, the neck of her T-shirt pulled up over her nose.

"It's fine," I managed, trying not to breathe while I spoke.

I turned and urged Lou away from this impossible disaster. "I can drive with the windows down. We just need to get it home."

What I was supposed to do then, I had no idea.

I followed Lou's car back out of Hagerstown, her long braid just barely visible through her rear windshield for the hour-plus drive back. The spray from the still-wet highway covered my left side, inside this place that was like my second home, my future, and I struggled every few moments to keep from retching.

And all I could think, with the street spray and the stench stinging my eyes, was *Why?* Why was everything I had being taken away from me?

Because my grandfather, my everything, had saved the life of one hate-and-fear-filled asshole from an even bigger hate-and-fear-filled asshole's lethal, cowardly tantrum.

And now I was left with nothing.


I couldn't even comprehend the task ahead of me as we pulled back into town. Couldn't imagine how I'd even *start,* as Lou parked along the sidewalk in front of the apartment and I went around the block to pull into the alley.

But when I rolled to a stop outside the open garage door, there they all were.

Jorge and Jesus. Javy. Josie. And their mom and dad and aunt.

Maggie and Juliet. Winston, his leash tied to a table leg inside the garage.

Lou's mom.

Mrs. Bixler. Mrs. Crockett. Even freaking Terrance.

The dumpster lids were open in the alley, and a hose and a pressure washer were hooked up from the garage. Trash bags. Buckets already full of suds, scrub brushes, and sponges. Everyone in rubber gloves.

I slid out of the driver's seat, openly sobbing, onto the patchwork asphalt of the alley, just as Lou walked up the alley behind me and put her arm around my shoulder, leaning her head against mine.

I think I let out more of an animal snort than an actual question. But Lou just squeezed and said, "I told them I needed a favor."

## CHAPTER THIRTY-FIVE

# A FEW LAST HOOPS

MAGGIE ASSURED ME THAT EITHER SHE OR JULIET WOULD BE
there with Farfar at some point every day during the day—that
was the only way I'd agree to go back to school for the last two
weeks before graduation. But the guilt of being away from him
all day was crippling, and the thought that it was just to burn
some hours each day inside a school building, for a few more
weeks of pointless formalities, only amplified the feelings. And
I still couldn't see anything beyond that arbitrary finish line at
the end of May.

Mrs. Bixler helped convince me, though, too, to regain some
small sense of normalcy—even if it was my least-favorite part of
"normal"—and to make sure I was present for everything leading up to graduation, though I didn't care about that, either. But
it mattered to them, and it mattered to Lou, and they didn't have
to tell me that it would matter to Farfar, so I went.

Mrs. Bixler worked it out that I'd spend pretty much all my
time in her room. There was no way I could pretend to care about
English or anything else. There was no way I could calmly sit
through final meaningless lessons and jump through pointless
hoops, thinking about the tubes and monitors keeping Farfar
stable or nurses moving him to prevent bedsores or what I was

supposed to do on the other side of those stupid hoops. So the other teachers compiled what they deemed "necessary" for me to complete their classes, and I'd work my way through what I could in Mrs. Bixler's room.

On that first Wednesday, after they'd let me start with two half days on Monday and Tuesday, Mrs. Bixler showed up with a small stack of folders and laid them on the counter in front of me: my compiled work from the other teachers.

I let out a sigh, but Mrs. Bixler just stood there grinning at me until I finally opened the first folder, then the second.

Every one of them had the same thing, written on a piece of notebook paper, each in different pen and scrawl:

FINAL ASSIGNMENT: Cupcakes (please! ☺)

Lou still showed up every fourth period, and she'd stay through lunch, when Terrance somehow managed to keep getting lunch detentions with Mrs. Bixler. But by that point, they had little to say and mostly left me alone to work. I mean, what *was* there to say after a while? No changes, no updates, no indication that there would be anytime soon, other than just hoping.

I would throw my earbuds in and turn on Harry and just go—what I'd been complaining about *not* being able to do the entire year.

I was grateful for the teachers' unexpected kindness, the bubble Mrs. Bixler created for me. I was. And honestly, if Lou had broken the AP tests the two weeks before, I utterly annihilated my final assignments.

But part of me felt like it was just an empty token. That I knew I was on borrowed time now, and these hours churning out cupcakes were really just a holding pattern. Because then what?

I could whip out batch after batch of endless cupcakes—or donuts or muffins or crisp or whatever—because everything was *here*. Purchased, collected, delivered, just for me. Industrial ovens, mixers, limitless storage and stocked pantries.

I didn't do *any* of that. It was just here. Provided.

Like the stupid cupcakes weren't even mine. *None* of it was mine.

How was I supposed to do this in a few weeks? On the other side of that arbitrary finish line, without all this? Without Farfar?

Just a naïve kid and a truck he could barely operate?

Who would back that business?

The panic overwhelmed me as I stared into the oven one day, waiting for the timer to count down. It flooded my chest again, my hands gripping the oven doors to keep me upright, and I tried to steady my breathing without the others noticing.

I could see Lou in the reflection of the oven window, looking up from her notebook. Lou, who'd been taking care of every little thing she could to keep me going. Terrance, eating his meatball, glancing at me sheepishly between bites, wanting, I could tell, to say the right things, but not having the vocabulary for it. Mrs. Bixler, giving me space to brood and work, without interruption, but always nearby to rest a hand on my shoulder, to smile at what I was doing, to taste the buttercream.

*One of the first things you will learn, Gubben . . . how hard it is to find good help.*

It was all around me.

I couldn't stop. I couldn't just sit down in the woods, waiting for Farfar to come find me and hold my hand back to the path. At some point, I realized, no matter how this turned out, I was going to have to start clearing a new path—hack away the brambles and take the next step.

I could make donuts. And donuts were a start.

And if I could make donuts, I could probably make fries.

The timer went off and I pulled the cupcakes from the oven. Lou was still watching me when I finished setting the trays on racks to cool. I let out a deep breath and gave her a small smile. She smiled back.

"I think I want to start on some donuts next."

Terrance closed his eyes, still working on his sub, and raised a single fist in the air.


My biggest fear, honestly, throughout all of this, was seeing Bryce. That if I did see him, I might honestly kill him, with my bare hands.

I wish I were joking. But I'd dreamed and daydreamed about it more than once, alone in our apartment at night, in the Prius back and forth from the hospital.

The Brooding Baker, his forearms like steel cables from years of kneading and working, his fingers like vise grips around Bryce's thick neck.

I didn't know if my brain could separate fiction from reality if I happened to see him in the hallway, laughing with his friends, or in speech, flirting loudly with Teegan.

I might have killed him. All my dreams gone, just like that. Just like Farfar was stolen away in one tiny, single moment.

But Lou told me Bryce hadn't been in school the whole week I was out, and the rumor was that he wouldn't be back. I didn't know what that meant, really—if he was too embarrassed to show his face as the bigoted coward he'd always been, if he was too traumatized to return to classes, if he was too guilt-ridden. Maybe all of them. I didn't know.

I just knew I wasn't likely to bump into him.

Mrs. Sommers stopped in one day that second week, while I was pumping out cupcakes and other goodies with abandon, timers counting down the seconds to baked goods and the moment I could get back on the road to Maryland.

She just stood in the doorway and watched me for a few minutes, flying around the kitchen, whipping up specialized batches of buttercream.

"So, there is a final presentation for my class," she finally said, stepping completely into the room.

I looked up at her, a mixing bowl in the crook of my arm and a spatula in hand.

"Here's what I want you to do," she said, motioning for me to continue with my frosting work. "Talk me through it. Keep doing what you're doing, but talk me through it, like this is your show on Netflix."

I stared at her again for a moment while she pulled a stool up to the counter across from me and smiled, her eyes catching more light than I expected.

So I talked while I worked. And at first it felt a little weird, but after a while, she'd ask me follow-up questions, and before long, we were just talking—about baking, about my life, about my future. And it felt good, like little traces of the path were being swept clean again.

When she stood up a few minutes before the bell, while I piped lemon-infused buttercream onto a tray of cooled cupcakes, she let out a long sigh and smiled again.

"Oscar, I've learned through some of my colleagues in the faculty room this year that school may not be your favorite thing." I let out something between a laugh and a sigh of my own. "But I have to tell you, honestly, you are one of the most fascinating, engaging, genuine students I've ever met. I'm so sorry for what's happened, but I'm so grateful to have had you in my classroom this year."

And before I knew what to say in response, she wrapped me in a hug, and I felt those stupid tears stinging my eyes again.

"I would watch your show, Oscar Olsson."

------

## CHAPTER THIRTY-SIX

# EAT MUNKAR,
# SPREAD LOVE

"SO WHERE ARE WE TAKING THE TRUCK THIS WEEKEND?"

"What?"

The question came on a Thursday, that last full week of school before graduation the following week, as I was putting the finishing touches on a batch of cupcakes destined for the faculty retirement picnic. Extra credit for Mrs. Shue.

"It's Memorial Day weekend," Lou said, setting her book bag on her usual table at the beginning of fourth period—as crazy as it was, one of the last fourth periods we'd spend together. In fact, with seniors not even required to come in for classes that next week, it was almost my last fourth period, *period.*

"Don't tell me you don't even have a game plan for Memorial Day weekend!"

"Lou . . ."

"There's got to be, like, a thousand baseball tournaments and festivals we could hit."

"Lou . . ."

"Oscar." She was next to me then, in her last student council T-shirt, that braid hanging off her shoulder. She took the piping bag from my hand and set it down, licked the end of her finger and nodded, then squeezed my hand. "We didn't all clean the truck for it to stay parked in the garage. If this is what you want, you don't have to wait for . . . We can do this—*you* can do this." Then, "I think you have to do this."

I let out a deep breath and dropped my head, putting my hands on the counter.

"And when he wakes up, he's going to ask about the truck. I'm pretty sure I know what you're going to want your answer to be."

And because Lou has the ability to completely disable my vocal cords, all I could do was nod as she kissed the side of my head.

"I'll be over after school to help prep. Figure out where we're going."

"Wait, where are we going?"

Terrance shuffled into the room then, looking uncharacteristically bashful for interrupting our moment.

I glanced up at Lou, my eyes wet, one side of her mouth turned up.

"Aren't you, like, forty minutes early for lunch detention?"

"I'm on a bathroom pass," Terrance replied, holding up a familiar oversized Edward Cullen keychain as evidence. A keychain I knew was normally housed in a classroom on the other side of the building.


I knew where we were going. Farfar had already planned it out, had our spot registered, right here at home. I just hadn't expected to still *go*.

The Memorial Kick-Off Festival, the first of three days of events leading up to the Gettysburg Memorial Day Parade.

"Do you really think we can do it?" I'd asked Lou that Thursday night, riding back from the hospital in the OG Prius. We'd made our plans after school, and she wanted to tell Farfar the details in person, whether he could respond or not. How we'd taken stock: we had meat cones in the chest freezer in the garage; we were good on kebab sauces, flour and yeast, serving trays and paper sleeves, foil. Farfar had stocked up before the start of festival season, luckily, and I'd even found the number for his fry-oil guy and had him out a few days after we'd cleaned up the truck.

More traces of the path swept clear.

We'd planned the menu, made the shopping list. (And she was right—it felt good to tell him, but . . .)

"I mean, *literally*, can we actually do this? Can we pull this off without him? It's a pretty big festival—a lot of tourists come in for the weekend."

I glanced over at Lou in the passenger seat. The last sliver of sunset shone in through the back windshield, casting the side of her face in orange twilight. And suddenly she just busted out laughing.

"God, I have no idea, Oscar."

"That's not terribly reassuring."

"I just want him back so bad, and I can't even imagine how this must be for you, and I'm trying so hard to do the right thing to help, because I love you. Fuck, Oscar, I love you. And everything feels absolutely crazy, because how the *fuck* can senior year end like this? And I just want him back. . . . I want it all back."

Her shoulders deflated, and she was breathing heavy, haphazard, and her eyes were wild with desperation. Unraveling.

I glanced at her once more before focusing on the road again, approaching the edge of the battlefields.

"Hmm."

"*Hmm,* what?"

"I mean, I guess it can't go worse than last time, right?"

And Lou let out a laugh that was mostly a sob and rested her head on my shoulder, the two of us crying the rest of the way into town.

"I guess if it's too much," I said as I pulled into the alley, "we just close it up and drive home. No big deal."

We prepped all Friday evening, just like Farfar and I always had. Jorge and Terrance were there, hashing out everyone's roles. We even went down to the garage to practice our spacing and workflow inside the truck.

Lou would keep her role at the window, managing workflow and dealing with customers. Jorge was confident he could handle Farfar's kebab station, having watched him enough times. Terrance was happy with defined tasks in the middle: put potatoes through the slicer, assist with munkar-filling and rulle-kebab toppings as needed.

I'd handle the fryers and munkar station, like normal, since that tended to be the most relentless job.

Lou showed up early Saturday morning, after picking up Terrance from his house. I was up crazy early—like, Farfar early—and had pancakes waiting when they slipped in the door, yawning. Terrance inhaled his chocolate chip pancakes with meatball-level enthusiasm, and Lou gave Koopa some sorely needed Swedish baby talk, and we carried the last coolers down to the truck. (Jorge planned to meet us at the festival, of course.)

We were ready.


What we were *not* ready for, however, were the crowds. Like, *our* crowds. People showed up specifically for *us*.

I'd sent out a simple post on Instagram and Twitter and Facebook the night before, a picture of the four of us standing arms over shoulders in front of the truck and a quick line:

Hej Hej! back on the road tomorrow #KickoffGettysburg #eatmunkarspreadlove

I thought it was kind of cheesy and stupid, but (along with Lou asserting her authority over her myriad school and service organizations) it must've caught on overnight, and the word spread.

I just wanted to get the truck back out for me, honestly—for *us*—to see if I could really do this on my own. To be able to tell Farfar that I could.

But like I said, Farfar had become something of a national hero, and the truck showing up to serve after such a tragedy, well, it meant something much more to an awful lot of people.

By the time Jorge got there, more than an hour before the official start of the festival (*way* early for him, he wanted to make sure I pointed out to Farfar), there were already small crowds gathering, just to take selfies in front of the truck.

Lou would talk to them through the window, and every few minutes, while I was getting as much munkar as I could set up on trays to proof, she'd call me over to the window to meet someone—other truck owners, teens and college kids, parents, old people—who wanted me to wish Farfar the best, or offer him their prayers, or share their love.

And when the festival officially kicked off, we already had the longest line I'd ever seen at a festival.

"O, can we really do this?" Jorge said, slicing ribbons of kebab meat into a tray as fast as he could, five minutes before go time, sheer panic on his face.

Lou looked back and laughed, and it was all I could manage, too. "I have no idea."

But Terrance stepped in as official Hej Hej! hype man, grabbing Jorge by the shoulders and screaming, "We can do this! LET'S GO!!!"

Which, I'll be honest, actually seemed to work. Jorge flared his nostrils, nodded, and turned back to his station to slice more kebab meat.

And we went.


We had to close the window by two-thirty. We *literally ran out of food*.

A young photographer from the *Baltimore Sun* caught us— Lou and me crying in each other's arms; Jorge sitting on the ground, his back against the front tire, a hand running through his soaking-wet hair; Terrance standing between us with both arms in the air, screaming at the sky—all four of us beneath the sign Lou had written in Sharpie and taped to the window:

> OUT OF FOOD!
> THANK YOU ALL!
> SPREAD LOVE!

It was a pretty good day. Maggie saved the article. For when . . .


After the emotional high of the festival, I spent the rest of the long weekend with Farfar.

I'm proud of what we did, how we managed to run the truck on our own, but I'll be honest, the guilt is still overwhelming, spending so much time away from him.

*I should be the one here when he wakes up.*

I know, I can hear him. *Don't be an idiote, Gubben.*

But there's another part, too. A part I don't want to admit out loud, but . . . it was kind of a relief. To be away. Just for a little while. To feel a little bit of normal, a little bit of good, especially if . . . if it's going to be my new normal. Alone.

It's been a month, and . . .

Okay. I'm sorry.

God, I miss him.

There's a little more story to go.

A little more I want him to hear.

## CHAPTER THIRTY-SEVEN

# GRADUATION

THREE DAYS LEFT. THREE DAYS AND I WAS FINALLY FINISHED FOR-ever. No more packets. No more reading assignments. No more homework. No more arbitrary numbers tied to arbitrary hoops.

Everything I'd been waiting for, right? The chance to get started with my *real* life.

No classes for seniors those last three days, either. I kid you not, we only had to go in to practice walking in a line, sitting in a chair for a while, and walking in a line again.

I know he would've liked to see me walk in that line, though.

He didn't miss much, honestly. Thirty thousand high schools, right? Millions of us, all the same, walking in the same lines, to the same song, after jumping through roughly the same number of hoops. Not really that special, right?

I know that's not at all what he meant. I've just been brooding on that one for days. The whole thing seemed more *surreal* than memorable. Like I was a bad actor, trying to play the role of graduating senior, only I'd forgotten my script and just hoped no one noticed.

With all those people there, together, us squinting through the glare of the sunset in our rows of folding chairs on the stadium turf, families and friends craning to find us and waving from the stands, it was the most profoundly *alone* I'd ever felt.

Even when Meredith read my name to walk across the little makeshift stage to receive my diploma, and the crowd stood and gave me a long, heartfelt ovation. And yeah, I cried, and it was a beautiful gesture, but it was nothing compared to the kids with obnoxious families shouting embarrassing nicknames and blasting contraband air horns for them. And when I sat back down again between Emily Odachowski and Victor Ortega—two kids I'd never spoken to in my life—I scanned the crowd, wondering where he would've sat.

If he would've been one to sneak in an air horn, or one of Jorge's uncle's cowbells. If he would've bellowed "Today, Gubben!" in the lull between names.

I did iron my own shirt, at least, like he taught me—the same shirt and pants from homecoming, actually.

Maggie checked in that afternoon, right as I was finishing the first sleeve, and asked if I needed help. And when I told her I had it under control, she smiled, then wrapped me in a hug.

"We're gonna be okay," she said, her chin over my shoulder.

And I couldn't tell if she meant okay as in, he'll be home soon and everything will be okay again, or, look at you ironing a shirt—you're going to be okay surviving on your own.

It's ripping my heart apart, preparing for both.

Our boy Jorge was valedictorian in the end, though, and he gave a speech reminiscent of his Paper Bag Speech back in September—*generational sacrifice*—but even better. I glanced up at his parents and grandparents in the stands just once at the beginning of his speech, and I'm not sure I breathed through the rest of it. Farfar would've been a mess.

Farfar had already heard Lou's speech—she read it to him herself the night before. Starting with the best piece of wisdom she'd ever received: *Don't be an idiote.* . . .

At the end, after the caps were thrown and everyone was meeting on the field, hugging and laughing and crying and posing for pictures, I decided to slip out of the gates without my cap and drive home.

Most of the seniors would be headed to Hickory Falls later that night, where they'd be locked in together, with free rein over go-karts and laser tag and arcade games and everything else, for one last night all together—and to prevent any graduation-night tragedies. Lou was going, Jorge and Jesus. And I knew Farfar would think I was an idiote for not going, but I was done.

Lou's family had a little graduation party right afterward that I was invited to, before the Hickory Falls lock-in. Jorge and Jesus's family, too. But for some reason, I couldn't do it. I just needed to be at home.

"Still just me," I said to Koopa when I opened the door, my gown wrapped in a ball around my hand. I tossed it over her to the couch as she twisted frantically between my feet. She'd been a mess since Farfar had been gone, even with Lou's daily check-ins, clinging to me every step I took in the apartment.

She stuck with me, yowling at my feet while I changed into sweats and an old Hej Hej! T-shirt, joined me as soon as I sank into the couch, and settled onto my lap as I grabbed Farfar's old rubber-banded remote and turned on the old Wii—*our* Wii—purring so hard it almost just felt like trembling.

"I know," I said. "I miss him, too."

And I pictured him, lying alone in his hospital room, his chest still rising and falling to the rhythm of a machine, while I lay alone in his spot on the couch, in our apartment, thirty-five miles away, wondering what the hell I was supposed to do next. I knew decisions were coming that I was not prepared to make.

I don't know exactly how long I'd been scrolling through the Mii Gallery again, but it was after eleven when I heard a knock at the door. I assumed it was Maggie, checking in one last time for the night, since she hadn't seen me at the end of the ceremony.

"Hey."

Lou stood in the doorway in a white tank top and fleece pajama pants, pulling at the end of her braid.

"Don't you have to be at the lock-in?" I said, stepping back to let her in.

"I'm not really part of student council anymore," she said, scooping up Koopa from the floor. "I think they can manage without me."

"You don't have to—"

"Oscar. I'm exactly where I want to be." And she whispered Swedish nonsense into Koopa's ear, and god, I nearly dropped to my knees. How was I supposed to say goodbye to *her* in a couple of months, too? No. Not *too*.

I closed the door and followed her back to the couch, Koopa like an idling tractor in her arms.

She rested her head on my shoulder, her legs curled beneath her, and I picked up the rubber-banded remote again.

"So this is our big graduation party, huh? Making Miis in a dark apartment with a mourning cat?"

I looked down at her, grinning up at me, and I tried my best to mirror it back. When I felt my smile falter, I made a pretend party horn, uncurling a finger from my lips.

But Lou just smiled wider and leaned up and gave me the most un-celery-like kiss in the history of kisses.

"There might be a meat cone in the freezer," I managed.

"Is that a euphemism?"

"Uh . . ."

"Like, fill the munkar?"

"Wait, is *that* a euphemism?"

My ears went pink, and Lou leaned in to kiss me again.

"Wait. Should we turn off the TV? The Miis are all watching."

Lou laughed, her forehead resting against mine.

"Honestly, I'm more concerned with the cat in your lap." And on cue, Koopa meowed up at us. "That one's not a euphemism."

I tried my best not to think about Lou leaving, about Farfar leaving, and just melted into the couch.


"Seriously, you might have to make me munkar for real tonight," Lou said a little while later. We were stretched out on the couch together, the Miis back on the screen.

"I'll see what I can do."

We scrolled through the gallery, Lou asking questions about each one—especially the ones that Farfar had added later. She wanted to know the stories.

So I told her our stories.

# CHAPTER THIRTY-EIGHT

## OUT OF STORY TO TELL

SO, THAT'S IT. IT'S OVER. I'M OUT OF SCHOOL. AN ADULT.

Lou's in Savannah now with Girl Scouts, their final trip together. There's still five of them, in the same troop together since fifth grade. Jorge and Jesus went to Senior Week in Ocean City, staying in some dumpy, overpriced hotel room near the boardwalk with other senior soccer players.

Me, I've been here all week, with Farfar.

And I'm out of story to tell.

I've been thinking about *chapters* again. I started going through my room, cleaning up, clearing out, reorganizing for adulthood, you know? And I found this random stuff, tucked against the wall beneath my bed, some of it there for years, lumped together over time. And I thought about how sometimes chapters can overlap.

I brought some of it with me. Think of it as a really poorly organized Paper Bag Speech.

This thing, this is the old phone charger. It was still plugged into the outlet that's covered by the end of my mattress, the cord dangling in the dust bunnies beneath, even though it doesn't work with any of our phones now.

It's from that transition time, after Farfar stopped reading to me every night but made sure I could still hear stories if I wanted to—the audiobooks he'd continued downloading to my old phone. They were never as good as his voice, no matter who the voice actor was, reading in the sound booth.

And this, this is that old phone. I found it buried at the back of my nightstand drawer, its battery long since depleted to nothing. It's a Motorola I-have-no-idea-other-than-he-got-it-for-$35-on-Consumer-Cellular. It worked, though. Worked just fine, even if the audio could never quite match the rumble of his voice or his leftover Swedish creeping in as he got tired.

But it did the job.

I could "go onto the Interwebs" if I needed to, could pull up YouTube if I wanted to hear some song I heard other kids talking about. Though I usually thought they were stupid when I did find them, and I'd end up watching cooking videos lined up in my feed instead. I could get to *Angry Birds*, or that stretch where the twins and I played *Clash of Clans* all the time. And my secret favorite: *My Singing Monsters*.

If I plugged it in, brought the Motorola back to life, I bet my islands would still be on there. I bet I could load up the app—it might take an update or three—and find my Drumplers still drumming away on their globular bellies. My favorite, the Entbrat, still bellowing its Gregorian monster chant. It took me forever to finally hatch one from the breeding cave.

I'm not sure how Farfar didn't notice that I'd be staring intently at the screen, my earbuds in, definitely *not* listening to the audiobook he'd downloaded for me.

Well, some nights I was. Really.

It just wasn't the same, though.

And I listen better while I'm cooking, anyway. The way I listened better to him while munching on the apples he'd cut for me before bed.

This, this is one of my many stuffed Moomins, but it's not from Farfar. This one's from before he even knew I existed, when he was in an entirely different chapter. It's the one thing I brought with me from Åland, when we left, crying—both of us, maybe—at the very beginning of our chapter.

I mean, I'm sure I had other things—clothes, toothbrush, maybe a few other toys I don't remember—but Moomin's the one thing that's remained.

It may have been from my mom or my dad, I don't know. My guess is that it came from Farmor, though. It's her house that I still have glimpses of in my head—I guess what would have been *his* house, too, in another chapter altogether. Before I was born.

I wonder how different it all would have been had he been there. Had he stayed. I know that's something he's probably asked himself every day since he left.

This—this is the troll book. My favorite one from when I was little. He always picked the books he'd read to me at night—even the audiobooks he'd put on that phone later on. But this one—this flimsy paperback, *Favorite Tales of Monsters and Trolls*, from when *my* dad was a kid, which somehow found its way across the Atlantic with him so many years ago—this one is my favorite. And no matter how many books Farfar had picked out that night, he'd still let me sneak this one in, even if it was just to read "The Stone Cheese."

And then this—this little slip of paper from Lou. She gave it to me over a month ago, before the festival. It's just the name of a poet she's obsessed with, Shane Koyczan, and the title of one of his poems she said reminded her of us. "Heaven, or Whatever." The paper must've slipped down the crack between my mattress and the wall while I watched the video of it on my bed.

I've listened to it almost every single day since.

It's about his grandfather—*to* his grandfather, really—who raised him after things fell apart with his own parents. He talks about his grandfather's belief that heaven would be specific to each person—that each person's was different.

I don't get through it without crying anymore.

Farfar's heaven?

His heaven, I think, would be *Mario Kart*, game reset, every character and every track, every speed bike and Super Blooper still in need of unlocking. A Monster Thickburger, a beer, and an endless stash of black licorice.

There's no heartburn in his heaven.

His heaven would be Koopa, stretched out on the windowsill in the living room, warming in the sun after dinner. Her purr as he purrs Swedish endearments, scratching under her chin in that way she only lets *him* do.

His heaven would be Amir.

I wish I could have met him. Wish I could have seen the two of them together, laughed with them in the sweltering heat of the food truck in early September.

And I wonder if—in his heaven—our two chapters could have been woven together. If the life he's given me and the life he shared with Amir could have overlapped. I'd be happy to work the window in his heaven. To face the customers waiting in the heat, impatient for a little taste of their own heaven.

Would Farfar and Amir banter back and forth while they cooked? Would they laugh together while sweat soaked into their do-rags and orders blurred together into one endless roll of kebab?

Would Amir play *Mario Kart* with us?

I wonder if maybe Farfar's heaven would be steering his own kart, inside the game, his gray ponytail slowly flapping in the lessened gravity of Rainbow Road, cackling as a smiling puff-cloud fishes him out of the abyss after he goes sailing over the guardrails. I'd wave as I pass, careful as always, decelerating my standard kart around the sharp turns, just waiting for him to come barreling past me yet again.

It breaks my heart a little bit that I might not really know what his heaven would be. Because, as I'm sitting here, crying and smiling over hypotheticals and random junk from my room, I realize that it's really *my* heaven.

This chapter. This life. With him.

And maybe it's stupid, a little selfish, that I worry about being just one chapter in his story. But I don't know if it's the chapter he'd choose to go back to again and again, stretched out on the couch, in those moments before sleep. Reading and rereading his favorite part of the story. And I'd like to.

Listen. I know the longer he's in this, the less chance he has of waking up. I know that. That my *someday* may have already gotten here, in a way we never planned, never imagined, never wanted.

I just want him to know, no matter what, I think I at least have some things figured out. That I may have found the path again. That we're—*I'm*—gonna be okay.

But you know—if he's hearing all this—it'd still be okay if maybe *someday* could stay *someday* just a little while longer. If maybe this chapter had a few more pages.

Just . . . *please.*

*Open your eyes.*

# EPILOGUE

THE GLASS DOOR SWINGS OPEN, AND SIX MEMBERS OF THE Gettysburg College men's soccer team file inside the small café. They have practice in a couple of hours, but that's plenty of time to digest an order or two of goat cheese poutine. Probably a few rounds of homemade donut holes, too—*munkhål*, they're called here—while they do schoolwork or study at their usual tables by the front window. The things are dangerously addictive, right out of the fryer. Some of the guys still can't believe they can use their student IDs here, like they're swiping into the school cafeteria a few blocks away.

It's an interesting combination of foods, but the local college community is well acquainted with their offerings. Faithful staff and students still rush to greet the café's food truck when it rumbles onto campus, which is not as often, sadly, as it once did.

The sixth team member steps inside after holding the door, takes in a deep breath, and smiles. It's a little early for it, he thinks, but the inside of the café today smells like unrefined holiday cheer, and he joins his teammates, scanning the menu board at the counter.

"What's good, O?" he calls through the wide opening into the kitchen.

The young owner looks up from the industrial mixer he's running, nods, and breaks into a wide grin. Flour fingerprints are visible along the side of his black Orioles hat, turned backward like always.

The typical lunch rush has already passed, and he's trying

to get a jump on the next day's munkar dough. It's a little over-whelming, with two huge cupcake orders still to fill for two separate baby showers, on top of the trays of saffron buns he'd like to get into the display case *before* Thanksgiving this year— especially after the feature in the *Gettysburg Times* last year, right after the café's opening.

But the young owner, a few weeks shy of his twentieth birth-day, couldn't be happier.

He sets a timer and comes out to chat with his customers, his friends, wiping his hands on a dish towel. He's got good help, too, he thinks, as he watches his employee drop two baskets of fresh-cut potatoes into the fryer and do a tiny, pelvic-heavy dance—dude's matured a lot in two years, actually.

"Is she home for break yet?" his friend asks at the counter, just as the bell above the door dings again.

He can see her, smiling at him from the sidewalk, holding the door wide. Her long, dark braid falls in front of her sweat-shirt when she turns her head away, talking to someone behind her by the art gallery next door. He spots the cane first, shaky but still improving, before the girl holds the old man's arm and the two of them take a careful step inside the café together.

"Hej hej, Gubben."

# HEJ HEJ! CAFÉ MENU

---

## RULLEKEBAB

**Original (Rullekebab)**—*shaved seasoned beef,
fresh flatbread, lettuce, tomato, cucumber, kebab sauce*
**Blue Kebab (Rullekebab med blåmögelost)**—
*Original Rullekebab with blue cheese*
**Shroom Kebab (Rullekebab med champinjoner)**—
*Original Rullekebab with mushrooms*
**Hej Hej! Special Rullekebab**—*Original Rullekebab
with pineapple, blue cheese, jalapeños*

## HAMBURGARE

*Hand-patted, local grass-fed beef, homemade buns*

**The Classic**—*beef, choice of cheese, bun*
**The Gettysburger**—*caramelized shallots, mushrooms,
blue cheese, bacon, balsamic glaze*
**The Farfar**—*two patties, four slices
of American cheese, four pieces of bacon*
**The Gruff Burger**—*goat cheese, fries (on top!),
caramelized shallots, poutine gravy to dip*
**The Valedictorian**—*pepper-jack cheese,
bacon, guacamole (from Rosa's)*

# POMMES FRITES

*Fresh-cut fries*

**Plain**—*with cheese or gravy to dip*
**Loaded Kebab Fries**—*fresh-cut fries,*
*chopped kebab meat, red and white kebab sauces,*
*crumbled feta, diced jalapeños and tomatoes*
**Goat Cheese Poutine**—*fresh-cut fries,*
*house-made gravy, goat cheese crumbles*

# MUNKAR

**Äpple Munk**—*fresh donut, cinnamon sugar,*
*filled w/ apple and sweet cream*
**Bär Munk**—*fresh donut, sugar, seasonal*
*berry jam, sweet cream*
**Munkhål**—*baby donuts (holes), cinnamon sugar*
**Special Munk**—*daily and seasonal specials*

# CUPCAKES

Vanilla Wedding Cake, Devil's Food, Lemon,
Strawberry Cheesecake, Weekly Specials

# SEASONAL TREATS

Homemade Apple Crisp à la Mode
Apple Fritters
Pumpamunk
Saffron Buns

# COFFEE & SPECIALTY DRINKS

*Proudly serving Merlin's Coffee,*
*Hanover, PA—organic, fair-trade, locally roasted*

Coffee—*daily light and dark roasts*
Lattes & Mochas
Chai Latte
Hot Chocolate
** Gratis munkhål om du beställer på svenska

# ACKNOWLEDGMENTS

I owe so much to so many.

The first fresh bär munk to my superhero agent, Laura Crockett, who does nothing but put good into this world. I think about how lucky I am every single day. And donuts to Uwe Stender and the entire team at Triada, agents and authors alike—it truly feels like a writing family.

An enormous äpple munk to Erin Clarke, my brilliant editor, whose insight and patience are unparalleled. I am forever grateful. Warm saffron buns to Jeff Hinchee and Ray Shappell for a cover that is so utterly perfect and gives me so much joy. I still can't believe there's a tiny Moomin poster hiding inside that truck. Another tray from the oven for Barbara Perris, Lisa Leventer, and Artie Bennett. And steaming mugs of glögg for the entire amazing team at Knopf.

Trays of warm apple crisp to Dr. Aileen Hower and Dr. Mona Kerby for their unending support and for granting me opportunities I never thought possible.

Monster Bacon Thickburgers to my brothers, Matt and Nate, and to my friend Ryan for demanding to read the earliest, messiest manuscript and giving me nothing but heartfelt encouragement.

A Special Rullekebab to my dear friend and brother André Friman for being my source for all things Swedish, and for making Åland part of my life, too. Any mistakes are strictly my own.

To my students, who have endured so many mentor sentences about Oscar and Farfar and *Mario Kart*. Their enthusiastic support means more than I could ever adequately express. Munkhål all around. (It's already been approved by the nurse.)

Fresh-cut fries to Mom and Dad. There will never be enough fries to repay your endless love and encouragement. But we should try.

Limited-edition pumpamunkar to Maddie and Mabel. I am in awe of the joy and the beauty you create every single day.

And, of course, all of the things, always, to Dawn, the gravy to my poutine. You make me so much better.